"YOU RAN AWAY FROM ME THAT NIGHT SIX MONTHS AGO. I WANT TO KNOW WHY," ADAM DEMANDED.

"I . . . I left because I thought it was time to go," she murmured, blushing furiously.

"Oh, really? Do you make it a habit to leave your dates frustrated?"

"We weren't on a date," Ariel responded indignantly.

"You mean, if I *had* been your date, you wouldn't have heated me up to the boiling point and then bailed out at the last minute? Is that it?" he asked, controlled anger evident in his voice.

"What am I supposed to make of a question like that?" she shot back. "Besides, my social life is not under discussion here. I'm sorry if you were . . . inconvenienced, but I didn't want to stay with you and I left. That's all there is to it."

"That sure wasn't the message you'd been sending me all evening," Adam said in a low, angry tone.

CANDLELIGHT ECSTASY SUPREMES

HIDDEN CHARMS

Lee Magner

A CANDLELIGHT ECSTASY SUPREME

Published by
Dell Publishing Co., Inc.
1 Dag Hammarskjold Plaza
New York, New York 10017

ISBN: 0-440-13596-6

Printed in the United States of America

First printing—August 1985

To Our Readers:

Candlelight Ecstasy is delighted to announce the start of a brand-new series—Ecstasy Supremes! Now you can enjoy a romance series unlike all the others—longer and more exciting, filled with more passion, adventure, and intrigue—the stories you've been waiting for.

In months to come we look forward to presenting books by many of your favorite authors and the very finest work from new authors of romantic fiction as well. As always, we are striving to present the unique, absorbing love stories that you enjoy most—the very best love has to offer.

Breathtaking and unforgettable, Ecstasy Supremes will follow in the great romantic tradition you've come to expect *only* from Candlelight Ecstasy.

Your suggestions and comments are always welcome. Please let us hear from you.

Sincerely,

The Editors
Candlelight Romances
1 Dag Hammarskjold Plaza
New York, New York 10017

CHAPTER ONE

Ariel had been feeling uneasy all through Dr. Norris's post-breakfast speech, but she kept trying to ignore it. She told herself that it was just a delayed reaction to the nightmare. She'd had it again, just when she'd begun to think that she was getting over it too. A nightmare would explain her jitters, as well as the hair that felt like it was standing up on the back of her neck and the wholly unaccountable urge she kept having to wet her lips.

She glanced nervously around the room for the fifteenth or sixteenth time, keenly aware that her pulse was beating a little too fast for someone sitting and eating breakfast. Caffeine in the coffee, perhaps?

The longer Dr. Norris droned on, the worse she felt and the harder it was to believe her own perfectly logical explanations. She was beginning to feel like a deer in a thicket that was on the verge of being uncovered by a very hungry carnivore.

She tried to concentrate on what he was saying, but something about the glowing description he was delivering was unsettling her even more.

". . . and we are fortunate indeed to have as a colleague and collaborator a man whose name is fast becoming synonymous with engineering sophistication and architectural artistry . . ."

Her employer hesitated in mid-accolade and turned toward the stranger seated across from him. The subject of Dr.

9

Norris's praise had his back to her, and he was only partially visible through the forest of people seated at the closely packed tables.

Ariel couldn't see enough of him to tell what he looked like exactly, but there was something vaguely familiar about the set of his shoulders and the dark brown color of his hair. Something familiar and . . . upsetting.

The audience was laughing politely at a joke, but Ariel had missed it. She'd been concentrating so hard on the stranger's aura of familiarity that she had rendered herself temporarily deaf.

". . . And then, of course, he's also a very shrewd businessman who knows how to drive a hard bargain when he wants to. Some of you will be discovering this for yourselves in the next few days when you find out how much time you'll be expected to spend on his project."

There was more polite chuckling and murmuring. Ariel glanced around the room. The women didn't look the least bit worried about it.

Ariel frowned a little.

". . . He's the founder and chief executive officer of the consulting firm that bears his name. . . ."

Dr. Norris hesitated, playing out the suspense for all it was worth before executing the coup de grace.

"Ladies and gentlemen, I would like to introduce you to Mr. . . ."

And suddenly Ariel knew with appalling certainty the name that was about to be uttered.

"Adam . . ."

It hadn't been the recurrence of the nightmare that had set her on edge at all.

"Locke."

It had been her instinct; she'd sensed his presence even before seeing him.

Her heart froze in place, clenched along with the rest of her in an icy fist.

"No!" she murmured weakly. "You can't be here!"

10

Her faintly whispered protest was swallowed up by the wave of polite applause rippling through the room. She stared at the dark-haired man who was now standing in order to acknowledge the pro-forma clapping.

"How can you be here?" she asked rhetorically in a soft, strained voice.

He had turned toward the audience, and for the first time she got a good look at him. There could be no doubt about it; it was the same Adam Locke, all right.

He was as ruggedly handsome as she remembered him to be. All hard planes and roughly sculpted features and smoothly leashed strength. She knew that she was staring at him, but she just couldn't help it. She had had the same reaction to him the first time too, she recalled defeatedly. He had been thoroughly captivating then. Unfortunately she had ended up being the one who was captivated. It wasn't precisely what she had planned at the time. That night-run-wild had been haunting her ever since. Unfortunately now it was haunting her in person, in broad daylight and in front of an audience!

Ariel watched his predatory gaze methodically sweep the room. He reminded her of a Roman conqueror searching a defeated kingdom for the spoils of war.

She sank lower in her chair.

Well, she would probably qualify as spoils, she thought miserably. For the millionth time she wondered how she could ever have been so stupid as to have done what she did.

Her features tensed in anger at her own impulsive, poorly thought out actions. Why on earth had she done it? One night out of her whole life when she had kicked over the traces, and now it was coming back to get her. It would all catch up with her for certain this time.

She sank her teeth into the inside of her lower lip.

"Catch up with her" wasn't quite the right phrase, she decided. It had never let her go. Not a day, nor a night, had passed without her thinking about him . . . and the feelings that he had aroused in her.

But she was willing to bet that he hadn't lost any sleep over it. He wasn't the type. She had learned that the hard way.

Well, hell, she thought angrily. *If you can take it in stride, so can I.*

Her dark brown eyes flashed, and she lifted her chin defiantly. She'd be damned if she'd slink off in embarrassment over it. No one had ever accused her of being a coward. She wasn't about to start trying out for the label now.

He had finished perusing the table to her left and was beginning a quick survey of hers. David he dismissed practically without looking at him. Lydia's short blond hair he dispatched with equal speed. But when he reached Ariel, he hesitated.

Cool eyes flickered over her hair, tightly coiled at the nape of her neck. Then they passed on to her carefully expressionless face and the soft, cream-colored shirtwaist's traditional styling.

For a heartbeat she thought he looked confused; then he turned his attention to the table to her right. Ariel breathed a sigh of relief.

So, he hadn't recognized her after all. She wondered why she didn't feel elated. Oddly enough, her relief was tinged with disappointment instead. Disappointment, of all things! She decided she must be out of her mind.

Ariel's expression softened, a rueful look dampening the fire in her eyes as the beginnings of a grin tugged at the corners of her shapely mouth.

So much for making a lasting impression on a man, she thought wryly. It just goes to show, Ariel, that you'll never make it as a femme fatale!

She blinked the object of her reverie back into focus. When she did, she discovered that he wasn't scanning the room anymore. A peculiar look had settled on his face. Doubt? Disbelief? And then he was turning back to look straight at her. Her heart sank, lead apparently having replaced its muscle.

His slate-blue eyes locked her soft brown ones in a shaft in which time and space had been suddenly suspended. They stared at each other, pursuer and pursued, while an unseen bond forged its links across the distance separating them. Unseen, perhaps, but not unfelt.

Triumph flared in Locke's eyes for a second before he ruthlessly smothered its flames. It was the triumphant gleam of a hunter who had found his quarry. Or that of a male who at last had within his grasp the female he wanted.

As the images formed and took root in Ariel's mind, her stunned dismay grew. The idea was flabbergasting, to say the least. Adam Locke just could not be pursuing her. Well, maybe he would have considered chasing the other Ariel, the one she'd conjured up with long flowing hair who'd tried to . . . No. This long afterward? Who was she kidding? It was too ridiculous even to consider. He wasn't looking for her. He just happened to be here, and he was surprised to see her. What could be more natural? That had to be it.

But it wasn't.

Adam Locke wasn't just surprised to see her. He had indeed been looking for her. And now that he'd found her and could practically taste victory, he intended to savor every minute of it.

A smile tugged at the corners of his hard, chiseled mouth.

He hadn't recognized her at first with her hair neatly pulled back into a chignon and those oversize, tinted glasses hiding the velvety brown of her eyes. And that dress had been good camouflage, too, he decided, lazily studying the demure curve of the collar and the diminutive buttons that were placed in a neat line up in the middle of her bodice to the discreet V just below the center of her collarbone.

He thought that she had looked surprised to see him for a moment before the cool mask had slipped into place. That suited him perfectly. A woman off-stride was always easier to bring down.

Adam Locke fully intended that Ariel Radnor stay off-stride for the indefinite future.

The funny thing was, he'd always had the nagging feeling that she had been off-balance that first time they had met.

That had bothered him at the time, though not enough to prevent him from getting involved with her. Unfortunately it had been bothering the hell out of him ever since as well. He intended to put a stop to that immediately.

Dr. Norris was speaking again, and Locke sat down. A sea of torsos interfered with their view of each other; eye contact was broken.

". . . and I hope that you've found these weekly staff breakfasts as informative and as enjoyable as I have."

Informative and enjoyable were hardly the words that Ariel had in mind at the moment. More like . . . trapped and caged. She was trying to figure out if there was a way she could get out of the place without being seen. Before she had to come to a decision, however, there was a great rustling of bodies and a scraping of chairs as people collectively got up to leave.

She caught a glimpse of Locke snapping to his feet, his eyes trained on her now. Before he could take a step, however, he was swallowed up in concentric circles of employees eager to say hello to him.

Hurray! she crowed silently, grabbing her purse and bounding out of her chair.

"I've got to run," she tossed over her shoulder to her astonished friends.

David and Lydia stared after her as she disappeared into the crowd.

"So I see," Lydia observed humorously.

"Bye," David shouted. He turned to his sister and asked in a more conversational tone, "What the devil's gotten into her?"

Lydia looked at the spot in the crowd where Ariel had vanished.

"I haven't the foggiest idea."

Ariel heard none of their parting comments; she had already reached the exit and was well on her way out of the building.

* * *

She spent the morning trying to get organized. By lunchtime she'd given it up as hopeless and simply sat and stared at the walls for an hour. If she was going to be miserable and preoccupied, she decided that she might as well throw herself wholeheartedly into it.

An hour of that was about her limit, she discovered; so, she switched to organizing her desk and clearing out the clutter on her myriad bookshelves. The telephone rang several times, providing her only respite from her own company. One call was from Lydia, inviting Ariel to a late lunch at the Athena Inn. Ariel declined, pleading a heavy workload. Lydia found that excuse a little hard to swallow, but she didn't push it.

By four o'clock Ariel was finally beginning to crawl out from under the blanket of doom that she'd wrapped around herself. She even entertained the possibility that she might not be asked to get involved in Locke's project. Why, she might be able to avoid him altogether, praise be. Especially if she hid out in her office as much as possible for the duration.

She stopped pushing her pen aimlessly over the dark-brown leather blotter on top of her large desk. A slight smile lifted the corners of her mouth, lightening her expression. The idea was so cheering that she actually began to feel like getting some work done.

Ariel reached for the letter on top of the pile in her incoming mail tray. She was about to open it when a sound at the door caught her attention.

"Afternoon, Ariel."

Dr. Norris's genial salutation reached her just as her finger slipped beneath the flap sealing the envelope.

She looked up, her brown eyes alight from surprise. As soon as she saw the man that Dr. Norris had brought with him, however, her heart plummeted, taking the sparkle with it.

"Good afternoon, Dr. Norris," she murmured. Her eyes remained trained on the older man.

"I wanted to introduce you to Adam. Adam Locke, this is Ariel Radnor, our resident translator and linguist. I'm sure you recognize Adam from the meeting this morning, don't you, Ariel?"

"Yes, of course," she murmured. And other places, she added silently.

Dr. Norris rolled on, oblivious to the fact that her unblinking eyes had been glued to him since he first opened his mouth.

"You'll be working quite closely together for the next few weeks," he was saying.

Oh, great, she thought. This must be how Lot's wife felt when she was turned into a pillar of salt for her sins.

"We will?" she said weakly.

Out of the corner of her eye she could see that Locke was watching her. He looked completely relaxed and a little amused by it all. He would. Warm color tinged her cheeks, anger painting its warning signals.

"Yes," Dr. Norris said, a little surprised at her reaction. "Didn't you get my note?"

He frowned. Then he saw the envelope in her hand.

"That's it. You haven't opened it yet. Had another busy day, eh?" He was the complete sympathetic father now, all but patting her on the head affectionately.

"Uh, yes, sir," she said faintly.

Locke murmured a word of sympathy she couldn't quite make out.

Ariel stared blankly at the long white envelope. Quickly she slid her finger under the back lip, neatly tearing it open. Unfortunately she also sliced her finger open in the process.

"Never mind, Ariel," her boss was saying. "I can tell you what's in it."

Locke had seen her flinch and had strolled over to her desk. She felt the room closing in on her as he came to a halt not a foot away from her.

"Let me see that," he ordered firmly, seeing the thin ribbon of red appearing on her finger.

He didn't wait for her to comply but picked up her hand and began examining the injury instead.

His lean, hard fingers felt smooth and warm against her skin. She tried to snatch her hand away, but he tightened his grip as soon as he felt her tense up. She couldn't do anything more to free herself short of engaging in a major battle with him. Not wanting to get into something like that in front of Dr. Norris, she resigned herself and sat stiffly in her chair.

"It's nothing," she protested, looking unhappily at her small hand lying palm-up in his.

"It looks like it hurts," he said casually. "Do you have any antiseptic or bandages with you?"

"No. Look, Mr. Locke . . ."

"Adam," he ordered.

She ignored his command to familiarity.

"I don't think—"

"We should put something on it."

What kind of a conversation was this to be having with a man she was not even supposed to know? she thought wildly. She ventured a glance at Dr. Norris. He didn't seemed surprised. Amused, perhaps. Ariel's brows drew together in annoyance.

"Well, you're in luck, Ariel, because I happen to have what you need with me," he announced.

Her eyes snapped to his. He was looking thoroughly pleased with himself, and there was a dangerous gleam in his slate-blue eyes. A familiar gleam. She leaned back away from him and pursed her lips.

"You do?"

"Yes."

Their eyes locked in combat for a split second.

He pressed his thumb down against the cut on her forefinger, stopping the trickle of blood that had begun to drip onto her blotter.

"There. As long as I keep pressing down you'll be okay. Come on. I'll fix you up. You'll be as good as new in no time."

"I'm as good as new now," she complained tightly.

He straightened and gently tugged on her hand.

"I can't go right now. I've . . . got some things to finish up. But thank you just the same."

She tried to pull her hand away, but his fingers merely tightened their steely grip.

"You won't be able to do much as long as you're dripping blood all over the place," he pointed out calmly, steamrolling on in spite of her protest that it was hardly an artery that they were talking about. "Anyway, while I'm patching you up I can tell you what you'll be doing with me for the next three weeks."

Ariel opened her mouth to say that she would be doing absolutely nothing with him for the next three weeks. Then she recalled that Dr. Norris was standing there listening to all of this. She made a quick change of topic. She would say that she couldn't go with him today. She'd run over to her cottage . . .

Dr. Norris outflanked her in the midst of her elaborate planning.

"Great idea, Locke!" he said enthusiastically, turning on his heel and making for the door. "I've got some things to wrap up myself this afternoon, anyway. You two go on and get acquainted." He glanced over his shoulder at Ariel. Locke was still standing protectively by her side. Dr. Norris's grin could hardly be misunderstood, even by the most naive. "Don't worry about your other assignments, Ariel. Make Mr. Locke your top priority."

And, with that charming exhortation, he left.

"Excellent advice," Locke murmured dryly. "I hope you're in the habit of following his instructions implicitly."

Ariel looked stonily at the broad, well-shaped thumb pressed firmly against her finger. The back of her hand felt hot nestled in his, and her knuckles were being pressed into his palm by the relentless pressure of his fingertips on the sensitive center of her hand.

"Would you let my hand out of that vise?" she asked pointedly.

He laughed softly.

18

"Not a chance! I've noticed that you have a tendency to run under pressure. I wouldn't want to give you the opportunity to escape."

"I'm not under pressure," she lied.

He grinned. She could see it in his distorted reflection on the surface of the ceramic coffee mug sitting on her desk.

"No? Do you always avoid looking at people to whom you're being introduced?" he asked interestedly.

He pulled her chair around so that she was forced to face him. With his free hand he tilted her chin gently upward. The light touch of his fingers sent a flurry of pleasurable sensations across her jaw and down her slender neck.

"Then you can look at me?" he inquired with just a hint of challenge.

She had focused on the top button of his charcoal-gray vest. She couldn't let the softly voiced challenge go unmet, though. With great deliberation, she lifted her eyes to his. Unwavering, she stared into the gleaming eyes.

"Of course." she said calmly.

"And you didn't run away from me this morning?"

"No."

"And that disappearing act you pulled six months ago wasn't running away, either?"

"Of course not."

Her eyes were darkening with suppressed anger at his inquisition. He obviously wasn't going to leave it alone. He was going to dig it up and flaunt it in her face. Didn't he know that gentlemen weren't supposed to do that? She glared at him in defiance and was surprised to see his skepticism and amusement fade into mild surprise.

He looked absently at her hand, lifting his thumb from the injury and gently pressing her own thumb onto it in his place. He traced a firm line across her palm with his thumb, watching without really seeing it as he softly caressed her palm. Back and forth. Back and forth. The delicate pleasure spiraled into her arm. Suddenly she became aware of how close they were. His warmth was heating the air next to her. And the warmth was beginning to spread. She tried to pull her hand away again. He held her fast.

"Okay. You don't run away," he agreed in a more serious tone.

He studied her for a moment, as if searching for something not readily apparent on the surface. He smiled gently, but his face had become strangely shuttered. She couldn't read his intentions.

"I still intend to patch you up and talk to you," he said firmly.

He stepped backward and pulled Ariel to her feet. She retrieved her purse from her desk, resigned to having to go with him by now. She looked straight at him.

"Lead on," she said with a sigh.

He nodded his head, the humor back in his eyes. But he held on to her hand as he led her to the door. Ariel hesitated.

"Now what's the matter?" he asked, frowning for the first time.

She looked significantly at his grip on her hand.

"I'm holding the cut closed," she reminded him. "You can let go of my hand now."

"I can, but I'm not going to," he replied. He didn't appear to be the least bit interested in discussing it further.

He turned to leave, but she dug in her heels and balked again.

"People will think we're holding hands!" she hissed angrily.

"We are."

"We are not! You're holding me prisoner. But no one knows that but us. What will they think?" she asked, trying to control her ire.

"That I work pretty fast and have good taste in women, probably," he replied with an easy grin.

He was halfway through the door, and several employees saw them as they walked by. They looked at Ariel and Locke with unconcealed interest.

"Coming?" he asked politely as he pulled her firmly along after him this time.

There was no way that she could free her hand, refuse to go, or keep on arguing without drawing a crowd, something she dearly wished to avoid. She smiled sweetly at her associates as she stumbled quickly after him. Well, holding hands wasn't a crime, after all. It would all blow over in a few days. She hoped.

Ariel had assumed that Locke's antiseptic and bandages were in an office located in the same building or perhaps in one of the neighboring office complexes. She was surprised, therefore, when he walked out of the main administration building and across the short distance to the Athena Inn.

Well, sometimes visitors were given offices on the ground floor or first floor, she told herself stoutly.

She forced herself to ignore the startled look of virtually every person they passed. She made it a special point to ignore the desk clerk when they passed through the lobby and got into the elevator. But when Locke jabbed the button for the top floor, she ran out of innocent explanations and bravado.

"Just where do you keep your antiseptic and bandages?" she asked suspiciously.

"In my dobb kit."

He was grinning again. She could hear it in his voice. She kept her face toward the closed elevator doors, like a woman carved in stone.

"Oh." She felt a little weak in the knees.

Serves you right for being so weak in the head, she told herself sharply, severely annoyed at having gotten herself into this situation.

The elevator doors opened, and Locke stepped out. She followed him, hurrying to keep up with his long, even strides.

"Look, this may be very amusing to you, but it's not the least bit funny to me," she snapped. "I can't go into your room."

He fished a key out of his jacket and inserted it into the lock. With his free hand he opened the door and motioned her in as if he hadn't heard her.

21

"Relax, Ariel. This is just my office," he explained easily, pulling her into the room and shutting the door after them.

"Your . . . office?"

She didn't bother launching into the list of reasons she had for not going into his hotel room with him. The suite obviously had been set up as an office. It was an elegant office, to be sure, but office, indeed, it was.

"This is where you're going to be working?"

He nodded, dropping the key onto a large, round coffee table.

Drafting tables and supplies were arrayed in front of the windows and the doors to the balcony. Sunlight was streaming in, making it easy for him to work there during the day. Computer equipment occupied a corner not far from the drafting materials, and there was a large desk along one wall. It was already covered with papers and reports.

Locke was removing his jacket and tossing it over the back of an overstuffed chair close to the coffee table. His shirt and vest had tautened over the well-defined muscles of his chest, shoulders, and arms as he did so. Ariel watched them bunch and stretch in spite of her resolve not to look at him any more than absolutely necessary.

It was difficult to hold on to that resolve. She enjoyed looking at him. He was good to look at.

She lost another small battle with herself as her eyes drifted over him from head to toe. The perfect fit of his trousers could not conceal the strong, masculine contours beneath.

Ariel's mouth began to feel dry, and then she realized that her breathing had become shallower and more frequent. So he looked good in a three-piece suit, she thought irritably. Well, he looked good out of one too, her mind added without her permission. She closed her eyes in silent misery. When she opened them again, barely a second later, he was looking at her rather oddly.

"Are you all right?" he asked, clearly concerned. "You're not feeling faint?"

She shook her head and smiled ruefully.

"Over a little cut like this? Don't be silly!"

He looked unconvinced, but he shrugged and paced over to the door on one side of the room. He opened it, hesitating to give her a parting word of advice.

"Go sit down."

He nodded toward a large semicircular couch curled around half of the coffee table.

"I'll be right back."

Sitting down didn't seem like such a bad idea under the circumstances. Ariel knew that when he returned, her cut was not the only topic that would be up for discussion. The others that came to mind were better contemplated while seated.

She dropped her purse on the coffee table and sank onto gold velvet cushions. It was nearing five o'clock. Maybe she could get out of here then. That was, after all, the end of the workday for her. Not that she ever made it out of the office that early here. But then, Locke wouldn't know that. She relaxed a little. Yes. That ought to get her out of here fairly quickly.

"Ready?"

Locke had returned, supplies in hand, and was sitting down beside her. His knee brushed hers lightly as he did so. The dark gray fabric was drawn tautly across the hard curves of bone and sinew. Where it had grazed her nyloned leg, Ariel felt her flesh seared by a strange hot-cold sensation. She slanted her legs away from him, knees together.

Locke had placed everything on the table and was reaching for her hand. In a few deft strokes he applied the stinging antiseptic. Then, to her surprise, he lowered his head to blow gently across the injury, easing the pain.

Ariel stared at his dark head bent over her hand, and her gaze wandered over his broad shoulders before she could force herself to think of something else to take an interest in. He was only inches away; the warmth from his thigh was enveloping her leg and marching upward toward her hips and torso. It was too much.

She felt herself being gently swallowed up by a dangerous

23

lethargy. The circumstances were too intimate for her to be safe from him and the memories he brought to mind. But it was such a temptation to linger a moment, to enjoy looking at him. He couldn't see her, and she let her eyes drift over him, remembering the feel of touching him that other time.

How perfectly the clean, strong lines of his neck and shoulder had fit under her hand as they had danced that night. And the firm ridges of muscle layered across his back . . . how warm he had felt. . . . She could still feel the smooth, powerful sensations that had seemed to emanate from him.

The striped dress shirt he was wearing today hid nothing from her. She saw him through the lens of her memories.

He straightened and turned toward her.

She snapped back to the present, her guard up again.

''Better?''

A light current of electricity thrummed just below the surface of her skin as he spoke. Better was not quite how she would have characterized the sensation. Disturbing was more like it. But he was referring to her finger, of course.

''Yes. Thank you.''

He shrugged, dismissing her gratitude as unnecessary. He leaned back, stretching his long legs out under the coffee table and draping an arm casually over the sofa in back of her. A half-smile played across his lips.

''It's quite a surprise seeing you like this,'' he said, having allowed several moments of silence to stretch between them first.

His eyes traveled dispassionately over her from head to toe, as if assessing for possible changes.

So, he had been surprised to see her this morning. That searching look that he'd treated them all to at breakfast hadn't been for her at all. Of course, she'd been telling herself that all day, but until he had said it, she'd secretly nurtured the fantasy that he might have actually come looking for her.

Not that she would have liked that any better, she told herself quickly. But after all, what woman likes to be easily forgotten? It's always sweeter to inspire a little pursuit!

Ariel clamped down on her errant thoughts and took a stab at holding up her end of the conversation.

"I could say the same thing."

He was studying her glasses, and she had the impression that he hadn't quite heard all of her comment. What was he thinking?

"How long have you worn glasses?"

He ran the tip of his finger across the dusky coral frames. She could feel the vibrations from his touch in the bones of her shoulders.

"For about ten years."

The finger hovered at the miniature silver hinge.

"You weren't wearing them the last time."

His voice was quiet and smooth; it alternately soothed and innervated her. Warmth was enveloping her completely this time, and her arms were beginning to tingle suspiciously.

"They didn't go with the costume," she managed to say in a reasonably normal voice.

"Tell me, are you hiding behind them now? Behind this?"

His questioning glance encompassed her entire outfit.

"I don't know what you mean."

Too late she read his intention and tried to grab his hand.

"Wait!" she said sharply, to no avail.

He removed her glasses with a quick flick of his wrist, leaving her fingers touching the air.

"It doesn't matter," he said easily. "The same woman is underneath all the camouflage."

He deposited her glasses on the table. Ariel shrank back to put some distance between them. Unfortunately she wasn't fast enough. The arm behind her locked onto her shoulders.

"Isn't she?" he asked softly, so close to her that the word brushed across her lips.

Somewhere a tiny rational cell buried deep in her brain was pleading to her to say no and escape. It didn't have a chance against the rest of her, which couldn't move a muscle to save her life at the moment.

She stared at his lips, so close, so tempting. It had been so long since he had kissed her, since she'd felt the magic. She'd tortured herself so often with the memory. Just one kiss to seal the memory . . . maybe it wouldn't be as good as she remembered. Just one kiss. What harm could it do?

He saw her mesmerized stillness through the unexpected haze of his own uncertainty. Should he kiss her, or would that drive her farther away? She hadn't been exactly thrilled to see him by all appearances.

Locke wanted to approach this logically, carefully, like a business contract or a social conquest, but she was too close for him to think anymore. That elusive scent she wore was clogging his senses, and the soft warmth of her nearness was fogging his mind. He couldn't think of anything except the intense need to press his lips against hers.

His mouth grazed hers lightly, experimentally at first, brushing softly from side to side, spreading an exquisite sparkle through her lips and into the interior of her mouth. Gently he increased the pressure, and Ariel relaxed into it. Vaguely she felt the touch of his hand at her waist, and she spread her own against the welcoming strength of his chest. She had meant to push him away, but there didn't seem to be enough strength in her arms to do it. The gentle suctioning he was applying to her mouth felt too incredibly good to interrupt, and the feel of him under her open palms was making it all the better.

His initial gentleness had disarmed her, and the tension had eased away. His insistence was clear but unthreatening, and her mouth softened in response, parting a little under the hardening pressure of his. The tentative invitation was too good to pass up, and Locke responded immediately.

His arms tightened, and he pressed her back into the cushions. His tongue began caressing the inner rim of her lips, teasing and cajoling and arousing her until her whole mouth ached for its touch. She half whimpered with frustration, and he plunged into her, massaging the velvet contours into ecstasy.

Ariel wriggled her aching arms from between their chests and slipped them around his back. He groaned against her mouth as she began to caress him. Suddenly he broke the kiss.

She felt his heart pounding against her. Or was it hers? Both of them were breathing unsteadily and were almost hot to the touch.

"Oh, yes," he said unsteadily. "You're the same woman all right."

A vision of her lying half dressed underneath Locke's equally undraped body flashed through her mind. And then another memory came fast on its heels. A memory of humiliation and worthlessness.

Ariel wriggled loose from him and managed to get unsteadily to her feet. Locke remained half sprawled across the couch, trying to figure out what in the devil had happened, making no effort to straighten his rumpled clothing.

She smoothed the simple lines of her dress, searching desperately for her sense of control.

"No. I'm not the same woman at all." Could he hear the hint of desperation hidden behind her firmly stated retort?

She grabbed her purse and glasses and flashed toward the door.

Ariel was quick, but Locke was quicker. He slammed his palms on the door on either side of her, trapping her with his body.

"Oh, no, you don't," he growled over her shoulder. "This time you're not running away from me. This time you're going to stay and tell me what this is all about, damn it!"

CHAPTER TWO

Ariel swayed against the door, resting her cheek on its cold, wood-grained surface. Her eyes closed, shutting everything out for a moment as she struggled to come up with her next move. He had trapped her. Now she had to give him an explanation of some kind.

The seconds ticked slowly by.

"All right," she mumbled, sighing reluctantly, her voice barely audible.

Locke rolled onto one shoulder, giving her enough room to escape if she wanted it. She didn't bother to take advantage of it at first. The added breathing space alone was rapidly restoring her equilibrium, but moving physically away from him didn't seem especially crucial to her now. Somehow the man seemed to fill the room as far as she was concerned. She never felt far enough away from him to do herself much good.

"I don't intend to lean on this door throughout a lengthy conversation," he pointed out evenly.

Since her face was turned away from him, she couldn't see him, and by his words alone, she wasn't sure exactly how to take his statement. There was the hint of something serious underlying his deceptively neutral comment, but she wasn't quite sure what it was.

"Why don't you sit down?" he suggested, annoyance tingeing the command masquerading as a question.

It wasn't such a bad idea, she had to admit. As soon as she

stopped leaning on the door she realized how rubbery her knees felt. They walked back to the couch without talking, Locke trailing behind her slightly, Ariel still clutching her glasses.

"I said I wanted an explanation," he remarked dryly. "Nothing else."

He eyed her stiff little figure seated primly on the edge of the couch and clenched his teeth in annoyance. He sat down in the chair across the table from her and waited for her to begin.

Ariel felt the blood rush to her cheeks. He was nothing if not perceptive. How she hated it, too, now. He could read her anxiety by looking at her. She had no idea how to defend herself from his shrewd assessment, but she couldn't bear the thought of his knowing just how much he affected her. Anger boiled up as a defensive shield, and her eyes darkened with hostility.

"Frankly, I don't care what you want," she retorted. "The only reason that I'm giving you any explanations at all is because you've trapped me into it." She emphasized *explanations* as if it were a poisonous species.

One dark eyebrow lifted sardonically.

"I'm forcing you to do it?" he asked doubtfully, his body suspiciously still and tense.

"Yes."

She glared at him, daring him to deny it.

He stared at her, his slate-blue eyes dueling with her angry ones.

"And do you think I forced you to do it the last time?"

His voice was soft, but it contained a hint of controlled anger that was new to the conversation. A ripple of alarm trickled down Ariel's spine in response. He sat watching her, waiting for her answer.

It was very difficult to stare back into those hard eyes, but Ariel refused to succumb to the temptation to drop her gaze. It seemed like admitting defeat, and Ariel had never liked to

29

lose. She lifted her chin proudly. She'd look him straight in the eyes if it killed her, she thought defiantly.

"No."

Her voice was firm in spite of the fact that she felt as if she were breaking apart like shattered glass inside. Very slowly. If she could keep herself together until this was all over . . .

Locke stared at her without speaking, trying to see into her soul. Her unflinching response to his scrutiny brought a flicker of respect and admiration to his flint-hard gaze. It was rapidly followed by uncertainty.

He expelled a long, tired breath and stretched out his legs, crossing them casually at the ankle. He loosened the knot of his tie and then the top button of his shirt, giving every appearance of a man preparing for a long siege and fully intending to be as comfortable as possible for it.

"Thanks, Ariel."

She hadn't expected an expression of gratitude.

"For what?" she asked blankly.

Incredibly, amusement was lurking in his eyes. It lightened his expression unbelievably. Ariel hardened her heart, anyway.

"For not trying to take the usual way out and blaming me for what happened the last time," he explained, a little surprised that she needed to have it spelled out for her. He smiled humorlessly. "Women have been doing it with remarkable predictability for thousands of years."

Ariel crossed her legs defensively at the knee.

"I'm not 'woman.' I'm me," she said a little crossly, simultaneously pleased by his backhanded compliment and annoyed with herself for being pleased about it.

His eyes never left her face.

"That's very true," he said softly.

His unrelenting gaze was becoming quite disconcerting, and Ariel pushed her glasses back on, as much in an effort to hide a little behind them as out of force of habit.

"Now tell me . . . exactly why did you leave?" he asked, frowning at the return of her glasses.

She could have played coy for a while, fencing with him

over what he meant by that and then tiptoeing around the real reasons. But Ariel had neither the energy nor the personality to construct a performance of that magnitude.

Better just to get it all over with, she thought fatalistically, groaning inwardly before plunging into the bath of fire that she feared awaited her.

"Basically I left because I thought it was time to go," she said for openers.

He was obviously not impressed with her opening salvo.

"Your sense of timing certainly left a lot to be desired," he said, barely veiling the sarcasm. "Do you make a habit of taking off and leaving your dates frustrated?" he challenged.

Why did she have to keep blushing? she wondered despairingly.

"We weren't on a date!" she retorted sharply.

His eyes narrowed speculatively.

"You mean you heated me up to the boiling point and decided to bail out at the last minute, but your dates you treat more considerately?"

"What am I supposed to make of a question like that?" she shot back furiously. "Besides, my social life is not under discussion here. I'm supposed to be explaining what happened."

"Go on."

"An opportunity presented itself." She shrugged. "So I took it. I'm sorry you were . . . inconvenienced."

He laced his fingers behind his head and continued to stare at her as she talked. He looked so laid back that Ariel relaxed in spite of herself. Now that they were fully engaged in talking, she'd almost forgotten the intimacy of the topic under discussion.

Her eyes wanted to wander over him, seeing if he was as attractive as she remembered. That brought her back to reality with a start. If there was one thing of which she was now certain, it was that she should never relax in Adam Locke's presence again. It was much too dangerous. She hugged her purse to her stomach.

"I'd have left soon, anyway," she added.

Disbelief chased across his features.

"Do you expect me to believe that?" he asked incredulously. "We were—"

"I know what we were doing," she said, interrupting him sharply.

"Surely you don't think that I would have needed more than a few more minutes to peel off your slip and underwear?" he argued. A confident grin slid over his handsome features.

"No. I'm sure you're quite proficient at it," she agreed sourly. "I just had no intention of personally sampling your technique."

He laughed, tossing his head back a little and struggling to regain his composure.

"That certainly wasn't the message you'd been sending me all evening," he said at last, his hard eyes at odds with the laughter he had finally contained.

Ariel had never felt quite so humbled. She sighed and dropped her gaze to the bare surface of the coffee table.

"I know. I'm sorry. I changed my mind. What else can I say?" she acknowledged stiffly, sensing his surprise at her naked admission.

"Thanks again," he replied, his voice now quiet and sincere.

She looked up sharply at him, a little confused by his gratitude under the circumstances.

"For being honest," he explained. "You're not trying the coy-damsel-in-distress or the outraged-virgin routines."

Ariel cringed inwardly at his choice of words. Maybe when she finished her little speech he'd want to retract his thanks.

"All right," he continued equably. "You' changed your mind. But what I'd like to know is why?"

How could he be so cool and businesslike about this? she wondered, extremely annoyed that she couldn't be. How could she tell him it was because she had never done anything like that before? Or that she had been so humiliated when . . . He'd laugh at her naïveté, for sure. Her courage waned in the face of his sophistication. Maybe it would be better to

32

skip the part about her own feelings and get to the part about his other visitor.

She became aware of the death grip she had on her purse and forced herself to loosen it a little.

"You . . . had someone else to see," she reminded him awkwardly. "And then, I had promised to be back much earlier in the evening. I really had never intended to get so involved with you. It just . . . happened," she ended lamely.

He had looked blank at her mention of his having to see someone else, but as soon as she made reference to her own need to go home, anger darkened his expression.

"Someone was waiting for you?" he inquired coolly.

"Yes."

That was true. Candy Laslow, the friend in whose apartment she had been staying while she was in Washington, had been expecting Ariel to return much earlier indeed.

Somehow Locke didn't look quite as laid-back to Ariel anymore. She sensed a subtle tension in him that added an aura of electricity to his very masculine appeal.

"Why didn't your friend come with you that night?"

Ariel detected a peculiar inflection at the word *friend*, but she dismissed it without too much thought. In her present state she didn't particularly trust her powers of perception.

"We worked in different worlds . . . led separate lives. We each had something else planned that night."

"What's your friend's name?" he asked casually.

Ariel hesitated. She really didn't want to get into this much detail with him. She just wanted to make her statement and leave, hopefully for good. But he was holding her with the force of his interest, in spite of the casualness with which he had asked that question. She had the feeling it would be easier simply to tell him than to fight about it. After all, what's in a name?

"Candy."

"Your friend's name is Candy?" he repeated, his eyes clearly dubious.

"Yes." Ariel was a little piqued by his perseverance. "Candy Laslow."

Locke was silent, but Ariel was certain that she had glimpsed a deep flare of anger in his hard, blue-gray eyes. Whatever it had been, he doused it before she could be sure.

"C. Laslow," he said aloud but not for Ariel's benefit.

"You were staying with this . . . Laslow?" he persisted unemotionally.

"Yes." She frowned. "How did you know?"

"Lucky guess," he muttered half to himself. Then, after a moment, he elaborated, "At that hour of the night I would hardly expect you to be going to meet another date. You'd be going straight home."

Something about his attitude and appearance of familiarity with Candy's name bothered Ariel. He didn't give her time to think about that, however.

He unlaced his fingers and unfolded his length from the chair, roosting instead on the arm, one foot firmly planted on the floor, the other swinging a little in the air.

"So . . . you were at loose ends that night, and I was your entertainment for the evening."

Stated so baldly like that, it sounded even worse than it had been.

"That wasn't exactly the way it was," she protested unhappily.

"Then exactly how was it?" he asked in razor-sharp words.

Cold, hard eyes pinned her to her seat. Ariel swallowed. "I don't know if I can explain it in a way that will make any sense to you. I had been invited to the party in Georgetown that night as a part of my job. But when the business-related contacts had been taken care of, Dr. Norris told me to stay and enjoy myself."

"He left?"

"Yes."

"Does he know you met me that night?"

"No," she said, too sharply. His eyebrow curved upward at her obvious discomfort.

"Go on."

It wasn't that easy, she thought, discouraged by his clearly unsympathetic scrutiny. The sooner this was over, the better. She plunged on.

"I had a few drinks and became thoroughly sorry for myself." She ignored his momentary look of surprise and edited the story down to its bottom line. "I had been feeling rather low and was wondering how the women at the party managed to look so glowing and so wildly successful with the men." She steeled her resolve and added, "I wondered what they had that I didn't."

She wet her lips, ignoring his startled disbelief.

"When I saw you"—this was definitely the hard part—"I wanted to see if I could . . . attract you," she said, faintly at the last. That wasn't quite it, but it would just have to do. It was close enough to the truth, as close as she could get at the moment.

Locke was staring at her, perplexed by her nervousness, her almost painful shyness in talking about all this. She certainly had shown little enough of it the last time.

"Let me see if I've got this straight," he said carefully. "You were in Washington on business." She nodded. "You were staying with your friend." Did she imagine the hardening of his features? "And you were at loose ends the night of the Carnaval, and you tried to pick me up as a sort of . . . test of your abilities?"

Only his eyes gave away his carefully controlled anger, but Ariel saw it. She faced him without flinching. What could it matter at this point, anyway?

"Yes. That's more or less it."

He scowled at her confirmation and stood up to pace across the room to the glass doors leading onto the balcony. Silence stretched out painfully for several minutes. Keeping his back to her, he posed another question.

"And what was your excuse for kissing me a little while ago?"

His question was so unexpected, she was speechless for a

moment. Finally she began to admit that she had been testing to make sure he really couldn't affect her in broad daylight in the real world, the way he had in the dark in the middle of a masquerade party. Fortunately her brain caught up with her mouth before the words were uttered. She couldn't tell him that. Because he *had* affected her. The test had been an abysmal failure, and she wasn't about to tell him so.

Since flight was still a little out of the question, she chose fight as her retaliation.

"You aren't particularly interested in other people's feelings, are you?" she snapped. "A gentleman wouldn't waste his time or mine doing postmortems on every meaningless encounter we've had. Don't you think that you could possibly discover enough civility to drop this whole conversation?"

Ariel felt distinctly small and at a disadvantage seated on the couch, so she shot to her feet, towering at her full five feet four inches. The fury boiling in her dark eyes had little effect on Locke's broad back. This lack of success merely served to fuel her fires.

"Meaningless encounters?" he echoed tightly. "Is that how you feel about it?"

It was all Ariel could do to keep from gaping at him. Who did he think he was, anyway? Here he was, a total stranger, asking her to bare her innermost thoughts and feelings to him, a man who had shown only a passing interest in her and was unlikely ever to cross her path again in the future! She couldn't believe his audacity. And she wasn't so naive as to give him what he wanted.

"Yes."

Her face tilted defiantly, underlining her succinct reply.

"I see."

She hadn't meant it to go like this. What had happened, anyhow? She had fully intended to tell him that she had set out to seduce him but that she had lost her nerve at the crucial moment in the farce. If he had been polite and friendly about it, she had even been prepared to mention the fact that Raquel's waltzing into his bedroom had been a factor in the speed with which she had exited his home. But, no, he had started grilling her and telling her how refreshing it was that she wasn't acting like an outraged virgin! He'd never believe that she was simply . . .

Locke turned and looked at her as if studying some rare species of bird about to take flight.

"Tell me . . . do you have many?" he inquired in a voice bordering on the disinterested.

"Many what?" she asked in confusion.

"Meaningless encounters."

The color receded from her cheeks. So. That was what he thought. Ariel didn't stop to wonder why she was becoming so upset at the implication. She was too far gone by this time to recognize the shields of anger shooting up around her as his comment struck home.

All right, if that's what you think of me, fine! she thought, seething. *But the person you'll be shooting at will be one I make up, just like the other me you ended up in bed with!* If he wanted to dislike her, it wouldn't be the real her.

"I manage to keep busy," she said enigmatically.

She walked toward the door like a woman who was fully prepared to pass through it this time. As a result she didn't see the stunned look in his eyes.

Ariel glanced quickly at her watch and opened the door before he could cross the room to deter her. Not that he was making any attempt in that direction. He was rooted to the spot, staring at her as if he had never seen her before.

"I've got to be going, Mr. Locke," she said, hesitating in the doorway.

"Adam," he growled, glaring at her as if affronted by her use of his last name.

"Adam."

Her breath caught in her throat as she practically stammered his name. Don't lose your nerve now, she told herself.

"We've still got some unfinished business," he reminded her coldly.

His lips curved a little at the corners when he saw her blank expression.

"We still have to discuss your role in my project," he pointed out.

She'd forgotten all about that.

"Of course," she said faintly.

"I'll see you tomorrow morning in your office at nine o'clock."

She acknowledged his clearly nonnegotiable appointment with a slight inclination of her head.

"Good-bye," she muttered.

He watched her rather rigid exit without further comment, but she felt as if the middle of her back had been branded by his silent parting look.

CHAPTER THREE

Dawn was creeping over the bluffs above the river as Ariel began to twist and turn in her bed. Her rigid fingers clenched the sheet as she tossed her head from side to side in mute, anguished protest. She moaned incoherently, her body tensed and knotted with pain as her past reached out to squeeze her in its relentless grip. Her legs caught in the sheets, but no matter how hard she struggled, she couldn't escape. Humiliation began to swamp her, and she was once again dragged into an excruciating, bottomless, black abyss. She gasped for breath, reaching . . . reaching . . . reaching out. . . .

But her fingers closed on emptiness. She was falling down, down, down . . . into the horrifying darkness. . . .

Just as the confused, agonizing dream had become unbearable, consciousness seeped in and gently freed her from the nightmare's awful grasp.

For a moment she could only lie, twisted and stiff, one foot dangling over the edge of the bed. Dry dream-tears still ached unshed in her eyes. After a while she managed to coax her trembling body upward. Slowly she sat up amid the damp tangle of bed covers. She felt awful. She always did after the nightmare was over. Her jaws still ached from clenching her teeth too long and too hard.

She bent her forehead into the sweat-dampened palms of her shaking hands. A half suppressed sob caught in her throat.

"Why are you doing this to me?" she cried out softly.

39

"Why can't you leave me alone? I thought I was beginning to forget. It's been months . . . I. . . ."

She closed her eyes and lay back in momentary defeat.

"I won't let you haunt me like this," she whispered fiercely.

Anger welled up forcefully, a tidal wave that completely washed away her overwhelming sense of loss and vulnerability.

She forced herself to breathe slowly, deeply. In. Out. Gradually the tension began to ease. It drained from her exhausted body, leaving her feeling hollow and weak at first. Breathe in. Breathe out. Inhale. Hold it. Exhale. Again. The rhythmic, detached litany calmed her, steadied her, returned her sense of control.

She rolled up onto her elbow and stared sightlessly at her pale, yellow gauze curtains as the sunlight streamed through the window.

She'd be damned if she would let the memory of that night keep tormenting her like this! She would deal with it if it was the last thing she ever did! Somehow she would erase him from her memory as if nothing had ever happened, she vowed defiantly.

Ariel punctuated the thought with a sharp jab at her pillow, imagining that it was his midsection. It made her feel immeasurably better.

Adam Locke hesitated, his razor poised over one of the few patches of shaving cream left on his face. For a moment he didn't see the bathroom anymore. His wandering thoughts had blanked everything out. All he saw was Ariel—the way she'd looked in the breakfast meeting.

She'd looked so contained, so reserved, so carefully polite on the outside. The picture of a demure young lady of what used to be called "good breeding."

He pulled the razor down one stripe of foam.

But in her eyes he'd seen a flash of shock and dismay before she could conceal it. His mystery lady was turning out to be mysterious indeed, he thought, trying not to smile as he eliminated another thin stripe of white froth.

40

With a last, deft stroke of the razor he finished shaving and rinsed off the blade. Still wondering what lay beneath that lovely surface of hers, he wiped his face with a damp cloth and walked into his bedroom to look for a shirt.

For months he'd told himself he was too old to become obsessed with a woman he'd spent only one evening with. When he had come to Annapolis several times during the summer, he'd told himself that it didn't matter that she was here. He wasn't hoping that they might accidentally run into each other someplace. No. Adam Locke wouldn't do something like that.

In a pig's eye.

He grinned as he finished buttoning the striped club shirt and looped a tie around his neck.

Well, damn it, she had fascinated the hell out of him! C. Laslow or no C. Laslow. Disappearing act be damned! He wanted to see her again, and he sure as hell was going to.

He'd gone to quite a bit of trouble to win this contract so that he could spend some time here. Half of his staff were still trying to figure out why the boss was taking this on personally instead of delegating the project to one of his subordinates.

He tightened the knot on the tie, his grin fading.

Let them wonder, he thought in annoyance. This was just one of those things he had to do. Once he had finally admitted that to himself, he had wasted no time in devising a means to accomplish it.

He shoved his wallet into his back pocket and put on his jacket.

After all, he hadn't made a success of his business by hanging back, he thought laconically.

He picked up his key on the way to the door, and within a matter of seconds, he was down the hall and waiting for the elevator to arrive.

Adam Locke moved fast when he saw something he wanted. And he had every intention of moving as fast as possible with

41

Ariel. After all, he had only three weeks to work with. He intended to make each one count.

The elevator doors glided open with a soft hiss. Adam Locke took two brisk steps into it, turned, and jabbed the button for the lobby.

Ariel locked her cottage door and walked quickly up the path that led to the sprawling complex of buildings that were spread across the rolling green hills of Anne Arundel County. Normally she enjoyed the walk to her office. The grounds of the Athena Corporation were quite beautiful, and the stone pathway from Ariel's cottage was especially so, since it ran along the forested cliff overlooking the Severn River.

Today she didn't even see the trees.

"Ariel! Wait for me!"

Lydia Carrollton's cheery voice reached Ariel just as she was crossing in front of the Athena Inn on her way to the main building.

"Hi, Lydia."

"I didn't see you at lunch yesterday," Lydia said with her usual forthrightness. "And David stopped by your office after work, but I guess he missed you. . . ."

Ariel smiled at a passing co-worker.

"I left a little early," she explained, pushing open the door to the main building and stepping through, ahead of Lydia.

"Hmmm." Lydia eyed her friend's back speculatively. "Out with friend Darryl?" she inquired blandly in spite of the humor lurking in her gray-green eyes.

Ariel groaned and started searching for her key in her purse as the came to a halt in front of her office door.

"Please," Ariel murmured in a pleading tone. "Don't even say it in jest!"

Lydia grinned and followed Ariel inside, flipping on the light switch as she went.

"Sorry. He isn't going to win any prizes for getting the message when a girl tries to give him a gentle refusal, is he?"

Ariel merely shook her head and smiled ruefully. She

42

dropped her things on the desk and went to start the automatic coffee machine in the corner.

"I've got to get some water for this thing, Lydia. I'll be right back," Ariel explained, grabbing an empty pitcher and leaving in the direction of the staff lounge.

When she returned, she found Lydia comfortably ensconced on the chair next to Ariel's desk.

"Got a big day?" Ariel asked as she poured in the water.

Lydia ran a finger along the edge of Ariel's gunmetal-gray desk and watched it glide by the piles of books and reports as Ariel sat down.

"Not too bad," she replied with a shrug. "You know Dr. Norris! There's never a dull moment around here. But today is really pretty straightforward." She glanced at Ariel, her finger halting in its travels. "Not like yesterday."

Ariel glanced through the half glass wall separating her office from the technical library next door. Everything was dark. Darryl wasn't here yet. Well, that was something, at least.

"You had a busy day yesterday?" Ariel ventured, hoping the conversation wasn't going to go the way she thought it was. She reached for her purse and started searching for her glasses.

"No," Lydia replied. "But I thought perhaps you might have had one."

Ariel put on her glasses and tore off the top sheet of paper on her desk calendar. She looked hopefully toward the coffee machine. Unfortunately it wasn't ready yet. No escape in that direction, she thought resignedly.

"Not really," Ariel murmured faintly.

Lydia leaned forward expectantly.

"Ariel," she said with that fascinating blend of authority and cajoling that had made her such an outstanding administrative assistant to Dr. Norris. "Why did you take off like a rabbit in hunting season after breakfast yesterday?"

"Like a rabbit in hunting season?"

Ariel tried to laugh it off, but the startled lift of her eyebrows didn't put Lydia off the scent.

"I asked myself all day what could have provoked my friend who never has a hair out of place or a droopy hemline? Why did she look like she'd been shot out of a cannon?"

"You did?" Ariel asked faintly.

Lydia studied Ariel like a cat studying an especially fascinating mouse.

"Do you know what I think?" Lydia offered with a mischievous gleam in her eyes.

Ariel was dimly aware that the trickle of water through the coffee filter was slowing to a drip. She got up and started filling a Styrofoam cup with hot coffee.

"No. But I have the feeling that you're about to tell me."

"I decided that it must have something to do with our good-looking new arrival, Adam Locke."

Lydia looked quite sure of herself, but she said it in a way that left Ariel an out. If Ariel chose to deny it, Lydia was willing to go along with her, even if Lydia wasn't about to swallow the denial.

Ariel was tempted to tell Lydia everything. Maybe it would help to talk about it. And Lydia was a good friend. Ariel knew that Lydia would honor the confidence, and besides, Lydia had a levelheaded, no-nonsense approach to male-female relationships. She probably could come up with a helpful insight as well as some reassuring observation.

Right now Ariel felt that she could use a little reassurance. She gave Lydia a reluctant smile. Then she nodded her head in assent.

"I'm right?" Lydia exclaimed, mildly surprised that Ariel was willing to admit it so easily.

Ariel was usually very reserved about herself, but, of course, she was warm and friendly. Lydia had liked her right away. But Ariel wasn't the type to spill her guts or air her problems at a moment's notice. Ariel was the type that kept it inside.

"Uh-huh," Ariel admitted ruefully. "Would you like a cup of coffee?"

"Sure. Thanks."

Ariel glanced at her watch. Eight forty-five. She couldn't get into an extended conversation now. Locke would be here in fifteen minutes.

"Why don't we go into Annapolis for dinner tonight?" Ariel suggested as she handed Lydia her cup. "I'll tell you about it then."

Lydia's eyes lit up.

"Great! I can't wait!"

"Can't wait for what?" asked a tentative male voice.

They turned to watch Darryl Fontaine hover in the doorway that connected the library to Ariel's office. Lydia then glanced at her watch and smiled cheerfully at him as she got to her feet.

"I can't wait to get to work!" she improvised. "I want to make sure I've got everything under control! You know what a mess some of the engineers around here can make of things: heads in their diagrams . . . no thought for the rest of us. . . ."

Darryl and Ariel stared at her, thoroughly perplexed. The slightly stoop-shouldered librarian smiled wanly and waved weakly as Lydia made a beeline for the exit.

"I'll call you later," Lydia called out with a conspiratorial wink as she sailed through the doorway.

"Okay," Ariel said, wishing that Darryl would disappear too. She needed her energy for the man who would be stepping into her office any minute now.

Ariel knew, however, that Darryl would not disappear. Since he made a habit of paying no attention to directly spoken rejections, she wasn't really surprised that he wasn't picking up her silently telepathed hope that he'd go back into his own office and leave her alone.

"Mind if I have a cup of coffee?" he asked hopefully.

Sometimes Darryl reminded her of a lonely puppy hoping for a handout. He certainly got a lot of mileage out of that approach, she had to admit.

"Help yourself, Darryl," Ariel replied, reaching for a report. Maybe if she started working, he'd take the hint.

He didn't. Instead he meandered over to her desk and leaned solicitously over her shoulder to see what she was doing.

"Ummm," he began awkwardly, sipping his coffee as if stalling for time. "I, uh . . ."

She ignored him and flipped a page, scanning it rapidly using her index finger as a speed-reading guide.

"I'm sorry I couldn't get back yesterday," he practically stammered.

Ariel looked up at him, her face as blank as her mind. Why in the world was he apologizing?

His brow creased in anxiety as he hovered.

"About lunch yesterday . . ." he added, clearly disappointed that he had to explain.

Lunch. Ariel frowned. Then it came back to her. She could remember his having said something vague about their going to lunch together as soon as he got back from his trip. Yesterday had been his first day back. Or it was supposed to have been.

"Oh, that's no problem," she said lightly, giving him a reassuring smile.

Ariel hoped that she didn't sound too relieved. She decided she probably hadn't when she saw the anxious look on Darryl's face dissolve into a bright smile.

"I was held up at the last minute Sunday night. Mother had an unexpected relapse just as I was getting into the car," he explained quickly, slipping into the chair by her desk, the same one Lydia had just vacated.

"Oh, I'm sorry, Darryl. I hope she's better. . . ."

Ariel put aside the report and gave him her full attention. Darryl was close to his poor, frail mother. He tried to visit her as often as his vacation schedule allowed. Ariel looked at him sympathetically.

He waved a hand helplessly.

"She's about the same as she was when I arrived last week."

He sounded so despondent that Ariel leaned toward him and put her hand on his arm in a gesture of comfort.

"I really am sorry, Darryl," she murmured kindly.

She knew that the poor man was just about at his wits' end. Darryl never discussed his personal problems with any of the other employees, but he had confided in Ariel on several occasions. Her warm heart and nearly constant availability because of the proximity of their offices had given him the courage to talk to her about it. Unfortunately for Ariel, that wasn't the only thing he had mustered up the courage to try.

"Well . . . there's not much to be done about it, I guess," he said tiredly, trying to terminate an obviously painful discussion.

He looked up at her hopefully.

"But since I couldn't meet you for lunch yesterday, perhaps we could, er, do it today," he suggested cautiously.

Ariel's face froze midway between the expression of sympathy that she had been wearing and the expression of dismay that she was trying her darnedest to swallow before it showed.

Oh, dear, we're back to that, she thought.

She really tried not to encourage him, but he soaked up the slightest display of kindness like a man dying of thirst in the desert. Recently she had found herself becoming increasingly uncomfortable with poor Darryl. The relationship that he was so tentatively, if perseveringly, trying to nurture with her was most definitely not the one she wished to have with him!

Ariel had just opened her mouth, desperately hoping that by the time she had to utter a sound, something intelligent—hopefully a good reason for turning him down—would have occurred to her.

As it turned out she had nothing to worry about.

"Do what today?" interrupted a masculine voice from the door.

Poor Darryl was so startled that he nearly spilled the remains of his coffee over Ariel's desk. Ariel jerked back her hand to avoid being scalded. Since there wasn't enough coffee to spill over, neither she nor her desk ended up unexpectedly christened.

Locke's eyebrows lowered slightly as the movement caught his attention. What in the devil was she doing touching him like that? he wondered, taking a closer look at the man seated next to her.

Darryl managed to get his wobbling cup under control, and he and Ariel glanced in the direction from which the voice had come. Locke, however, was no longer there. He was striding purposefully toward the two people staring at him wide-eyed.

Ariel's mouth snapped closed first. It must be nine o'clock, she decided fatalistically. The day had gone from awkward to bad and looked like it was heading downhill at breakneck speed, she thought, watching in surprised fascination as the two men sized each other up.

That is, one of them was sizing up the other. While Adam was giving poor Darryl the once-over, Darryl was trying to figure out why this tall stranger was acting as though he had every right to stride into Ariel's office and behave as if he were in charge.

Darryl rose awkwardly to his feet, wondering who this man was and how to ask without sounding uninformed.

Locke put out his hand.

"Adam Locke," he introduced himself in a firm, no-nonsense way.

Darryl switched his coffee to his left hand and shook hands.

"Darryl Fontaine," he said, reciprocating.

Locke shot a narrow-eyed look at Ariel, who was still seated at her desk and waiting for the next shoe to drop.

"We have an appointment at nine, if I remember correctly. Are you ready to start?" he asked, indirectly dismissing Darryl as clearly as if he had physically ushered him to the door.

"Yes," she said coolly.

The sooner I get this over with, the better, she mentally added.

"Ummm . . . I'll see you later," Darryl said, backing around the desk and heading toward the connecting door to his office in the library. "Uh . . . I'll talk to you later, Ariel. . . ."

Ariel smiled her warmest smile at him. She hated to see anyone bullied! She was willing to bet that Adam Locke had never had an insecure day in his life! How dare he treat Darryl so insensitively!

Never mind, Darryl, she telegraphed as she waved her fingers good-bye when he reached the door. *I'll make it up to you! Don't you pay any attention to this gorilla!*

"Would twelve-thirty be all right, Darryl?" she asked in her most gentle voice.

"Twelve-thirty would be just great, Ariel," Darryl responded enthusiastically. "See you then. Nice meeting you, Mr. Locke!" he added politely, closing the door behind him as he practically tripped out of her office.

Locke frowned and watched the departure of the man in the plaid sport jacket. He now seemed overjoyed. From the thin slices of conversation that he'd overheard since arriving, Locke concluded that they would be "doing it today" at "twelve-thirty." He wondered if "it" was some form of work. Not too likely. Locke never recalled seeing a man so thrilled at the prospect of doing some work, even if it involved a pretty woman like Ariel.

He decided that his first instinct had probably been correct. They'd been arranging a date. And he, like an idiot, had stood by while they concluded their plans!

"I'm ready whenever you are, Mr. Locke," Ariel pointed out, wondering why he was still standing in the middle of her office with a scowl on his face.

"Adam," he growled.

She stared at him in surprise. My, he was touchy first thing in the morning, she thought. Maybe he'd gotten out of the wrong side of the bed.

He shot her an unreadable look, then strolled over toward her coffee machine, temporarily ignoring her prod to get on with it.

"Is this free for your guests or should I put some money somewhere?" he inquired coolly as he poured himself a cup and looked around her office.

"No charge," she replied stiffly. "Help yourself."

She could have kicked herself for the faintly sarcastic edge to that last, needless comment. But there was something extremely annoying about seeing Adam helping himself to her coffee. Sharing your food and drink with someone was one of the most ancient forms of communicating friendship, hospitality, welcome, or, at the very least, a truce in any hostilities.

Ariel did not want any form of communication at all. Least of all friendly.

She pushed the report she had been looking at earlier into her metal "out" box and searched for a pad of paper and something to take notes with. Why in the devil was the man strolling around her office like a leisurely tourist, anyhow, she fumed. Her fingers closed over a slender ballpoint pen. She stabbed it into working position and looked at Locke expectantly.

Adam knew he was stalling for time, but he slowly perused her office, anyway. He needed a minute to decide what to do with the meeting now, in light of the unexpected turn of events when he had arrived. Besides, you could learn a lot about a person by looking over their office, he concluded mentally.

Her office, like the woman who worked in it, was elegantly arranged. It was also completely professional. The bookcases that lined the walls were filled with references needed by a linguist translating technical treatises in several languages.

She had a large desk, which was laden with papers and reports, but everything appeared to be carefully organized and neatly filed. There was no mess or clutter here. Neither was there anything of a personal nature, he realized. That was what had been bothering him since yesterday when

50

he had first seen her office, he realized with a sudden spurt of insight.

Most people put pictures of their family on their desks, some art or decoration on a wall, even a knickknack on a shelf somewhere to relieve the tedium of the office environment. It made it more personal. There was something of themselves there. It made the place you spent half of your waking hours in a little more your own.

He walked over to her desk. There was a single bud vase with a lone red carnation in it. A gift from the stumbling wonder next door, perhaps? He eyed the disreputable flower in annoyance.

The minute he had seen Ariel leaning tenderly toward that plaid-coated bozo, his breakfast had curdled in his stomach. In all these months he'd never pictured her with another man.

Intellectually, of course, it had occurred to him that she might be dating, might even be . . . involved, with someone. But somehow it hadn't been real before. Now it was real. There was at least one flesh-and-blood man, however pale that blood might be, who seemed to play some role in her life.

Much to his surprise, Locke found he didn't like it. He didn't like it one bit.

"Cancel it," he said firmly.

Ariel looked at him blankly.

"Cancel what?"

She hadn't the foggiest idea what he was talking about.

"Your luncheon date with Fountain," he explained curtly.

"Fontaine," she corrected automatically, too flabbergasted at the unorthodox demand to add anything else at first. That problem didn't last too long, however.

"Don't be ridiculous. Why on earth should I?" she flashed at him.

"Don't get huffy," he ordered calmly, sitting down in the chair her two previous visitors had so generously warmed for him.

Ariel felt herself puff up in annoyance.

"I'm not being the least bit huffy!" she snapped. "I simply fail to see what business it is of yours with whom I should have lunch today!"

She glared at him through the soft coral haze of her glasses, seeing red. The lazy grin spreading across his features merely served to further inflame her.

"Normally it's none of my business whatsoever," he replied agreeably, although there was a hard quality in his gaze that seemed at odds with his tone.

"Well, then, I fail to see—" she began, sputtering.

"In this case it's a matter of business coming first," he interjected.

"Business!" she exclaimed, disbelief written all over her face.

He took a swallow of the coffee.

"I need a lot of your time for the next couple of weeks, maybe more," he explained, ignoring her outburst.

"Well, that's too bad, Mr. Locke—"

"Adam," he said, correcting her and frowning again at her persistent refusal to use his first name.

She disregarded his correction.

"Perhaps you don't grant your employees any personal time for such luxuries as eating lunch," she sailed on, "but fortunately for me, Dr. Norris is more tolerant of such human frailties."

Ariel couldn't believe how angry she'd become. The man hadn't been in her office for more than ten minutes and she was already set to skin him alive.

Her heated delivery was nearly eclipsed by the fires of anger burning in her eyes. Her ire didn't put off Locke in the least. On the contrary, it drew him like a moth to the flame. He shifted his position in the chair and finished his coffee.

"Don't forget," he said, dropping the cup into a nearby wastebasket. "Dr. Norris has given me top billing for the next month here. Any resource I need I can have. As soon as I want it."

Their eyes locked.

"You need me?" she asked, forcing the words through unwilling lips.

Slowly he nodded his head.

He leaned back, stretching out his legs and crossing them casually at the ankles.

"And I'm tolerant of lots of human frailties," he added softly.

Ariel felt the heat rush to her cheeks.

Something invisible flowed between them. Electricity. The heat of anger. A struggle of wills. A remembrance of things past . . .

Ariel felt as if he were staring straight into her, seeing the essence of her.

"You are?" she asked weakly, barely conscious that she had spoken the words aloud.

"Oh, yes. Very tolerant."

His eyes narrowed slightly.

"But I'm also a businessman, and I'll need most of your time for a couple of weeks to get this contract completed by the deadline."

And besides, he'd be damned if he'd share her time with anyone else after the trouble he'd gone to in order to be here!

"I'll keep track of the overtime you put in, and when we're finished, you're more than welcome to take all the compensatory time you've accrued," he suggested, a rather charming grin taking shape on his face.

"I'm a professional," Ariel pointed out. "Athena's professional staff don't take comp time. We merely work overtime," she tacked on in mildly acid tones.

"Well, I'll be happy to recommend an exception in this case," he offered. "And I guarantee that you won't be forced to go hungry."

He certainly seemed pleased at the prospect of keeping her nose to the grindstone night and day, Ariel thought, thoroughly put out and wondering how she could wriggle out of this trap.

"How much have you been told about the project?" he asked.

"Just that you're in charge of it and I'm to give you any assistance you require."

"Well, then, let me fill you in on the details," he said, proceeding to do so at a brisk pace.

Ariel took a few notes as he outlined the project's scope and purpose, but mostly she listened. A well-known land developer from northern Virginia was paying them to design a variety of energy-efficient, moderately priced, single-family homes, which could be built partially or entirely underground. The houses were to be aesthetically pleasing, with the maximum range of architectural details possible, so that each could be customized . . . one of a kind as far as the exterior was concerned. The developer intended to use the plans to design planned communities in various sections of the country where hilly terrain had left the area untouched by local urban sprawl.

"And I want you to review some European publications for us, translating or summarizing everything that pertains to the type of housing stock. I've already arranged to have some materials sent to you," he explained. "And I've got access to more on my terminal."

His computer terminal? She started drawing tight little circles along the edge of her notes. She had the sinking feeling that for her to use his terminal, she'd have to be in his office.

"Fine," she said, lying through her teeth in her most businesslike voice. "When will you need the translations?"

"As soon as possible, but just keep the material coming until we run out of time. There's quite a bit. I doubt that you can plow through it all in three weeks. . . ."

"I'll do my best," Ariel replied, feeling distinctly challenged to rise to the occasion and prove him wrong since he was so clearly pleased with his generosity in giving her no specific deadlines to meet. She'd finish the stuff in lightning speed!

Another thought hit her at that point. As soon as she'd finished his translations, she wouldn't have to see him again! What a delightful prospect!

Locke's gaze drifted over her desk, noting the cream-colored ceramic mug nestled between her incoming mailbox and her desk calendar. He rose to his feet and looked at her quizzically.

"Tell me," he said abruptly. "Why do you drink out of a Styrofoam cup when you've got a mug on your desk?"

Ariel looked at him in surprise.

"Well, I don't want to ruin it."

"Ruin it!" He laughed, eyeing her in amazement. "But that's what it was made for. Presumably that's why you bought it," he pointed out.

"That has nothing to do with it," she grumbled defensively. "I like it the way it is, as beautiful as the day I got it," she added before getting up and heading for her door. She put her hand on the doorknob. "Besides, why are we discussing my mug, anyway?"

He grinned at her disarmingly as he walked across the office at an unhurried pace.

"Just making conversation," he said innocently.

Ariel was tempted to tap her toe in annoyance. Then she remembered her vow. Work as fast as you can and kiss Mr. Locke's project good-bye as soon as possible. Her look of suspicion was transformed into a sweet smile.

Locke stepped a foot away from her and checked his watch. When he looked up and caught the expression on her face, he frowned. What did that smile mean? She'd been annoyed with him all morning. He had the feeling that that smile meant trouble.

"I've got to be going," he said sarcastically, giving a significant look toward her hand on the now ready and open door. "Be at my office at twelve o'clock today. We'll go over the computer access I referred to."

He was back to all business, no play in the flick of an eyelash.

"Today!" Ariel protested.

"Yes. Today."

"But I have an engagement—"

"I know all about that," he said dismissingly. "As I told you, break it," he ordered curtly.

With that felicitous command echoing in her ears he walked out of her office.

"Break it, he says," she fumed, returning to her desk.

She sat down and began angrily tapping the point of her pen against the notepad.

"I'd like to break something, all right, but my luncheon date with Darryl isn't it!"

CHAPTER FOUR

Darryl took the news stoically.

"Oh, that's all right, Ariel," he said reasurringly. "We can do it tomorrow."

Great! Just what I need . . . another reason not to get out of bed tomorrow, she thought wryly. Well, sooner or later she knew she'd have to have lunch with the man, so Ariel didn't waste any time feeling guilty about canceling. The delay wouldn't really hurt Darryl.

It was just so infuriating to be told to break it by that arrogant so-and-so! She was still doing a slow burn on that subject when she showed up at Locke's office at noon.

Their meeting went smoothly enough, considering that one of them was as mad as a wet hen and the other didn't seem to be the least bit perturbed about it.

". . . and if you want to ask the computer to display both indices at once," he explained, leaning over her shoulder to press a key on her right, "you just do this."

The indices under discussion instantly appeared on the split-screen format now displayed by the monitor.

"I see," she said, jotting down the sequence of instructions so that she could use the computer herself later.

Later? What a horrifying thought!

"Why do you look do disgusted?" he asked in surprise, moving around to her side and peering into her eyes. "You *have* used a computer before, haven't you?" he asked suspiciously.

"Of course I have!" she snapped. "Now, is that all?"

He straightened up and shook his head.

"My, my . . . you *are* testy today." He leaned against the wall behind the computer terminal. "I'd better feed you some lunch before you start to foam at the mouth."

Ariel gave him an annoyed look, but the word *food* had been heard by her anxious stomach. Her stomach, having absolutely no sense of discrimination about whose food it took, growled.

Locke grinned triumphantly.

"You see. I knew you needed to be fed."

She was about to say that she didn't care to eat his food no matter what mistaken impression he had formed, when a knock at the door interrupted them.

"Excuse me," he said with a slight bow of his head.

A few moments later a caterer from the kitchen was wheeling in a tray of sandwiches and a pot of coffee. After ushering out the room service, Locke sat down on the sofa and selected a sandwich from the platter, which had been placed on the coffee table.

"Come on, Ariel," he coaxed. "You work too hard. Remember, all work and no play . . ." He trailed off with an eloquent shrug before taking a healthy bite.

All work and no play! Well, if that didn't take the cake!

"If you will recall, Mr. Locke, it wasn't my idea to work through my lunch hour," she pointed out sweetly.

"Adam," he reminded her, looking her straight in the eyes and daring her to call him Mr. Locke again.

Ariel cleared her throat and tried to look away from the tray of food. It certainly looked good, she admitted reluctantly. She felt her stomach pleading for a little taste. Well, maybe just one little bite wouldn't hurt. She got up rather slowly and wandered casually over to the coffee table, sitting down primly on the edge of one of the overstuffed chairs.

"Want some coffee?" he asked encouragingly as he poured himself a cup.

"Please," she replied politely as she picked up a tasty-looking ham on rye.

As she reached for the coffee she told herself that she wasn't being in the least bit friendly by taking food from him. Just in case he might misinterpret the situation, however, she decided to frown through every bite. Then he wouldn't think that her breaking bread with him indicated a willingness to be friends.

Of course, he would be no more interested in forming a friendship than she was, she reminded herself sternly.

After they had finished eating Ariel gathered her notes and marched back to her office, burying herself in work for the remainder of the day. By the time she escaped to her car to drive into Annapolis for dinner with Lydia, she was ready for a break.

"So tell me," Lydia urged, leaning forward conspiratorially over her dinner. "What's going on?"

In between bites of salad and steak Ariel told Lydia what she wanted to know.

"But that's fascinating," said Lydia, wide-eyed. "How romantic!"

"It wasn't the least bit romantic," Ariel grumbled, pushing her plate away. "A female friend of his dashed into his house and headed straight up the stairs looking for him."

"So?"

"So it was two in the morning!" Ariel exploded.

"Well . . ." Lydia waved an arm, as if to say that there might be a very simple explanation for that.

"She went into the bedroom," Ariel clarified with a warning voice.

"Well, he is a bachelor, Ariel. . . ." Lydia's mind was churning, but for the life of her, she couldn't come up with an innocent explanation for that. Her protest in his defense had sounded rather weak, even to Lydia.

"So . . . I left before he could come back upstairs with the wine," Ariel concluded in disgust.

She put her fingers to her temple. Recalling how stewed

she'd been by then, after an evening of carousing with him, brought back vivid memories of the hangover that had greeted her the next day.

Lydia put down her fork and folded her napkin.

"But, Ariel," she argued as the waiter cleared away the plates, "he's one heck of a good-looking man. You don't imagine that he's been living the life of a monk, do you?"

The idea of his well-built body in the robes of a monk was pretty ridiculous and almost made Ariel smile.

"Of course not!" she snapped. Why was she so touchy about this, anyway?

"Well, don't overreact to a *faux pas* that he had no control over," Lydia counseled.

Ariel stared at her friend in disbelief.

"What are you saying?" she asked in astonishment.

Lydia's eyes narrowed, and she drummed her fingers on the table.

"If you had enough of a yen for the man to go home with him that night, why don't you take this opportunity to get acquainted with him?" She ignored Ariel's openmouthed speechlessness and plowed on ruthlessly. "After all, you have your own little fortress to go to. The setting is work, not a cocktail party. There are lots of people around during the day. You should feel perfectly safe. What could happen? Why don't you see if you can figure out why you chose Adam Locke to be your target for seduction that night?"

Ariel closed her mouth and suddenly felt very weary. They put their money on the small tray left by the waiter and placed a tip on the table.

"I know why I chose him," she said dispiritedly. "That was to have been . . ."

Lydia gave Ariel a comforting look as they put on their jackets.

"I know that was to have been a special night for you," she said sympathetically. "But I don't think it was just because of that. No matter how hurt you were that Andrew had let you down, I just don't think you'd have gone with Locke that night if there hadn't been more to it.''

Mention of Andrew and his abandonment was not helping Ariel's self-esteem any. She pressed her lips together and tried to put it out of her mind.

The last thing Lydia said to her before they went their separate ways was equally disturbing.

"You know what I think?" Lydia asked provocatively.

"What?"

"I think that you're hiding behind Andrew's betrayal and your belief that everything that happened that night with Locke was the result of your unhappiness about his marriage. I can see you flirting with a good-looking man because you were depressed over the end of your engagement. I can see you trying your talents as a seductress to boost your ego a little, to prove something to yourself. But, quite frankly, I cannot see you going home with him to boot, unless at some point during that evening you forgot why you had tried to attract him and just got really interested in the man.''

Lydia added softly. "Just ask yourself this, Ariel: Of all the attractive men at the party that night, why did you pick Adam Locke to work your wiles on?''

Ariel remained silent, and Lydia gave her perplexed friend a warm hug.

"Good luck, kid,'' she said with a grin.

"Bye, Lydia.''

All the way home Ariel told herself that Lydia's inferences were all wrong. What she had done that evening with Locke had nothing to do with him as a man, and everything to do with the fact that she had been depressed and despondent and wanting to prove that she was an attractive woman.

It had nothing to do with Adam Locke's good looks. Nor his charm. Nor his amusing conversation. Nor the way he looked straight at her when she talked, making her quiver.

She jammed her key into the lock and slammed the door shut after she got inside.

It had nothing whatsoever to do with that, she told herself.
Nothing whatsoever.

On Wednesday a good-looking, six-foot blond, who looked
like he could bench-press three hundred pounds without even
breathing hard, delivered Ariel's mail.

He glanced down at her name on the top envelope in his
hand.

"Good morning, Ariel Radnor," he said with a friendly
grin.

She smiled back.

"Good morning."

"I'm Jim Reeves," he said easily, dropping some mail into
her "in" tray.

Ariel wondered what happened to the girl who usually
delivered her mail. Jim must have read the question on her
face, because he answered it before she could ask.

"Your mail girl got another job," he said helpfully.

"Oh."

That came as a surprise to Ariel. She didn't recall Carol
ever mentioning that she was looking for another job.

"It probably paid better," he said conversationally, looking over her office with admiration.

"When did you start, Jim?"

"Monday. But it took a couple of days of orientation
before they trusted me enough to turn me loose on my own.
This is my first solo mail run," he offered. "There sure are a
lot of people working here!" he added with mock exhaustion.

Ariel smiled sympathetically.

"And we all get a lot of mail!" she said, thinking that he
was probably better equipped to push the stuff around the
complex than Carol had been.

"Nice meeting you, Ariel."

"Bye."

He certainly had an easygoing charm, Ariel decided as she
watched him saunter out the door. He seemed nice enough.
But he probably had an inflated ego. He struck her as the type

who was accustomed to wrapping ladies around his little finger without overexerting himself in the process.

She smiled in amusement and attacked the stack of work that she'd set aside for the day.

And did she ever work!

When Darryl poked his head in for a friendly coffee break, he wandered out a matter of minutes later, having been unsuccessful in getting Ariel to put aside her work. She barely looked up when David stopped by to see if she wanted to go to lunch with him. When Locke stopped by in the afternoon, she handed him a sheaf of translations and started thumbing through her dictionary.

"I didn't see you at lunch," he said, standing in front of her desk.

Ariel's eyes were running down a page of the reference book in her hands. *Courge. Courir. Couronne.* There it was. *Couronne . . . géométrie . . . Ouvrage de fortification de forme semi-circulaire . . .* It was difficult to ignore the fact that he was still standing next to her desk, so she gave up the effort to do so. She closed the dictionary abruptly and put it down.

"Lunch," she murmured, swiveling her chair around and searching for another dictionary. "No, I didn't have time," she added vaguely.

She located the volume that she needed and swung back around to her desk with it.

Locke frowned slightly.

"Are you always this much of a workaholic?" he asked, watching her search anew.

Ariel kept her eyes trained on the book, but her concentration had pretty well been destroyed by now.

"No," she sighed in resignation. "I thought you needed this information as soon as possible. Surely you're not complaining that I'm working too hard!"

Locke saw the half smile playing on her lips, and for the life of him he couldn't think of anything effective to say to that. He wasn't particularly pleased about being caught in his own trap like this. He'd dumped the work on her to give them an opportunity to talk, to see each other a few times. It was extremely disconcerting that she was using it to keep them apart!

"No," he admitted dryly. "I guess I'd better not set any precedents like that." He turned to go, adding, "Thanks, Ariel."

She couldn't resist looking at him as he walked out, wondering if it was just her imagination or if he had been wanting to stay and talk for a while. She stared vacantly at her closing door. What would he have wanted to talk about? Surely nothing but work . . .

The memory of the night they had first met seeped back into her awareness, against her more rational nature's entreaties for it to stay put in the deep recesses of her mind. She remembered talking to him. They had laughed and teased and told each other interesting, if outrageously tall, stories. . . . For a brief moment Ariel regretted not encouraging him to stay and talk for a while. A few minutes surely would have been harmless enough. After all, they were in her office . . . they were working together, for heaven's sake! People had friendly little conversations with each other all the time. Maybe she should have . . .

She looked out her window at the opposite end of the room from her door. She could see him walking briskly across the square, then disappearing into the Athena Inn.

Ariel shook her head slightly. What kind of thinking was that? She went back to the translation and worked steadily until seven-thirty that night.

The nightmare plagued her again. On Thursday morning it roused her from sleep, leaving her sweat-soaked and exhausted. Determined to shake it off and regain some control for the day ahead, she went to the small gymnasium Dr. Norris had set up in a neighboring cottage for use by the staff. She knew that the exercise would help, and it always honed her concentration to a fine edge.

Thursday went more or less as Wednesday had, except that

Locke called her twice to talk on the telephone as well as stopping by her office once in the afternoon. Maybe she should try talking to him a little, she thought as he left. After all, he wasn't putting the make on her, and some of her initial embarrassment had definitely worn off since his arrival. How long could she sustain feeling that humiliated in his presence, anyway?

But something else happened on Thursday. Jim Reeves stopped in to try to strike up a conversation in between his twice-daily mail drops. He was turning out to be as friendly as Darryl. But, unlike Darryl, Jim Reeves clearly knew his way around women. Ariel couldn't put her finger on the reason why, but somehow, something bothered her about Jim. There was something about the way he smiled so charmingly at her, as if he were trying to manipulate her into a friendship.

Deciding that her lack of sleep and turmoil over whether to have a more normal relationship with Locke was warping her feeble mind, Ariel firmly tried to think of nothing but the work she was doing.

But the nightmare wouldn't go away. It came back again Thursday night. Ariel sat amid her rumpled bedclothes in the dark, early hours of Friday morning telling herself that she could get through this if she could just hang on and grit her teeth hard enough. She sincerely hoped that she was right. Nothing seemed to be getting any better. Since Adam Locke had showed up, she felt as if her life had begun to shred at the edges.

"Is something the matter?" asked David Carrollton later that night.

He bent his head to look with concern at the young woman gyrating gracefully in front of him to the beat of the music.

It was a good thing that they weren't dancing in each other's arms, or he would have felt her lose the beat for a moment, Ariel thought with a grimace.

"No. I'm just getting tired, I guess. I'm sorry, David."

She kept moving to the music as she spoke, and the apologetic wave of her hand probably looked like part of the dance to any interested bystanders. Not that there were any bystanders or that they could have seen through the wildly undulating crush of bodies filling the center of the ballroom. The dance floor was very crowded now, and David had led her to the center of it.

"Tired already?" he exclaimed in genuine surprise. "I've always thought of you as a girl with endless resources and full of energy! Been burning your candles at both ends, Ariel?" he teased.

David gave her a friendly, suggestive leer in spite of the fact that he really was becoming a little concerned about her. There was the suggestion of shadows under her eyes, and he thought she looked a little washed-out.

Ariel tried to laugh it off. The music helped to mask the forced sound of her laughter, fortunately.

"Me?" she asked as if mildly shocked at the suggestion. "The girl who rises at dawn and goes to sleep when the sun goes down? You've got to be kidding!"

He grinned at her affectionately.

"All right! All right! So it's not your candle ends! How about your meals? Been forgetting to eat?" he persevered helpfully.

Ariel opened her mouth to deny it but thought better of it just in the nick of time. It was true in a way. She'd certainly lacked an appetite all week, ever since Monday morning's breakfast meeting, to be precise. Friday had been an exceptionally busy day too. She'd skipped lunch again in order to wrap everything up.

Besides, if she let him believe that it was just a case of low blood sugar or hunger pains, maybe he'd stop asking questions. After all, David knew her well enough to have sensed that she was upset, and he was smart enough to ferret out the cause as well.

She slapped her forehead gently with the palm of one hand.

"That must be it! I can't remember having anything since . . . breakfast, I guess. . . ."

David raised his eyes heavenward and lifted his palms in supplication, hips still swinging to the beat.

"Lord help you, woman! How have you survived all these years without a keeper?"

"Just lucky, I guess," she murmured as the music ended and he led her from the dance floor in the direction of the buffet.

"Dr. Norris certainly knows how to entertain," David observed admiringly as he piled some shrimp and dip onto his plate.

"I thought that Mrs. Norris took care of the catering at the parties here," Ariel countered, although she honestly wasn't certain which of the Norrises had actually arranged tonight's festivities. Considering Dr. Norris's boundless enthusiasm, it was conceivable that he had for once planned the buffet himself.

Ariel put a few canapés and hors d'oeuvres on her plate for show.

"Exactly!" rejoined David with a smug grin as he lightly touched her elbow and steered her toward the far end of the table where there were some vacant seats at the moment. "He chose a wife who could take care of little things like this. He delegates well, don't you think?"

"Little things like this?" Ariel's eyebrows arched in exasperation. "There must be a hundred and fifty people here! And I'll bet she didn't see any fine print in their marriage contract saying that she'd have to arrange these little soirees, either!"

David polished off a few shrimp as she voiced her feelings on the subject, well entertained at having gotten such a rise out of her.

"Well, I, for one, think it's a nice gesture for the boss to hold a party for us all every once in a while." He looked up at her mischievously. "Say, do you know your eyes start to sparkle when you're irritated?" he teased.

The sparkle became more pronounced.

"They sure do," drawled Jim Reeves as he sauntered up to them, beer in hand.

"Hi, Jim."

"Reeves."

The mail carrier grinned at them and took a healthy swallow from his glass. Just then Darryl spotted them and waded carefully through the crowded buffet to Ariel's side.

Just as Fontaine had reached Ariel, Adam Locke, accompanied by Dr. Norris, entered the ballroom.

"So, anytime you want to have Carrollton design that computer model for the ventilation system, just ask him. I've taken him off the other project for the next two weeks. He'll have the time," Dr. Norris was saying. "Well, so much for work! Now it's time for a little relaxation!"

Locke looked over the crowd, and his gaze stopped as it fell upon the cozy little tête-à-tête for four at the far end of the buffet.

"If you'll excuse me," Locke murmured, looking steadily at the auburn-haired woman in the champagne-colored cocktail dress, who was surrounded by attentively admiring males.

Norris followed the line of vision of his companion and smiled benevolently.

"Of course. Ariel's a much more entertaining companion than I am," he remarked with a chuckle. "And there's Margaret!" he exclaimed, brightening as he caught sight of his wife.

He turned away, still chuckling at the expression on Locke's face. The man looked distinctly annoyed at the prospect of having to wait in line for Ariel's favors. Somehow he couldn't see Adam as the waiting-in-line type. That was all to the good, as far as Dr. Norris was concerned. Ariel always had had a tendency to get involved with the waiting-in-line variety of male. And it certainly had brought her nothing but heartache, he recalled sadly. Well, good luck, Locke! he added, welcoming his wife and turning to his other employees.

Ariel was just beginning to wonder which fate would be

worse . . . dancing with the swaggering, overconfident Reeves or the stumbling, self-effacing Darryl. She was certain from the way that Jim was grinning and how Darryl was hovering that they were both preparing to ask her to dance.

She turned to put her plate on the table, wishing that she had stayed home tonight, when they both put the question to her at the same time.

A shadow fell over her, and she had a strange feeling she knew whose it was.

"Sorry, gentlemen. Ariel promised me a dance earlier," said Adam Locke in the smooth-styled delivery of one who fully expects compliance.

Reeves shrugged good-naturedly and muttered something congenial about his loss being Locke's gain. Darryl cleared his throat, blushing slightly as he mumbled something to the effect that Ariel might dance with him later.

Ariel turned to face him and found Locke standing there, his hand outstretched.

"May I have this dance?" he asked softly.

His voice was firm enough, but Ariel thought she saw a flicker of uncertainty in the recesses of those slate-blue eyes. It seemed to melt some of her own ambivalence about him, oddly enough.

She smiled up at him and put her hand in his.

"It would be my pleasure," she replied, rising to follow him to the dance floor, forcing the rather tenuous smile to keep its place on her face until they were surrounded with people.

Dr. Norris and his wife had beat them there, and with the Norrises' arrival on the dance floor, the band had eased into a medley of slow ballads.

"My favorite kind of music," Locke murmured with a half-smile as he turned Ariel gently into his arms.

He didn't hold her close at first, using only the light pressure of his arm around her waist to guide her.

"You know," he said quietly, "You're still the best partner I've ever danced with."

Ariel looked up warily at him. She found no humor, no teasing, no superficial bantering gleam in his eyes. He meant it. His honesty helped ease her ambivalence about dancing with him. Maybe she could get reacquainted with the man. Only this time it would be in a normal way—talking together in the real world, not in the hazy wonder of her self-created fantasy. . . .

"You said that to me once before," she reminded him, taking her nerve in hand and trying to relax.

"I meant it then too."

They were dancing in a small circle in one corner of the crowded floor. The lights were dimmed and the press of other couples were gradually pushing them closer together.

"Oh, hell," he muttered, pulling her snugly into his arms. "Come here."

Ariel felt one last moment of panic, but his arms were reassuring and felt so good holding her close again. Gradually she relaxed against him. Just as she had before. It was like coming home to an old friend, and it made no more sense to her this time than it had the last.

But life doesn't always make sense, she told herself as she closed her eyes and rested her head against his. The softly intoxicating scent of his after-shave was clean and fresh. There was something intimate about it too. She hadn't been aware of it before, not until he pulled her close.

They moved as one in slow, smooth steps, blending with each other with each sweet lilt of the melody. It was good to be with him again, she admitted, in spite of everything that had happened. It brought it all back to her so vividly. She'd never met anyone with whom she'd felt such instant rapport—on the dance floor or off. It was wonderful and frightening at the same time.

Of course, forewarned is forearmed, she reminded herself. *I'll know when I'm getting in over my head this time. I can walk away before I do anything foolish. . . .*

"I wasn't sure you'd dance with me," he said softly, his lips brushing her ear gently as he spoke.

"Really?" she replied in a husky whisper.

"Especially after I climbed out on a limb and said you'd already promised me a dance," he elaborated, grinning ruefully.

Ariel's lips curved in genuine amusement for the first time that evening.

"Then why did you take the chance?" she asked curiously.

He tightened his hold on her right hand and pulled it in close to his chest.

"Because for six months I've wanted to dance with you, and I wasn't about to stand by and watch three other men have that pleasure first," he said with a growl. The hardness turned to brief laughter. "And I couldn't think of another reason on the spur of the moment that would allow me to steal you from under their eager noses."

"Oh," she said faintly.

She looked at him and lost herself in his blue-eyed gaze. The warmth she saw sent a welcome stroke of happiness straight to her heart. This is risky, a small voice said from the deep recesses of her mind. She ignored it and rested her cheek against his jaw. Surely she could take this one small risk. Dancing with him couldn't hurt. . . .

"I've told you why I asked. Now tell me why you accepted," he asked quietly. "You haven't been exactly eager to spend any time with me that I could notice," he pointed out reluctantly.

Ariel took a breath and stared vacantly into the crowd.

"I've been telling myself all week that I . . . should relax and take this more in stride," she admitted cautiously. "Besides," she added with a slight smile, "you saved me from a fate worse than death."

He looked confused and turned to get a clearer view of her face.

"How did I do that?" he asked.

"I wasn't exactly dying to be the first woman here to dance simultaneously with two men," she explained.

He chuckled and tucked her head back against his.

"Anytime you need me I'm at your service," he said, laughter in his voice.

As it turned out, Ariel ended up taking more than one risk. Several dances later she was still enjoying it every bit as much as she had the first time. When the band finally started playing a fast tune, she couldn't help feeling a stab of disappointment.

"How about giving me a tour of the terrace," Locke suggested, guiding her with a light touch at her elbow through the ballroom to the terrace door.

Ariel could see Darryl searching the room, and she had no doubt that she was the target. Under the circumstances, she told herself reasonably, why not escape with Adam Locke for a few more minutes? Just a few more minutes wouldn't hurt. Then she'd go home.

"All right," she said, though by now it was hardly necessary.

They walked past a small cluster of people gathered close to the terrace entrance to the ballroom. In the stillness of the night people were talking quietly, smoking, and sipping drinks.

The terrace was dotted with small love seats sheltered by potted shrubs and miniature trees. Here and there a table for two or three could be found, each with a glowing candle in a dark red or burnt-orange bottle. Several couples had found secluded spots to continue their own conversations with greater privacy.

Locke and Ariel walked to the edge of the terrace, stopping at the low brick wall that rimmed it, gazing out across the nearby cliff and down into the river below.

At night it was difficult to see. The river was not well lit. There were no wharves or yacht clubs along this particular stretch of the Severn. Only two tiny, flickering lights signaled the presence of a sailboat anchored not too far from the bank. The full moon and stars gave a silvery cast to the water. It looked like a ribbon fashioned out of a dark, twinkling strand of liquid mirror.

"It's beautiful, isn't it?" Ariel asked quietly, staring into the silvery darkness.

"Yes. Quite beautiful," he agreed, turning half toward her, watching the moonlight cast its soft, white light over her hair and skin. "Very beautiful," he murmured, half to himself.

Ariel heard the quiet laughter of the group of people they had passed at the door. It was a relief at the moment to hear it. It reminded her that she wasn't alone with him. There were lots of people around. . . . .

"Have you ever been down there?" he inquired, his eyes running slowly over her profile.

"You mean, on the Severn?" she asked, surprised.

"Yes."

"No," she answered.

"Have you ever been sailing?"

She smiled into the darkness.

"A long time ago. Not here."

He was silent a moment, as if weighing a decision.

"The Severn is one of the best rivers around here to sail on," he said. "And when you think about the sailing opportunities around the Chesapeake Bay, that's quite a compliment."

"It certainly is beautiful to look at from up here," she said agreeably.

Locke watched her enigmatically. He sensed that for some reason her reluctance to have anything to do with him had lessened. He wasn't sure that the explanation she'd offered was the whole truth, but he wasn't about to quibble at this point. He knew that for the first time this week he had an opportunity to get through to her. Now, if he could just do it without arousing her defenses again . . .

"It's even better from down there," he replied. He turned to look at her. "Could I talk you into sailing on it with me tomorrow?" he asked casually.

CHAPTER FIVE

"Sailing?" she echoed faintly as the blood rushed to her feet. "I don't think . . ."

Locke's jaw hardened.

"Don't tell me it's not a good idea," he said, his voice softly warning as he watched her carefully. "What are you afraid of, anyway?" he challenged, pinning her with the intensity behind his question.

She knew he wanted an answer this time. A real answer.

Ariel looked away. She couldn't bring herself to tell him face-to-face what he wanted to know. She needed a little distance from him in order to say it. Even if it was just not having to look directly at him . . . she needed that much.

"It isn't a good idea," she said, ignoring his warning. "And you're right. I am afraid," she added, anguished.

He stood by, waiting for her to collect her thoughts and go on, readying himself to find a weak link in whatever chain-mail defense she might decide to don.

Ariel was overwhelmed. She was sorely tempted to tell him the truth. In doing so, however, she would strip herself of her own defenses. She would be emotionally laid bare to this man for whom she felt a terrifying fascination. How could she protect herself afterward?

She covered her cheeks with her hands, letting her head tilt forward slightly.

Locke saw the gesture and read the pain in it correctly. He sighed and slipped an arm gently around her shoulders.

"Look," he confided awkwardly, "this isn't a hell of a lot easier for me than it is for you."

She looked up at him in confusion, the anguish still filling her eyes.

"It isn't?" she whispered.

He smiled ruefully and looked into the starry night.

"Before I came I knew that you would be here, Ariel," he admitted quietly.

"You knew that I worked for Athena?"

She was genuinely surprised at that.

"Yes, I knew."

"But how . . ." she asked faintly.

He released her shoulders and leaned against the terrace wall before answering.

"The morning after you so precipitously left my house," he replied, "I called the hostess of the party where we'd met. I described you to her, and she told me that you had arrived with Dr. Norris and worked as a translator for the Athena Corporation."

He studied her carefully as she took in what he had said.

"Then," she began slowly, "when you came here, you knew that I would be here. . . ."

"Yes."

"And that first day at breakfast . . . when you saw me . . . you weren't surprised?"

"No."

There was something unnerving about the way he was gazing at her so steadily and giving her bulletlike confirmations as she clarified the implications. She blinked as the next thought occurred to her.

"Were you looking for me that day . . . the first day you were here?" she asked weakly.

Slowly and very deliberately he nodded his head.

"Yes. I was."

"Oh," she whispered, her mouth dry as anxiety began to overwhelm her. She vividly recalled his predatory gaze searching the dining room. For her? A chill ran down her spine.

75

"And I want to see you, Ariel," he added in that low, compelling voice that she found so hard to resist. "I'd like to spend some time with you while I'm here."

She turned away and looked down at the river.

Tonight had been a big, big mistake, she decided, rather belatedly. She never should have come. She shouldn't have dressed like she had. She shouldn't have danced with him. And above all, she should never have risked coming out onto the terrace with him. The temptation was too great. . . .

"No," she managed to say.

He reached for her hands, which were clenched together in front of her. Gently he warmed them with his own.

"Why, Ariel?" he asked, infusing the question with a steely imperative that she could not ignore.

"Because . . . you do something to me," she whispered unsteadily. "I never felt like that before . . . never. That night was like nothing I've even dreamed before."

The words were practically choking her. They came straight from her heart, flowing through the thin crack in her defenses. For a brief moment her resolve to hide the truth had been drowned by her need to let him know.

His hands had been frozen at first. As her words sank in, however, he tightened his grip.

"It started all wrong," she went on, unsteadily. "Dr. Norris had left. There I was in that costume with a room full of virtual strangers. I wanted to prove something to myself. . . ."

Her voice dwindled into nothingness.

"Why?" he asked, still surprised that she had been willing to be so honest with him. Maybe there was hope yet.

She sighed. Her sholders sagged a little, and she pulled her hands free of his.

"That night should have been my wedding night," she said clearly.

Locke looked at her in stunned silence. *That* he had not expected. When he recovered from the revelation, he realized that it still hurt her to talk about it. He was torn between the

desire to comfort her and anger that she had been engaged
. . . and a very unique kind of anger that she might have been
using him to get even with another man.

"What happened?" he asked coolly.

"Andrew, my fiancé, met someone else. He called off our
engagement about two and a half months before the wedding."

Locke did some quick mental calculations.

"He broke your engagement around the first of the year,
then?" he mused aloud.

She nodded.

"New Year's Eve, to be exact," she said, remembering
the humiliating scene in excruciating, emotional detail. Her
shock . . . her parents' suffering for her . . . her friends'
pity . . .

"You never suspected that something was wrong?" he
inquired cautiously. His undercurrent of sympathy acted as a
welcome balm to her wounded pride.

"No," she replied with a self-deprecating grimace. "That
was the worst part. I'd known Andrew since I was a teenager.
We practically grew up together. We met in high school. We
dated in college. We wrote to each other and saw each other
on vacations when I was studying in Europe and he was in
graduate school on the West Coast."

She still couldn't understand what had happened to them.
But she had to admit that with each passing month it bothered
her less and less that she didn't. The pain of that experience
was, for the most part, anyway, definitely behind her.

"You'd known each other quite a long time," Locke observed thoughtfully.

Ariel sighed and lifted her shoulders slightly.

"Yes. Perhaps too long. We had a long engagement too."

"How long were you engaged?"

"Almost two years."

"You're kidding," he exclaimed, hardly believing his ears.

"No," she said, a little annoyed at this reaction. "We just
had to keep postponing it. We were working on our careers.

Our studies and our jobs kept taking us to different places," she explained defensively.

Locke stared at her, stunned at what she was saying.

"Did you love him?" he demanded.

"What kind of question is that?" she retorted. "Of course I loved him, and he loved me. . . ."

Locke snorted in derision.

"That, no doubt, was why he waited two years to marry you and then managed to get involved with another woman before he could tie the knot!"

"She was different," Ariel snapped. Then, more haltingly, she elaborated. "Andrew said that he had never known what people meant by the words *falling in love* until he met Cory. It was a case of love at first sight for him. Cory hit him like a thunderbolt, he said. She . . . captivated him from the moment he first saw her."

The words reverberated in Ariel's head, and her voice trailed off in embarrassment. Captivated. Odd. That was the word that kept coming back to her whenever she thought of that evening in Georgetown. Locke had captivated her so . . . from the moment she first saw him, and she had been so determined to do the captivating.

"So, you were depressed over the breakup that night?" he reiterated in a smooth, neutral voice.

He sounded as if he were studying an engineering design, she thought irritably.

"That doesn't explain what happened between us, though," he added pointedly.

"But it does," she protested rather desperately. "Don't you see? It was a bad time for me. I was vulnerable . . . susceptible to doing something foolish! You've got to believe me," she said earnestly, her face warming as the blood coursed into her cheeks. "I've never done anything like that before."

He pulled her chin slightly to one side, gently forcing her to look at him, his fingers branding her jaw where they lingered. He stared into her soft, brown eyes and saw the pain and confusion. This wasn't the face of a woman who made a habit of "meaningless encounters," as she had so unattractively termed their first meeting while arguing with him in his hotel suite. She had more the look of a frightened doe running from a stag . . . the look of a hunted female who was very determined not to give in yet.

"Would you believe that I've never done anything like that, either?" he asked softly, his eyes warming hers with the intimacy of his gaze.

For one brief, heart-stopping moment, they were suspended alone, just the two of them, in a place where time didn't exist. Nothing could penetrate the warm, private world that had enfolded them. They stared into each other's soul, mesmerized. . . .

Ariel shook her head and pressed her fingertips against her temples. What was happening to her? When she looked at him, she felt as if she had known him from the beginning of time, and this was just the most recent interlude in which their paths had crossed.

"It's true," he said seriously. "I've never followed a woman who gave me a come-hither smile in a masquerade costume. I've never even considered taking a woman to my home the first time I took her out." His voice deepened as he added huskily, "And I've never made love to a woman I've only just met."

Why are you saying this to me? Ariel wondered wildly as she felt herself falling more and more into the magical spell that bound them. I've got to fight it. He's too dangerous for me, a man out of my league altogether. It would be playing with fire to give in to this . . . this fascination. She forced herself to think rationally. *I can go back to my simple, uncomplicated life,* she told herself. *It's a life where I'm in control, where everything is smooth, peaceful, and predictable. . . .*

She stepped away from him, frowning, and carefully biting her lower lip.

Locke noticed the change. He didn't like it. Unfortunately he wasn't sure what to do to counteract it.

"All right. So neither of us makes a habit of doing things like that," she conceded, thinking hard. "And we'll probably never do it again. But you've got to accept that I was not the woman you thought I was. I made her up for the night. Please," she pleaded, "it was just a crazy night. There was just something about you that appealed to me at the time," she finished lamely.

"Why, thank you," he said in a voice that told her he hadn't taken her comment as such. She just as well could have been describing a cucumber sandwich, he thought in annoyance.

"Well, I can't help it if you're the type who stands out in a crowd!" she retorted crossly.

Ariel was wishing from the bottom of her heart that she could sink immediately out of sight in order to remove herself as quickly as possible from this dreadful conversation.

"You make it sound as though my fly were unzipped," he said, arguing and wearing a frown.

"There's no need to be offensive!" she retorted heatedly.

The color rose in her cheeks as she fought to keep her eyes off the aforementioned article of clothing.

"Say! I think I'm the injured party here," he protested with growing ire. "I've heard of damning with faint praise, but believe me, you're breaking new ground!"

Ariel turned to go, but he grabbed her wrist and held her fast.

"And you're going to stay here until we've sorted everything out," he ordered angrily. "Quit running away from me!"

"I'm not running away from you!"

Ariel was so angry at his thwarting her exit that she even believed her own hotly delivered denial.

He laughed humorlessly.

"We seem to be back at square one," he muttered, surveying her defiant face, flushed with anger. "If that's the case, I guess I have nothing more to lose tonight," he said enigmatically.

Roughly he pulled her into his arms. The darkness and his back cloaked them from any curious onlookers. By now, though, almost everyone had deserted the terrace for the warm environs of the ballroom. They were alone.

"What are you doing?" she cried in a strangled voice. The seeds of alarm were taking root in her dark eyes.

His face was close to hers as he crushed the front of her body against his.

"I'm going to kiss you," he said deliberately, holding her wrists behind her back as he lowered his mouth to hers.

"No," she said, moaning, then twisting her face away from him.

Instantly he released one wrist and grasped the back of her head, forcing her to hold still. She pressed the heel of her hand as hard as she could against his shoulder as his mouth touched hers. No matter how hard she pushed, he didn't budge. Then his hard, warm lips were on hers, and she found it harder and harder to push him away.

Ariel felt the anger in him as he branded her with the coldly premeditated kiss. But she also felt the emotion in him, the wanting so strong that it was almost palpable.

Her free hand stopped trying to push. The cold hardness of his mouth eased into the exquisitely pleasurable pressure she could not forget. As the sensation flowed through her, her fingers uncurled and spread over his shoulder. He slanted his mouth against hers and began to tease her lips with a barely perceptible alternation of pressure. She felt the textured warmth as he teased the edge of her lips with the tip of his tongue. Then he released her other wrist and pulled her tightly into his embrace as she leaned into him and, for a moment, forgot all her resolutions.

She felt all the anger drain out of him, leaving behind the growing fire of passion. As she pressed her body against him the blaze grew stronger.

Reluctantly he eased the kiss and lifted his mouth from hers.

"You know," he whispered huskily, kissing her cheekbones, "you're beautiful without your glasses. . . ."

Ariel opened her eyes and stared at him helplessly.

Something of her vulnerability got through to him, and he felt a stab of remorse. He relaxed his arms a little and shut his eyes. When he opened them a moment later, he looked down at her uncomfortably.

"I'm sorry, Ariel. I didn't mean it to go like this," he murmured. "I don't know how to get through that wall you keep putting between us. . . ."

She loosened her arms and slid the palms of her hands against his chest. The fine wool of his suit jacket was still warm from the imprint of her body.

"So you thought you'd try demolishing it headfirst," she said a little shakily.

"Something like that."

He cupped the side of her face with one hand.

"If you'll tell me how, I'll tear it down brick by brick to get through to you," he vowed.

"But why?" she cried out softly. "Why should you try? I'm not your type . . . we're from totally different worlds!"

Her vehement protest stunned him.

"What—" he began.

Before he could finish the question, they were interrupted. Several people were pushing through the doors to the ballroom, laughing and talking with great animation.

"Say! Adam Locke! Is that you?" boomed the voice of one of the senior environmental engineers.

Adam swore softly.

"I'll get rid of them," he said curtly. "Then let's go someplace where we can finish this with more privacy."

Ariel watched the party goers' boisterous approach. They didn't look exactly like the cavalry to her, but they certainly were serving the same purpose! She had been awash in her own conflict-ridden emotions, too overwhelmed to put up much more resistance to his insistence or his charm. In another few minutes she'd have been defenseless and ready to yield to his tempting offer.

Never one to miss an opportunity, however, Ariel shook her head and stepped away from him, backing toward the terrace steps.

"That won't be necessary," she said firmly. "We have nothing else to say!"

She saw his face darken as she reached out to grab her. Before his hand could close over her wrist, she whirled and ran quickly down the staircase.

"Ariel!" he shouted as the small throng closed in around him, restraining him from following her.

He watched the champagne-colored chiffon of her dress disappear into the darkness as she ran home, like Cinderella running from the ball at the stroke of midnight.

"Damn!" he swore under his breath, feeling much as the prince must have under similar circumstances.

"So!" exclaimed the jovial, well-lubricated man who had just slapped his arm around Locke's shoulders. "I hear we both went to the same school! Did you know Ray Pugliese, by any chance? Or maybe . . ."

Locke stared at the speaker, trying to quell the desire to knock his block off.

"No," he replied coldly, brushing off his newfound friend's unwelcome hand.

He couldn't see her anymore, but as he looked into the darkness where she had vanished, he made a silent vow.

This isn't the end of it, Ariel. We have a hell of a lot more to say to each other. And you damn well know it!

The night was quiet a few hours later. All had gone home to sleep. All but one.

A shadowy figure entered the computer room in the main building. Silently he surveyed the mainframe. A stiletto beam of light touched a nearby keyboard. He directed a pen-sized flashlight to the lock. The copy he'd made of the master key

83

slipped in easily. With a turn of the wrist, the terminal switched on.

He sat down at the terminal and began punching in the codes commanding the computer to access the confidential data banks.

"Now," whispered the intruder coolly. "Let's take a look at those files. . . ."

Information appeared on the monitor in front of him.

Project 10.84: Energy Efficient Housing Design. Project Director: A. Locke. Personnel Assigned Project Time: Carrollton, Graves, Radnor, Fontaine, Word Processing Unit: 160 hours, Computer Technicians: 30 hours.

He punched three more codes and the screen cleared. New information replaced it: the index of current research addressing the buildup and ventilation of toxic gases in energy efficient homes . . . the raw data for a computer model designed to simulate toxic gas buildup and ventilation . . . the index of eastern European studies done on a new form of housing insulation and its level of toxicity.

A keystroke here, another there. The data were deleted or changed to hide the truth.

The computer was shut down. Now . . . there were only the handwritten drafts to worry about. . . . Some undoubtedly had been destroyed, but it would be necessary to check the offices to make sure. . . .

Ariel stared at the ceiling of her bedroom, telling herself futilely to go back to sleep. It was Saturday morning. She was out of her mind to be wide-awake at this hour! The new day had just dawned, for crying out loud!

The sunlight cast a soft, golden glow throughout her room. It was the last straw. She kicked off the covers and got out of bed, heading straight for the oak dresser to find her leotards.

At least she hadn't had the nightmare again, she consoled herself silently as she stepped out of her cottage a short time later. She followed the stone path to a compact brick building couched in the remains of what had once been a flourishing garden. It was beautiful in the spring and summer, but now it was barren of color and rather overgrown and wild-looking.

That could just as aptly describe her this morning, she thought wryly as she unlocked the door and entered the sturdy, austere edifice. While she had not had the nightmare again, neither had she had much sleep. She was sure it showed. She had been too restless and tense to sleep. And all she could think of was how much she wanted to be with Adam Locke. That was hardly a soothing thought!

She shook her head, trying to dispel the images that kept invading her mind: Adam's voice . . . Adam's touch . . . Adam's kiss . . .

She gritted her teeth and lowered her head in determination. She'd get the man out of her system and her attention on other matters one way or the other! She refused to give in to this . . . this . . . whatever it was!

The air was cool and musty. It didn't do much to refresh her, but she hoped that a good workout might help. The practice should help her concentrate on something else for a while, if nothing else.

It was such a familiar thing to do. All the warm memories of years past came back to her when she stepped onto the cold, green mats that covered most of the old wooden floor. She pulled off her cream-colored warm-up suit, just as she had countless times before, and started touching her toes, remembering. . . .

She'd been a shy, eight-year-old girl when she'd first seen the inside of a gymnasium. It had been busy and well worn, located in the physical education building of the college where her father taught. He had gone there one day to talk to the gymnastics-coach about a mutual student, and he'd taken Ariel with him. Little Ariel, her soft, brown eyes as big as saucers, had been fascinated. She'd hugged the wall, hoping not to be noticed by anyone while the men talked. But all the while she had watched the students practice.

How could anyone be so strong and confident? she had wondered. The rapid-fire tumbling routines, the high-speed vaulting, the elegantly controlled flying rings . . . she had thought that she'd been ushered into another universe at first.

And the admiration, the approval they received when others saw their performances! She'd discovered that tantalizing fact when, a month later, her parents had taken her to see an interscholastic competition. Her parents had been completely amazed when she had hesitantly expressed an interest in going back again. The coach, however, had been more perceptive. He had seen the timorous hunger in her young face, and he did something about it.

Forty-eight. Forty-nine. Fifty.

Ariel stood straight and began rotating her head in a circular fashion, loosening the tight muscles of neck and shoulders. Slowly . . . smoothly . . . just until she felt a little pain, just the way her coach had taught her all those years ago.

The warm-up exercises toned and stretched her body until it was lithe and pliant and ready to go. They also helped to sharpen her mind and prepare it for what was to come. Like Pavlov's dog, who had learned to salivate at the sound of a bell, Ariel had learned to be confident and in control in the confines of a gymnasium. Every time she stepped into the familiar environs and warmed up or began a routine, she found once again those reassuring feelings. She treasured them and stored them up, hoarding them for when she might need them, remembering the admiration, the applause . . . savoring her own sense of achievement and mastery.

Stretched and warmed into condition now, Ariel looked over the equipment, trying to decide which piece to work on first. Maybe the balance beam, she thought, walking toward it, her bare feet sticking slightly to the cool, tacky surface of the mat.

She could remember how graceful the girls she had first seen perform on it had looked. How proud her parents would be if she could do that, she had thought wistfully, painfully conscious of her own childish awkwardness and skinny, knobby-kneed build. How proud her father would be. . . .

The pale wood of the beam was smooth and hard under the

palms of her hands as she stood in front of it, gathering her thoughts. Smooth and hard, like . . . She shook her head, forcing the forbidden thought out of her mind before it could be fully formed and take root.

She pressed down, pushing herself into a straight-arm support mount, her arms straight, her back arched, the front of her thighs against the beam. Toes pointed, she raised one leg until it was horizontal, then arced it gracefully over, straddling the beam.

Her mind cleared as years of training took hold. The iron leash of concentration commanded her mind now. There was no room for anything else. Or anyone else. There was just her supple body flowing into a balance seat, rocking into a back shoulder roll and through a shoulder stand. She worked the beam from one end to the other, with straddles, splits, runs, pirouettes, walkovers, leaps—her full repertoire of skills. Each successful execution made her self-confidence soar. With each step she felt it grow, and eagerly she cheered it on.

"Feel it in your head and let your body move into the space, like a shadow following inevitably behind," her coach had said. "That's it, Ariel. Control . . . ease through it . . . it's all yours . . . nobody can do it for you . . . That's it . . . Way to go, baby! Way to go!"

She was holding an English handstand when Locke first saw her, barely discerning her figure through the dusky windowpane. She was perfectly still, like a graceful statue. At last his eyes caught and held her, just before she arced her pointed toes downward, gracefully dismounting to one side of the beam.

Norris had told him about the gymnasium he had equipped and how Ariel liked to use it in the early morning. Locke was very glad right now that he'd stumbled onto that piece of information.

He hesitated there, wondering when would be the best moment to enter. As evasive as she was being, he wanted to approach her carefully, in a low-key way that wouldn't inflame her fears. In a way she reminded him of a small, scared animal. He didn't need her any more skittish than she already was!

The damp chill of the early-morning air penetrated to the bone as he stood and watched her move into a tumbling routine. God, but she was a graceful little thing, he thought. But underneath beat the heart of a rabbit. He grinned, ignoring the cold. Watching her move like that would keep him warm enough, all right.

She ran from one corner of the mat, building up speed and somersaulting into another burst of handsprings. He watched her lithe curves flex, admiring the gentle curves and wishing he could do more than just look at them. Touching would be a pleasure. He knew that for a fact. The memory of running his hand over her back, down the swell of her tight little bottom, and down her thigh was burned into his mind.

He felt his temperature rising and reminded himself that he was not going to push her too fast too soon. He could wait. For a while at least. He hoped.

He pressed his lips into a thin, grim line.

Round-offs, cartwheels, handsprings, somersaults, flips, twists . . . Ariel's feet landed squarely and authoritatively on the mat. Automatically she arched her back proudly and bowed with a graceful flourish.

He could practically hear applause. She held herself with the bearing of a seasoned competitor . . . not world-class, perhaps, but very good all the same. He tried to keep his eyes on her face. He failed miserably. His eyes traced the curve of her back and derriere, applauding mentally as his heart beat a little more quickly.

Ariel chalked up her hands and approached the uneven parallel bars. She was functionally deaf by now. All of her thoughts were turned inward, concentrating on her next routine, moving through it mentally. Her body would merely be following as a visible afterthought.

As a result she didn't hear the soft creak of the door or feel the slight stir of the air as a draft entered. She was only aware of herself—her hands reaching out to grasp the smooth wood, the feel of the bars flexing as she pushed into a cross-seat mount, the bar pressing against the back of her thighs and buttocks as she balanced momentarily in a seat rest. . . .

Locke tugged down the zipper on the jacket of his running suit. Inside, it was warmer by far in spite of the fact that it was not a heated building. Maybe it was the way his pulse had started racing when he'd stepped inside, knowing they were, at last, alone together again . . . or maybe it was the scent he'd inhaled, that elusive and tantalizing reminder of her. What the devil was it, anyway?

He watched her from across the open room in silence. She looked like she was in a trance. Maybe that was just as well, he decided. At least he could enjoy looking at her for a little longer without her being aware of it. He was beginning to think that he could enjoy looking at her forever.

The apricot and lemon colors of her leotard brought out the deep gold highlights latent in her dark auburn hair. Its clinging fabric molded her firm, rounded figure, leaving very little to the imagination . . . just the color and the texture and the taste of the body hidden beneath its glovelike fit.

Locke leaned against the wall, only dimly aware of the moment his shoulder touched the rough stone surface.

He watched her silently, almost hungrily now, as she moved in between the uneven bars. She swung into a crotch seat, straddling the lower bar, the fingers of her right hand closing over it while her left lightly retained its grasp on the higher one.

Ariel swung into a seat balance, her right foot resting in front of her, her left leg pointing upward. She felt a ripple . . . something. She forced herself not to break concentration and rotated the bar at her hips, straddled it, then dropped through to the lower bar. Her mind was still trying to wander, as if something was tugging at her from somewhere. She pressed her lips together, frowning, determined not to let her concentration slip. She wove back and forth—high bar . . . low bar . . . high bar, around and around, up and over, back and forth . . .

"That's it, Ariel!" her coach had cried jubilantly when she'd finally gotten the hang of it. Adrenaline pumped into her as she remembered how proud of her he had been. If he had only realized how much of her accomplishment had been the result of his own faith in her . . . He'd had enough for both of them. That had certainly been a good thing, too, because she'd had absolutely no confidence in herself at all.

Back and forth . . .

She remembered her parents' reaction after her first winning performance: "Honey, you look like a wood nymph up there, the most beautiful little girl I ever saw. . . ."

She moved into a side-cross handstand with her right hand supporting her on the lower bar and her left gripping the higher. She was looking straight down, aware of everything but seeing nothing. It was then that she knew he was there. Locke. Just thinking his name made her blood freeze.

She glanced sharply toward the far corner of the room. She nearly let go when his figure took shape in her line of vision.

"What are you doing here?" she asked, annoyed at how breathless she sounded. She told herself it was just that she was a little winded from all of the exercise. It wasn't that the sight of him had knocked the breath from her. . . .

He straightened and walked casually toward her without answering at first. A grin tugged at the corners of his mouth. Why the devil was she talking to him upside down?

Ariel's heart pounded as she watched his approach. It was peculiar looking at him. Then she realized why. He was upside down. Or, at least, she was. All of her muscles felt locked in place, she realized finally, fuming at the recognition that her brain had apparently short-circuited upon seeing him again. She could not for the life of her decipher his expression from her head-over-heels posture. But she was getting very strong vibrations from the purposeful way he was coming toward her!

She gave herself a mental shake and took a deep breath. This was utterly ridiculous! Who ever heard of freezing upside down at the sight of a man, anyway?

90

With great strength of will she managed to regain control of herself. She swung her legs down between the two bars, then up and over the lower one. In one fluid motion she turned her body and executed a graceful rear vault with a quarter-turn dismount over the lower one.

Locke stopped a few feet away and clapped.

"Why are you here?" she repeated more firmly now, facing him rather warily.

"I came to watch you work out."

She blinked in surprise.

"You knew I would be here?"

He shrugged.

"I hoped you would." He smiled at her perplexed expression. "Norris told me you come here almost every morning. I just took a chance that today would be one of those days," he explained.

"I see," she murmured, not at all certain that she did at the moment.

He took a step toward her. She moved a step back.

"I don't think you do," he replied, frowning at her retreat. "We have a few things to work out," he said in suspiciously neutral tones.

Ariel backed away, sidling toward her warm-up suit, which was puddled on the mat too far away.

"No, we don't," she argued stubbornly, trying hard to ignore the steady pounding of her heart. "I told you last night that we have nothing more to discuss." She groaned silently. Lord, how adolescent she sounded! Well, it just couldn't be helped. *Remember the lesson of last night,* she told herself sternly. *The man's dynamite. Play with him and you'll get hurt.* Trying a normal relationship with Adam Locke was not realistic.

"All right," he said agreeably, trying not to laugh out loud at the startled look on her face and doing his damnedest to watch neutrally as she snatched up her clothing and tugged on her pants. "Tell me . . . how's the work coming?"

Ariel was halfway through pulling on her warm-up jacket

91

and thought at first that she hadn't heard right. She grimaced and jerked it on, thrusting her arms angrily into the sleeves. He knew she couldn't refuse to discuss work with him. Blast the man for his perseverance!

Locke watched her firm breasts jounce slightly as she rammed her body into the suit. Desire surged through him, the more strongly for having been so tightly reined in while watching her earlier. He frowned, trying to quell it before she noticed.

"Everything is on schedule," she replied firmly, knowing full well that it was really far ahead of schedule. She'd buried him in a blizzard of translations every day, she recalled smugly.

He walked around the pommel horse, examining the handles in a desultory fashion as a crooked grin spread across his face.

"On schedule," he murmured in amusement. "I've got a building full of engineers in Washington who'd like to be able to say the same thing. . . ." He shot her a level glance. "You're really breaking your back on this," he commented, surprised as the idea hit him and sank in.

He walked around the piece of equipment and back toward her, a small furrow carving a frown between his eyebrows as something else occurred to him. He stopped a few feet away, really looking at her face and seeing it clearly for the first time.

"You look exhausted," he said bluntly.

"Well, I feel fine," she lied defiantly.

She turned toward the door, but he caught her elbow before she could move more than a step.

"Look," he began awkwardly, "I never meant to work you into the ground. Let's go through the assignments. We'll cut out the material that doesn't appear to be essential," he offered, his seriousness disarming her.

His hand on her arm was doing strange things to her, too, as usual, she thought grimly. She could feel her resistance starting to melt. His obvious sincerity was just accelerating the process. Ariel felt torn. It was so tempting to give in to the growing desire to respond to him. Damn his appeal, anyway!

"It's not exactly that," he said weakly, pulling away from him and looking wistfully at the door.

His hands fell loosely to his sides. Frowning, he stared at the unhappy young woman who persisted in rejecting his advances. He couldn't believe that he was going through all of this for her. He hadn't chased a woman like this since . . . He'd *never* chased a woman like this, damn it!

He leaned his back against the door. If she wanted to leave, she'd damn well have to go through him to do it!

Ariel glanced up at him in surprise. When she saw the fierce-looking scowl on his face, she automatically backed away from him.

Locke saw the slight alarm in her stance and the wariness that flooded her eyes. They only fanned the smoldering fires of annoyance and frustration that had been eating at him for what was beginning to seem like forever.

"What did you mean by that parting crack last night, anyway?" he demanded, crossing his arms in front of his chest.

It looked to Ariel as if he were planting himself there for the indefinite future. She backed into the room again, half tripping over the edge of the mat as she went.

"What crack?"

"About your not being my type and being from different worlds," he replied succinctly, giving a sarcastic frost to "my type" and "different worlds."

She bumped against the parallel bars and came to a halt.

"You're . . ." How could she explain it? "You're a well-known, successful, big-city businessman. You're used to the Washington cocktail party circuit, people using each other for their own ends, the ruthlessness of ambitious people and the importance of power. You've traveled everywhere . . . have women in every major city for all I know."

His eyebrows lowered further, if that was possible.

93

"I'm a small-town girl. The only politics I know about is the academic infighting at a college and the personnel gossip at the office. There's only been one man in my life, and even though we knew each other for years, I lost him. And it hurt. I never learned to be casual about relationships," she cried, hating how much he was drawing out of her. Hating how vulnerable it was making her.

"That's what all of this is about?" he said incredulously, straightening up quickly and unfolding his arms.

"You're used to a fast, classy social life," she added, waving her arm as though that helped to explain everything. "I live a very quiet life."

His stance was beginning to look combative now. His legs were stiff, his hands lightly clenched, his face grim. Why in the world was he acting like this? she wondered, a little wildly.

"Are you angry?" she asked, her soft voice trembling slightly.

Her words served to ignite the smoldering fires in him. With an exasperated growl he lowered his head slightly and stalked in a slow, straight line across the matted room to her.

"You make me sound like an international playboy with a calculator for a heart," he said, just banking his anger enough to keep it from frightening her more. "And you're painting yourself as a regular Pollyanna," he added, his voice hard and rough as he recalled talking to Laslow the morning after she'd disappeared.

She stared at him, so mesmerized by his burning gaze that she never thought to move away from him. He stopped a foot away from her, glaring down.

"Is that really how you remember me from that night?" he challenged, remembering the laughter, the pleasure, the surprising rapport between them.

Doubt flickered in her deep brown eyes. Triumphantly he knew that she was remembering too.

"I told you before that I would tear down that wall you've put between us, and damn it, I will if I have to camp on your doorstep for the rest of the year to do it!'' he vowed, grabbing her shoulders as she belatedly tried to duck away.

"Oh, no, you don't,'' he ground out as his hands burned into her. "You're not running off until I've finished what I want to say!''

CHAPTER SIX

He felt her stiffen and caught the warning flash of fire in her dark eyes. Insinuating that she was cowardly certainly seemed to have hit the mark, he thought in satisfaction, encouraged that he'd made at least some sort of contact with her.

"I'm listening." she pointed out, telling herself not to do anything irrefutably stupid such as gaping at him like a fish or melting at the man's feet.

If only her heart didn't keep going haywire every time he came near her . . .

His eyes narrowed thoughtfully as he stared at her.

"Something must have happened," he said quietly, as if thinking out loud. "When I left you on the couch in the study and went downstairs, you wanted me as much as I wanted you. But when I returned a few minutes later with the champagne . . ."

Ariel's heart sank as the old, familiar sense of humiliation washed over her.

His eyes never left her face, and he saw her turn pale. Something *had* happened, he realized with genuine surprise.

"What in the hell was it?" he growled in frustration. "Did lying there in my home bother you? Was it that you were wishing you were in bed with your lukewarm fiancé? Did you suddenly recognize that you weren't with him, you were with me?" His eyes darkened into a midnight shade as his anger burned more hotly in his veins.

Ariel wriggled, trying to free herself from his grasp. She

could feel the emotions boiling up in him just beneath the surface. He didn't frighten her. She had no fear that he meant her any harm. But the strength of his feelings made her weak and she longed to wrap her arms around him. She fought down the insane urge to lift her face to his and kiss him, tell him that it wasn't true, that she'd never thought of Andrew from the moment she'd first laid eyes on Locke. Her heart ached with compassion for the man holding her at arm's length while he struggled with his own powerful feelings for her. For it was obvious to her that he did have feelings for her—powerful feelings—and they were acting on her like an aphrodisiac.

She pulled back again, harder this time, trying to escape the inexorable grip of his hands. Locke pulled her against him, locking her arms against her sides as his own closed around her body like a vise.

His face, dark with feeling, looked down at her, his lips just inches away from hers, his breath caressing her.

"No!" she retorted hotly, her own temper flaring, furious at her own powerlessness, fighting her own weakness for him. "That wasn't it at all! I left because I had to escape before I lost my self-respect. I wasn't thinking of Andrew . . . I was barely thinking at all. There was nothing but you that night. You filled everything . . . my thoughts, my fantasies, everything. And I was so far gone that I would have been there waiting with open arms for you if that girl hadn't brought me back to my senses!"

Ariel was so angry now that she was practically unaware of what she was saying to him. The words poured out in a torrent, straight from her wounded soul, lashing at him—her last weapon. She spat the words at him like a cornered cat. He might be stronger and able to dominate her physically, but she refused to go down without a fight. He was too potent, too strong, too dangerous, and he was much too close, in more ways than one.

She saw the surprise as it registered in his face.

"Girl?" he asked blankly. "What are you talking about?

What girl?'' His question was hard and sharp. Like the edge of a razor.

She groaned so softly, it sounded more like a sigh than anything else. The cat was out of the bag now, she thought. No more shields. She'd admitted he'd really gotten to her that night. Telling him the rest didn't seem to matter much anymore.

She slumped a little as the fire died in her. Feeling the change, Locke let go of her. He had the impression that she would be staying of her own free will now. She looked so vulnerable. He reached out and tenderly smoothed a curly wisp of auburn hair away from her face.

Ariel looked up, startled at the unexpected touch and its gentle protectiveness.

"Tell me," he said softly. "Please."

"That pretty young woman from the Carnaval, Raquel Dos Santos, came running into your house," she explained tonelessly. "Didn't you . . ." Ariel's cheeks warmed as they were suffused by a delicate blush of color. "Didn't you run into her when you came upstairs with the wine?" she managed to ask.

"No," he replied absently, visualizing for the first time what had happened that night. "When I got upstairs and found that you weren't there, I called out for you. It took a couple of minutes before I realized that your coat and purse were gone. As soon as I noticed that, I left the house myself, looking for you."

She caught her breath in surprise.

"You followed me that night?"

He gave a short laugh and grinned ruefully.

"Damn right."

"Oh."

It was all she could say. Her eyes said the rest.

He felt a strong surge of protectiveness.

"If you keep looking at me like that, we'll never get to the bottom of this," he warned, half hoping that she'd be willing to waive further explanations for a while.

Ariel blinked, trying to shore herself up in the face of an

all-invasive weakness that was swallowing her whole. Maybe it would help if she could tear her eyes away from him, she thought vaguely, hanging on to the last vestiges of her intellect for dear life. She ducked under the parallel bars, adding a little distance between them.

"Sorry," she mumbled as she gripped the bar closest to her with damp, trembling hands. "I just never thought that you might have tried to follow me."

"That's not the half of it," he muttered darkly under his breath.

"What?"

He cleared his throat and ran a hand roughly through his hair as he quickly tried to organize his thoughts. Her unexpected piece of information had thrown a monkey wrench into his preconceived opinions about her. It was unsettling to have to realign his thinking on such short notice. There were too many strong emotions involved where Ariel was concerned.

"As I was saying," he proceeded crisply, sidestepping her question, "I left the house a few minutes after you apparently did, trying to catch you. I must have searched for you for twenty minutes or so. By then I'd decided that you'd had enough time to catch a cab and had probably gone on home. I went back and went to bed."

He remembered the shock, the dismay for lack of a better word, that he'd experienced. And the anger that had burned them away for half the night as he lay awake in his large, empty bed.

Locke noticed the slight stiffening that his last comment had provoked in Ariel.

"I went to bed alone," he ground out. "And I never saw heads or tails of Raquel," he added pointedly.

"By the way," he said, turning the tables on her a little, "how did you know that my visitor was Raquel, anyway? Do you know her?"

"I saw her when she passed through the living room and ran upstairs." Presumably to your bedroom. Ariel hesitated.

"And I remembered her from the party. Before you arrived," she explained a little stiffly. "She made quite a splash."

Quite a splash indeed. Raquel had walzed her way effortlessly through clusters of admirers, smiling beguilingly, flirting outrageously, charming everyone with ease. Even the women had found it hard to be put off by her, in spite of her obvious success with the men present. Raquel had had a soothing word and a heartfelt touch of her delicate hand for each of them. Yes, Ariel conceded begrudgingly, remembering it all more vividly than she cared to, Raquel Dos Santos was a femme fatale with class. She embodied qualities so elusive, there weren't any names for them. Of all the gracious, confident, beautiful women that night, Ariel had most wanted to be fascinating to a man in the way that Raquel was.

"What did she want?" Adam asked, intruding without preamble into her reverie. He sounded more baffled than curious.

Ariel stared at him in disbelief.

"I—she—well . . ." she said, stammering. Angry at herself, she harnessed her mouth with an effort. "I didn't stop to ask her," she replied shortly.

"Isn't that a little awkward to do?" he asked, eyebrows rising slightly. "You two just pass in the night, two strangers in my home, and don't even say hello in the process?"

"She didn't see me," Ariel pointed out. "I saw her."

He studied her thoughtfully.

"You didn't want her to see you there? Why not just put on your clothes and sit in the study until I returned?"

Ariel blushed.

"She ran upstairs into what I presumed was your bedroom, calling out your name as if she did it all the time," Ariel blurted out, gripping the bar until her knuckles were white. "I . . . It suddenly seemed very cheap and sordid to say nothing of embarrassing and humiliating for me to be lying half dressed on a settee in your library!" She inhaled sharply. "I . . . I just couldn't stay."

Her voice had faded into a whisper. When she stopped

speaking, the cold silence of the gymnasium cast a pall over them.

Locke took a deep breath and expelled it slowly.

"I see," he said, treading carefully with her now.

He reached out slowly, closing his warm hand reassuringly over her cold one.

"I'm sorry that happened, Ariel," he said softly, apologetically. "I had no idea it had. If you'd stayed instead, you'd merely have seen me escort her out of the house as fast as possible, none too happy for her unexpected interruption."

His voice was low and warm. She wanted to believe him. He sounded so sincere. But he was a man with plenty of experience under his belt, she reminded herself. Should she trust his explanation? Or was he just going to manipulate her into doing what he wanted, the way everyone at the party had been manipulating one another that night?

"I'd like to try to explain," he said, gazing steadily at her. "Please, Ariel. Give me the chance to do that much, at least."

She looked up at him again. Helplessness and doubt were engaging in a losing battle with a reluctant desire to soothe his obvious discomfort. Still . . . She hesitated. His hand tightened ever so slightly in a silent plea.

She stared at his earnest face, suddenly aware that they were standing on her turf. This was the one place in all the world where she felt strong, self-confident, victorious. Courage. The memory of it came back to her, infusing her with the will to take the chance.

"All right," she agreed, hoping with every fiber of her being that she wouldn't come to regret her decision.

Saturday evening found Ariel hard at work at her desk, trying for the millionth time to keep the events of the morning from creeping back into her mind. After she'd agreed to give Adam a chance to explain, he'd suggested they straighten it all out over dinner that night. He'd explained that he was going to be tied up all day working on the project and signing some papers for his company. A courier would be bringing them to his rooms at the Athena Inn any moment now, he'd added, looking at his watch.

Well, what could she have said?

They had walked back to her cottage together, barely talking. Not because they didn't want to talk. The silence had been strained. So much was being left unsaid. But the things they needed to say couldn't be squeezed into a five-minute walk in the woods. And somehow neither of them had felt like making small talk.

Adam had left her at her doorstep, giving her shoulder a gentle, almost awkward squeeze, and gazing at her enigmatically before turning to go. Ariel had watched him jog up the hill and out of sight. She'd felt oddly disappointed, as if something important needed to be finished.

A few minutes later, when she was changing her clothes and getting ready to take a shower, she could still feel the tingling sensation on her lips, the peculiar bubbling feeling that had invaded her body. She'd told herself it wasn't that she'd wanted him to kiss her again. Or hold her once before he left.

The light in Ariel's office was bright and strong. Quite a contrast to the settling darkness as evening came to Athena.

She stared at the article in front of her. Bewegen von Luft. Bewegen von Gasen. Toxisch . . .

Ariel shut her eyes and pressed the tips of her fingers against her aching forehead. Maybe she needed new glasses. Of course, it could be that she was getting tired of reading about ventilation systems, she admitted with a wry smile.

She stretched and stood up, gathering up the drafts she'd been writing all day. Coffee and snacks had managed to keep her going, but now she was hungry for some real food.

"I hope you've got a restaurant in mind that's known for its fast service, Adam Locke, because I'm starved," she murmured as she dropped the papers into a file and locked the cabinet.

She grabbed her purse and jacket and left. By the time she

got home, it was six o'clock. That gave her an hour to shower and change. Long enough, without being so long that she'd end up pacing her floor waiting for his arrival, she thought as she dropped her purse on her bed and started to undress.

In spite of her best intentions, however, Ariel was ready early. As it turned out, it was just as well. She was looking around for the report that she'd been planning on giving Locke and discovered that she'd left it at work. She glanced at a clock. Six-forty. She pressed her lips together thoughtfully. Well, that was enough time for her to walk back to the office and retrieve it.

She grabbed her keys and shot out of the door.

It was getting pretty dark by now. The trees and shrubbery dappled the hill in deep shadows. The warm, golden lights twinkling through the smoky glass of the Athena Inn were cheery in contrast. A few lights had flicked on here and there in most of the office buildings and cottages.

The main administration building was dark, except for a light in the hall, left on for security purposes.

Ariel unlocked the door and stepped inside, her tread falling softly on the carpeted floor just inside the entrance. The soles of her shoes made no sound as she made her way to her office. She reached her door, fishing out her key, unlocked the door, and opened it so quickly that she hardly had to break stride.

She had barely crossed the threshold when she knew that something was wrong. A bulky shadow had been darting off to her left as she'd stepped into the room.

Fear lanced through her. She whirled, backing a step toward the hallway as she did so. To no avail. It was too late. Before she could see him, he had lunged forward. She felt a hard blow land against the back of her neck. Blackness engulfed her. She slid limply to the floor, a cry dying unvoiced on her lips.

Locke's fingers rippled the keys in his hand. Again. And again. The metallic jangle was beginning to grate on his nerves. He knocked again. No answer. He didn't want to be a Peeping Tom, but he was getting pretty tempted to look through one of the windows in back of Ariel's cottage to see if she was back there.

Damn. Was she doing this on purpose? Making him cool his heels on her front step? He glanced at the illuminated dial of his watch. He'd been standing here for more than five minutes. That did it.

He walked around to the back, climbing past shrubbery and swearing softly as his expensive shoes sank into the soft ground a little.

Nothing. Her curtains were drawn, but they were light and gauzy, and he could see enough to tell that she wasn't there. He returned to her front step, gingerly sidestepping a few sunken areas this time. He knocked again. He tried the doorknob. Locked.

What in the hell was going on?

He frowned. He turned on his heel and started back up the hill toward the Athena Inn, his long-legged stride eating up the distance in no time. He took the steps outside the entrance two at a time, shoved open the door, and headed straight for the front desk.

"Has Ariel Radnor been here?" he asked.

The startled night clerk looked up blankly from his crossword puzzle.

"Uh . . . Ariel? No, Mr. Locke."

"Thanks," he said, not sounding particularly appreciative of the answer he'd gotten.

He walked slowly over to the glass doors and gazed outside. Gradually he became aware of the faint glow of a light emanating from the nearby administration building. The administration building . . . where Ariel's office was located.

What the hell, he thought. There was nothing to lose in going over and checking it out. Maybe she'd lost track of time and was still at her desk wearing those damned glasses!

He grimaced as he pushed open the door. Obviously she

hadn't been as preoccupied with him all day as he had been with her.

A few minutes after he had unlocked the door to the building, thanks to Dr. Norris's generosity, Locke arrived at Ariel's door. It was ajar. And it was dark inside. A chill of concern coursed through his chest.

Cautiously he pushed it open. Then he saw her, crumpled on her side on the floor. The chill became a heart-freezing cold.

"Ariel," he breathed, glancing sharply around the room even as he sank on one knee beside her limp form.

He felt for a pulse. His fingers trembled as he touched her throat. He didn't realize that he was holding his breath until he let it out when he felt the steady, reassuring beat pulse rhythmically against his fingertip.

"Thank God," he murmured.

He straightened up and flipped on the lights, quickly, thoroughly checking the office and adjoining library for an intruder with a hard-eyed visual inspection on his way to the telephone on Ariel's desk. Long gone, he concluded, punching out some numbers and looking at the still form lying a few feet away from him.

"Galway," he snapped. "We've got a big problem. . . ."

Light. A warm hand on her cheek. A dull ache at the back of her head. A strange, disjointed mixture of sensations greeted Ariel as she slowly regained consciousness.

"No," she muttered protestingly, opening her eyes and trying hard to focus on the owner of the hand.

"It's all right." Locke soothed as he knelt over her. "I'm here now. Galway and a doctor are on their way."

Ariel shut her eyes and tried to rest a minute. She felt so weak and shaky.

The sound of heavy footsteps approaching at a fast clip brought both of their heads around in the direction of the doorway. Robert Galway, the chief of security at Athena, bulldozed through Ariel's door just as his voice announced his identity. His ruddy cheeks were even redder than usual, from the chill air, the beer he'd been enjoying with his dinner, and the anger that something had dared to happen on premises protected by him.

"What happened?" he asked gruffly, looking at Locke before turning a more concerned expression toward Ariel.

Locke, who'd been preparing to get up in case the new arrival was the intruder instead of the security force, turned back to Ariel. He frowned as he saw her slowly push herself into a sitting position, but he slipped a supportive arm behind her back all the same.

"Somebody hit me on the back of the head," Ariel murmured a little shakily, wincing as her finger found the tender spot in question.

Galway muttered darkly and began questioning her. She answered as best she could while he carefully searched her office, seeking the explanations that it quickly became apparent she could not provide.

The physician Galway had called appeared fifteen minutes later in casual clothes and smelling of martinis. Dr. Robison lived on some property adjoining the Athena Corporation. Almost all of the employees were his patients. It hadn't taken him long to get there. It took even less time for him to complete his examination of Ariel.

"I'd say she's okay," he said brusquely, talking to the two men as he stuffed his ophthalmoscope into his little black bag.

He turned his attention to Ariel.

"Is there someone who can stay with you tonight, just in case there's any dizziness, bleeding, or nausea? If you experience any of those symptoms or otherwise feel worse, you should contact me at once," he said bluntly.

Ariel's numbed mind had formed the mental image of Lydia Carrollton's cheery face as he spoke. Before she could open her mouth, Locke had spoken for her.

"I'll see to it that she's not left alone," he said firmly. "Can she go home now?"

"Yes. Someone should go with her, of course," replied the slightly balding man as he snapped shut his bag and turned toward the door.

"Do you feel like getting up?" he asked her quietly, turning to Ariel.

Ariel nodded. He helped her up from the chair she'd been sitting in throughout the exam.

"I'll call you tomorrow, Galway," Locke said, nodding good-bye.

The security chief acknowledged the farewell with an understanding nod of his own head. He watched in silence as Locke shepherded a flustered-looking Ariel out of her office toward home.

"Poor kid," he muttered before turning back for another check of her office.

The temperature had dropped. Ariel began to shiver halfway across the courtyard between the administration building and the Athena Inn. Adam, who had been lightly touching her elbow, slipped his arm protectively around her shoulders.

"You need a warmer jacket," he pointed out needlessly. "What are you doing wearing that filmy thing?" He glanced sharply at her as another question occurred to him. "And what in the devil were you doing at your office at this time of night, anyway?"

Ariel stopped dead in her tracks and clapped a hand over her mouth to stifle a gasp. Adam cursed as he struggled to stop quickly enough to avoid toppling them both onto the stone-paved path.

"Are you going to get sick?" he questioned sharply, casting a suspicious look at the hand smacked against her mouth.

"No." Ariel replied with frustration. She let her hand drop limply back to her side. "I just remembered that I forgot to bring a report home with me. Again."

"What report?"

Now he was beginning to shiver. He'd left his overcoat in his car earlier, and his sport jacket wasn't helping much anymore. He took it off and slipped it onto Ariel's shoulders. Maybe at least one of them would be warm, he thought.

"The report that I went back to the office for earlier this evening," she explained crossly. "This makes the second time tonight I've forgotten it," she added in disgust.

Locke stared at her in disbelief.

"You got dressed to go out with me and then dashed back to your office in order to give me a report?" he asked incredulously.

"Yes." Why was that so strange? she wondered, getting a little defensive about his attitude.

She turned toward the administration building but quickly found herself twirled back and pointing toward home. A firm hand gave her a meaningful shove in that direction.

"What . . ." she sputtered.

"You're going home," he announced, rather more forcefully than he had intended. "Straight home. Do not pass 'Go.' Do not collect two hundred dollars. And *do not*, under any circumstances, even *think* of going back to your office to pick up a translation for me tonight!"

Ariel fumed and protested to no avail as he marched her straight down the hill and into her cottage.

"Uh . . . um . . ." Ariel stammered nonsensically as he locked her door behind them and headed for her kitchen.

She followed him and sat down on one of the two second-hand wooden chairs at her small kitchen table. She still felt a little wobbly. Now that he wasn't half holding her up and hustling her along, she realized just how wobbly.

"How's the head?" he asked as he looked into her refrigerator and searched through her cupboards.

"My head's just fine, if you don't count the sensation of a hot poker banging against the back of it," she replied with a sigh of resignation. "Just what are you doing, anyway?"

He had put a small skillet on the stove top and had taken some bread and eggs out of the refrigerator.

"I thought I'd make us some dinner. Are you hungry?"

He turned and gave her a concerned look. She thought

about it. She certainly had been hungry earlier. Her stomach still had a decidedly hollow feeling.

"Yes . . ." What was she saying? After all, going out for dinner and conversation was one thing. Adam Locke fixing her dinner and looking after her in her own cottage was quite something else! "Look, you don't have to bother," she protested, getting up on somewhat less shaky legs. "This wasn't what either of us had in mind for tonight. Why don't we just call it an evening."

He turned away from the counter top and looked at her.

"Forget about this evening?" he asked, surprised.

"Well, yes." This evening . . . the next few weeks . . . the past six months. Forget the whole thing, she thought numbly. *If only I could find a nice shell to crawl into, somewhere safe and peaceful where my heart doesn't beat like this, where I don't feel these terrifying feelings that I can't seem to dampen, where I can just be the person I used to be before I met you, Adam Locke.*

She looked away, afraid he'd see too much in her eyes.

Locke frowned and walked over to her.

"You," he said quietly but firmly, "go take a nice warm bath. See if that helps the head. Get into something comfortable . . . your favorite old clothes to relax in. I'll fix us a little supper. We'll eat and talk a little. And then you're going to sleep."

Ariel felt the heat flood her cheeks.

"I think I'd better call Lydia," she said nervously, trying to muster the strength to follow through on her idea.

"Nonsense," he said dismissively.

He led her to her bedroom and brought her inside.

"How did you know where my bedroom was?" she asked, startled.

He grinned at her.

"The place isn't that big, for one thing, and we just walked through the two other main rooms. Besides, I peeked through your bedroom window earlier this evening."

He said it with such a straight face that his explanation

didn't register with her at first. When it did, she blushed and flashed him an angry look.

"You what?" she asked in angry disbelief.

"When I came to pick you up," he explained with a chuckle. "I knocked but got no response. So I walked around back to see if you were hiding from me again."

"Well, of all the nerve!" she exclaimed, nearly speechless. "Hiding in my bedroom! Why on earth would I do something as ridiculous as that?" she protested, blushing a little as she realized what a nice little shell her bedroom could be.

"She doth protest too much!" He laughed, putting up a hand of surrender when she prepared to argue the point. "All right, I take it all back," he said gallantly. "By the way, are you feeling well enough to try a bath? I don't want you to pass out in there. Feeling dizzy or anything?"

He looked and sounded genuinely concerned. Ariel felt a warm inner glow of happiness. Well, after all, it was nice that he cared at least that much. Not that it amounted to anything of any significance, she hastened to tell herself.

"I'm fine," she said firmly. "Believe me, I've been knocked out a couple of times in the gym. I'd know when to worry."

He still looked a little doubtful.

"Well, be sure to tell me if you do."

"Agreed."

He closed the door after her and turned back toward the kitchen.

Get into something I can relax in? What in the world would that be? It had such a disquieting ring to it. Relaxation and Adam Locke just didn't seem to go together. She took a deep breath and searched her drawers for some casual clothes. A few minutes later she closed and locked the bathroom door behind her.

Her carefully selected outfit for the evening was stripped off, and it landed in a soft pile in the corner. So much for a mature, congenial evening, she thought fatalistically as she stepped into the shower for the second time that night.

But it did feel good . . . and the warm water *was* very relaxing.

By the time Ariel had finished showering and had donned her corduroy slacks and a soft, cotton work shirt, she could smell the homey aroma of bacon and eggs, toast and coffee.

"You really didn't have to do this," she said gratefully a few minutes later as she sat down at the kitchen table to join him for supper.

"It's the least I could do," he said with a shrug. "After all, I did invite you to dinner. I'm sure you were expecting better fare than this," he added with a grin. "Next time I promise you'll have a real chef prepare your supper."

Next time?

She took a sip of her coffee.

There was to be a next time? Was it fear or excitement, or maybe a little of each, that felt like ice water rushing through her veins?

She had been concentrating so hard on getting through this evening, she'd avoided thinking about what might happen next. She'd kept telling herself that they would clear the air between them. They'd share a few explanations, clear up any remaining misunderstanding. Maybe they'd even be able to laugh at the strange events they'd be caught up in. They would finally come to see each other as real people. Real people who had absolutely nothing of any consequence in common . . . two people destined to remain strangers. Somehow she'd believed that the magic that seemed to surround him would then dissipate and she would be free of him at last. She would go home at the end of the evening, back to her reality . . . free of him. Free of the haunting memory of him.

And in spite of his obvious interest in her, she had somehow believed that one evening would be more than enough for him too. He would see her as she really was. After all, she wasn't exciting. She wasn't glamorous. She was not a femme fatale. She wasn't the woman she'd pretended to be, the woman he had met six months before.

Next time?

"Eat your food before it gets cold," he ordered cheerfully as he buttered a slice of toast and reached for the jar of strawberry preserves.

Much to her surprise, Ariel discovered that she was still hungry. Before she quite realized what she was doing, she'd polished off every speck of food on her plate.

"Say! You really liked my cooking, didn't you?" teased her impromptu chef, both flattered and amused.

"I'll do that," she said, reaching to take a plate out of his hand. He ignored her.

Brushing off her attempt, he continued to clear away the dishes. When she continued to linger nearby, trying to take over the task of cleaning up, he whirled her around by the shoulders and literally pushed her out of the kitchen.

"I'll take care of this," he announced in a no-nonsense fashion. "Why don't you just put your feet up on the couch while I finish up. I'll be with you in a few minutes."

Ariel tried not to feel guilty, but the sound of him rinsing and stacking dishes was too much.

As if reading her mind, his voice called out reassuringly, "Remember, I did invite you out to dinner. Since we didn't go anywhere, I'll just make it up with a sort of in-kind contribution: free labor."

She shook her head. He was really a rather sweet man underneath all that smooth-tailored appearance. A rather sweet man . . . and a very peculiar evening.

Ariel put her feet up and smiled thoughtfully. She couldn't remember a man ever fixing her a meal before or serving her . . . certainly not washing dishes for her! And of all the men in her acquaintaince, Locke was certainly the last she'd have guessed would be willing to do something like that.

He joined her a short time later, looking fairly pleased with himself. He came to a halt in the middle of the small room. The look of satisfaction faded as he stared down at her.

As she swung her feet down off the sofa he put out a hand, indicating that she stay put.

"That's all right," he said, glancing suspiciously at the

small space on the sofa next to her. He looked around the room, relaxing as he spotted an old Windsor chair. "Keep your feet up."

He sat down, looking rather large and out of place with a hand-crocheted afghan nestled around him. Ariel had thrown it over the chair for added color and comfort. Under Locke it looked like a child's coverlet accidentally left with the adults.

"By the way," he said comfortably, stretching out his legs, "Dr. Norris called while you were in the shower. I told him that you seemed to be all right but that I would keep an eye on you for a while, anyway, just in case."

"Oh." Why couldn't she think of something more original to say than that? "Thanks."

Locke shrugged indifferently.

"Have they found anything? Or anyone?" she asked.

"No. Galway contacted Norris and then filed a report with the police. Apparently no one knows much more yet. But Galway ought to know by tomorrow whether someone broke through any of the security fences along the perimeter to get in or out."

He fell silent. A brooding look settled briefly over his features.

"What's the matter?" she questioned, concerned. Was he holding something back? "Is there something else?" she prodded gently.

He shook his head.

"Not really. I was just thinking . . . ."

Thinking that if the person who hit her on the head was an employee of the Athena Corporation, there would be absolutely no evidence of his or her entering or departing. But Locke wasn't about to say that. Not to Ariel. The idea concerned him enough as it was. He didn't want her worrying about it too. She'd had enough for one day.

He smiled faintly, trying to marshal enough energy to take up his next topic . . . one he didn't particularly relish.

"Now let's see," he began. "What were we talking about

this morning? Ah, yes. Now I remember. I was telling you that I wanted a chance to explain about Raquel."

At the sound of Raquel's name Ariel tensed involuntarily. Why did he have to say it? Somehow it sounded tender and treasured on his lips. Reluctantly she awaited his explanation. She felt like a prisoner going before a firing squad. Deep down she'd been hoping he would leave the explanations for last. That way, they could have had at least one pleasant evening together before the bubble burst again on her fantasies.

Regrettably it appeared that the evening would not be living up to her expectations. Again.

Absently Locke stroked the dark walnut arm of his chair with the tips of his fingers.

"Raquel is a memorable person," he began.

I already noticed that, Ariel thought, annoyed that he'd pointed it out.

"She's beautiful . . ." he continued.

Was it necessary to dwell on the obvious? she wondered as depression began to set in.

". . . And she has a special kind of warmth and vitality that reach out and envelop those near her."

Warmth and vitality, Ariel echoed silently. Wouldn't it be nice if you could buy it at the drug store?

"She's always been that way," he mused, as if seeing Raquel's life flash before his eyes in videotape as he spoke.

Known her a long time, have you? Ariel thought, knowing she didn't want to hear the rest of this. He'd already told her more than enough. Before she could decide what to say to stop him, however, he was talking again.

"I've known her for years. We met when her parents were assigned to the United States. They're from Brazil. We've both lived in Georgetown for thirty years." There was a barely perceptible hesitation. "I guess you could say we're both fairly well connected, come from well-known families, that sort of thing."

He shrugged it off as if it were of no special importance to him. Why, then, did it seem important to her? Ariel felt the same way she had that night six months ago. He was from a different world. She felt so alien, so inadequate.

Adam glanced up at her and guessed how she had taken his last remark. He shook his head and frowned.

"No. Don't think that. We're all made of flesh and blood. We all have hopes and dreams and disappointments. We all put on clothes to keep warm and drink cold drinks to cool off."

Their eyes locked.

"But you and your circle of friends put on ermine and mink and one-of-a-kind suits to warm yourselves, drink prizewinning champagne and imported bottled water to cool your palates," she protested, eyeing him defiantly and daring him to deny it, although she'd never before thought of it as much of a distinction. Not until now.

He didn't bother to argue the point.

"Sometimes. But that's a difference in degree, not in kind. Some people use it like a badge," he admitted. "If you flaunt your badge, they'll recognize you as a member of the same club. Some of the people at the party that night are certainly in that category. I'm not. And neither is Raquel, for that matter. She's a genuine, straightforward woman in many ways. She has friends in all income brackets and treats them all as if they were royalty."

It all clicked when he said that. That was it. Raquel made people feel like they were valued above all else, as if, for the moment, they had her full and total attention. It was hard to dislike someone like that. Even when you wanted what they had.

"I'm sorry," Ariel said softly, eyes downcast. "It's not necessary to say any more. Let's just forget it."

He didn't look any more comfortable with their conversation than she did, but his discomfort was for a different reason. He had more to say.

"No. I want to get this behind us. And Raquel is still bothering you. So, as I was saying, we both came from

115

well-off, socially prominent families. That was how we met. We've known each other a very long time."

He sounded almost awkward to her.

Ariel decided to take the plunge and ask the question that had been haunting her.

"And are you engaged?" she asked, forcing the words out.

Her heart plummeted as he seemed to hesitate in answering. "No."

But there was something. She was sure of it.

"Are you dating?" She was surprised at how easily the words formed this time in comparison to the last.

"Not exactly," he replied awkwardly, loosening his collar a little.

"Then, are you friends?" she proceeded to ask, hardly able to bring herself to believe it if he said yes to that.

"I wouldn't exactly say that," he admitted uncomfortably. "Raquel and I saw quite a bit of each other for almost a year. Her husband had died. . . ."

That did get Ariel's attention.

"He had been an old friend of my uncle. So I started taking Raquel to a few parties when her period of mourning had ended."

Ariel had the impression that he would have left it all right there. She leaned forward.

"And . . ." she said encouragingly.

"And we found that we were very attracted to each other," he said with a frown.

"What happened?" Ariel forced herself to ask, dreading the answer and trying to nurse the hurt his last revelation had inflicted on her. After all, it was totally unrealistic to expect that he wouldn't have cared for other women.

"Things . . . just cooled off between us. She wanted more than I could give her. We parted friends. We're still friends. When we run into each other at parties, we still talk to each other."

He smiled. But it was as if he were smiling at a woman

who was not there. He was smiling into the vision of his own memory of Raquel.

Ariel wanted to believe him, but it still didn't make sense.

"But why was she looking for you that night?" she asked. Stoically she awaited his reply.

He looked directly into her eyes.

"I don't know. When I returned to the house after chasing unsuccessfully after you, there was no one there. She never contacted me afterward. If you hadn't told me that she was there that night, I still wouldn't have known about it."

He studied her and sighed in frustration, rapping his knuckles once against the hardwood chair.

"I'm sorry it happened, Ariel. There's not much more I can say than that, when it gets right down to it. Raquel and I are simply old friends now. Nothing more."

The words should have been reassuring, but Ariel didn't feel reassured. Somewhere deep inside a small doubt gnawed away at her. Why couldn't she believe him? Why?

CHAPTER SEVEN

"Now, tell me about Ariel Radnor," he suggested, crossing his ankles and looking at her with an easy smile.

"Well, she likes it here," Ariel replied, trying to match his mood.

So they talked about other things. Innocuous, neutral things such as where they went to school and where they'd traveled and where they wanted to go next in life. What was it like to work at Athena? What were the challenges of running your own firm?

Over his protest she made them each a cup of tea and they listened to some music on her stereo. The earlier conversation faded away, and soon Ariel couldn't help but wish that he'd come a little closer, sit beside her on the sofa, put his arm around her, kiss her. . . .

But he didn't. Adam Locke was the model of propriety. He was charming and polite and just a little reserved physically. Exactly the kind of behavior she'd have expected from a date when they were sitting in her parents' living room.

The evening couldn't go on forever, of course, but Ariel felt a pang of regret when he finally brought it to a close.

"I think you'd better be getting into bed," he said firmly as he stood up and held out a hand to help her to her feet.

She tried to think of something clever and witty to say as he led her, unresisting, to her bedroom door. By the time he stopped in front of it her mind was still a blank.

He rested his hands lightly on her shoulders and gazed

down enigmatically at her. Their eyes locked for a moment. An unseen flame touched them. Locke cleared his throat and brushed a kiss lightly across her cheek. Then he drew back.

"Go on," he told her. "Go to sleep. I'll keep an eye on things here for a little while. If you feel ill, just call out. If you're still feeling all right in a few hours, I'll let myself out and lock up for you as I go."

She opened her mouth to protest that it wasn't necessary. He laid a finger softly on her lips.

"Remember what the doctor said? Go on."

He stood, waiting for her to go, but Ariel couldn't seem to move. She stared up at him, mesmerized by her own attraction for him.

His expression changed slightly, and he cupped her face lightly in his hands. Slowly he bent down until their lips met. The flame grew as his mouth touched hers, kindling all the yearning that had been smoldering there for so long. His mouth moved gently against hers, and she slipped her arms around his waist. When he reluctantly withdrew, she barely managed to stifle a groan of protest.

"Go on," he said huskily. "Go to bed."

He turned away and walked across the tiny living room, not stopping until he'd reached her front window. He stared out into the darkness, clenched fists jammed into the pockets of his trousers.

"Good night," she whispered unsteadily. What was it that happened to her with him? What did he have that sent her weak in the knees like this? she wondered helplessly.

She inhaled sharply and turned away from him, closing the door firmly behind her as she went into the bedroom.

Ariel lay down on her bed. She didn't bother to change clothes. Under the circumstances it seemed safer to remain dressed. She stared despondently at the ceiling, which was now barely visible in the darkness. Never in her life had she felt less like sleeping. She lay there for what seemed like hours. Every rustle and creak in the next room set her nerves on end. Just when she was beginning to think that she would never sleep again, she slipped into a restless void.

Darkness swirled about her. Only the darkness wasn't just black. It was gray and maroon and deep shades of purple and blue. Swimming images, blurred and unrecognizable, drifted in and out of the void that was black and not black at the same time.

The nightmare enveloped her once more. It was the same one that had haunted her for months, but that didn't lessen its impact. It came with greater strength than ever. And now she knew what would come next, and she hated it all the more because she knew she could do nothing to change it.

The dark, disturbing colors gradually gave way, only to be replaced by wild, grotesque, masked faces that flew at her from all directions. There was laughter and music, but the laughter sounded like shrieks of pain and the music was like a discordant *danse macabre*. Glitter and elegance was everywhere, but it hurt to touch and burned her skin. The glitter parted, and a raven-haired woman flowed effortlessly onto the scene. The ambience changed as all were drawn to her warmth and beauty. As they turned away from her Ariel felt herself wither and die.

With her last tiny thread of energy she managed to drag herself away, to a place that was quiet and peaceful and tender and warm . . . where she could be alone, where her beauty could return, where there was no raven-haired woman to destroy her.

And then he appeared. The dark-haired man with eyes like iron. He walked toward her slowly . . . so slowly . . . and she walked toward him. And each step was effortless yet it seemed to take an eternity. And, as they grew closer their souls seemed to touch, even before their bodies could.

When finally they were close enough, the dark-haired man reached out his hand to her. And she touched him, placing her trembling hand in his. And warmth and beauty and courage and trust were hers. And they were his too. Their beings seemed to flow together, flooding their surroundings with brilliant light and joyful sounds.

The iron-eyed man bent down as if to kiss her. She looked up and saw into his soul, eager to be united to him, mesmerized by everything about him. And when his lips were almost brushing hers and she could feel his warm, soft breath on her mouth, a terrible wrenching sound tore them apart. The raven-haired woman had called out his name.

Everything stopped. The kaleidoscope of beauty froze into ugliness. The woman stepped between them and pushed him away. Ariel could see the withdrawal in his eyes and was helpless to stop it.

She cried out to him, but he'd let go of her hand and was receding, backing away. Cool loneliness replaced his magical warmth. Her dream lover was leaving her again, as he had over and over, time after time.

The crystalline laugh of the raven-haired woman cut her like a razor's edge. And, in her dream Ariel cried out again as unshed tears ached behind her eyes. She reached out with both hands, pleading for him to come back to her, to forgive her for her plainness, to love her just the same, to forget the raven-haired woman who beckoned to him. But the more she reached out, the more he faded away, as if repelled by her forwardness.

Anguish tore at her heart. One last time she had to try to reach him. Just one kiss. Just one embrace to remember forever. And one last time she reached out and called his name.

"Adam . . ."

And this time he was there. The feel of his shoulders beneath her hands was such a relief and gave her such joy that she began to weep.

"Shhh, it's all right," she heard him murmur.

She sobbed his name again, but this time she cried out in joy. At last he was hers, if only for a moment.

She pulled him toward her and felt the length of his body pressed against hers. After such a long, pain-filled search, it was not close enough. He tried to pull away, but she held him fast, pressing herself against him, murmuring wordlessly her desire for him.

She felt him stiffen in resistance, and she cried out again.

"Please . . . don't go. Not . . . again. Please. Not . . . again . . ."

She ran one hand up across his back until she felt his hair fall softly between her fingers. She pulled his head down, and her lips found his.

Slowly the resistance melted in him as the kiss blossomed and grew, enveloping them both, cradling them in a world of exquisite delights. She felt his hands on her shoulders and wriggled against them, reveling in his first willing touch.

Ariel took his face in her hands and kissed his cheeks and eyes as his ragged breathing and groans of pleasure urged her on.

"Ariel . . ."

His voice was a strangled, agonized whisper. Gently he pushed her shoulders down, levering his body away from her.

"No," she cried out softly, as knife blades of pain pierced her heart, suddenly bereft of her dream lover.

"Please," she whispered, her heart in her voice as she clutched his hand in hers and drew it toward her mouth. Tentatively she kissed his palm. Then, instinctively, she caressed it with the tip of her tongue, thrilling at his ragged intake of air and muted protest.

As he tried to draw away from her again she pulled his hand down to her breast. She could feel the warmth of his hand through the soft cotton shirt. A smile of contentment dawned on her face. She lifted herself up a little to kiss the hollow of his neck, holding his hand in place.

She was only vaguely aware of his muffled voice as his arm encircled her waist and pulled her up against him. She smiled in pleasure at the feel of his grip. The hand she had drawn to her breast closed over the gentle swell, caressing her . . . as she had only dared to dream.

Then, wondrously, his mouth found her throat and trailed

fiery kisses across it, continuing upward until, at last, he found her lips. Her soft cries of pleasure and tattered breathing blended with his. His lips brought warmth and tenderness and a slender flame of passion to her. She was so eager for him, she couldn't bear for him to want her any less. And so she kissed him with a desperate hunger, and his resistance broke. He kissed her back, the way a man kisses a woman, the way she'd always dreamed of being kissed, the way a man kisses a woman whom he desperately wants to possess in every way possible.

The more they sought to assuage the gnawing emptiness and frustration that had tormented them for so long, the more they wanted from each other. The kisses that had been so sweet, so exciting, soon became almost frustrating. It was not enough.

She felt his hands on her body. She ran her hands down his back. The feel of his shirt seemed so strange, so out of place in a dream . . . so real.

She heard him murmur her name again, in an odd, strangled way. She hugged him and pressed up against him. But he was saying something. It was so hard to hear. His lips were no longer touching hers, and his weight was strangely stiff and still now. She lifted her head slightly.

"Ariel . . ."

His voice was so real. A tiny needle of consciousness slowly penetrated her drugged senses. His body felt too real. The heat from their bodies was too real. The sharp pressure of his belt buckle against her stomach was too real to be a dream.

Ariel froze.

Her eyes flew open. She struggled to focus in the darkness of her room as the dream receded and reality gradually filtered in.

It was not a dream. It was real.

He sensed the change in her and looked down warily into her shocked face. Her eyes were wide-open and vulnerable. She looked like she expected to be executed.

123

Ariel stared up at Adam in the darkness. It was the real Adam, not the Adam of her dreams. She opened her mouth to speak, but no words came to her. The taste of him was still on her mouth. The feel of his body was imprinted on hers. And it was no wonder. He lay sprawled across her. They were so closely entwined, even Ariel, in her innocence and barely awake, could not mistake the state of his arousal. It had not been a dream after all this time, she realized, as shock began to settle in.

Ariel's hands dropped to the bed, and she clutched nervously at the covers.

Adam exhaled raggedly, as though he had been holding his breath for a long time. Reluctantly he rolled off her, lying next to her for a moment in silence, gathering his thoughts. He stared sightlessly into space, rather shaken himself at this point.

"I . . . what are you . . ." Ariel choked.

". . . doing here?" he finished for her in a roughened voice. "I heard you cry out. I came in to see what the matter was."

He hesitated.

"Oh," she said weakly as embarrassment began to overwhelm her.

"When I touched your shoulder, you pulled me off balance, and things got a little out of hand," he explained, watching her thoughtfully. "Are you all right?" he asked softly.

Ariel felt the warmth in her face and knew it was shame, not desire, this time.

"Yes," she whispered in a tortured voice. "I'm sorry. I don't know what to say. . . ."

With every ounce of her being Ariel wished she would somehow miraculously be transported back into her dream, even if it did always end as a nightmare. Tonight's ending in reality was by far the worst one yet.

She tried to smooth her shirt a little. It was looking rather wrinkled and the tails were out.

"Why did you cry out?" he asked guardedly.

"I . . ." She stammered. What could she say? What had she already said? What a dreadful mess! "I was having a nightmare," she admitted, struggling to sound halfway in control of herself again.

He lay there so still and unmoving, as if her answer were of great importance to him.

"You called out my name," he said carefully. "Several times," he added when she did not reply to that. "Am I part of your nightmare?"

Ariel didn't know what to say. She couldn't tell him the truth. And yet, she couldn't tell him a lie.

He stretched out his arm and touched her cheek tentatively.

"Tell me, Ariel," he said in a low, compelling voice. "Do I frighten you?"

She tried to ignore the wonderful sensation his fingertips brought to her. It was impossible.

"Frighten me?" she echoed as her eyes slid closed and she leaned slightly into his open palm. "Yes. You frighten me. You make me feel things that frighten me. You make me want things that I don't understand. You make me need things that I never knew existed before."

His fingers splayed out and gently sank into the softness of her hair. She sighed with pleasure. They were in a dark cocoon. She had no more to lose. She had lost everything. He would never see her the way she wanted him to see her—as a cultivated, cool, well-crafted woman. He had already seen too much of the woman within her, the woman she had never known she was until she met Adam Locke.

"And you frighten me, Ariel Radnor," he murmured huskily as his eyes traced her features in the shadows. He half smiled at her surprise. "That surprises you?"

"Yes," she replied. She would have used the word *astonished*. "How can I frighten you?"

He traced the smooth line of her cheek with his free hand, leaving an arc of relaxation and delight in its path.

"For the same reasons that I frighten you. I never felt this

125

way about a woman before," he muttered, finding it difficult to admit the truth out loud to her. "You're driving me crazy. Do you know that?"

He leaned forward and pressed his mouth to hers, and Ariel was lost to him. She kissed him back automatically, without hesitation, without thinking. She needed the feel of his mouth on hers, as much as she needed food or drink . . . perhaps more.

He pulled back for a moment, gazing deeply into her eyes, as if trying to be sure of something.

"Are you sure you're awake now?" he asked softly.

She looked at his familiar features. He was real now. This was no dream. There were no phantoms to come between them. Her barriers were in rubble around her, destroyed by her own recklessness and desire. And yet she was still torn two ways. She wanted to hide from him and from all that he aroused in her. She wanted to walk away from those terrifying, wonderful feelings that he magically ignited in her. But a part of her wanted desperately to reach out and really know him, to follow him down the path of desire, to become a part of him, to make him a part of her.

"Yes," she managed to say. "I'm awake. I'm sure of it."

"There's something I have to know," he murmured, holding her face tenderly.

"What is it?" she breathed.

"Is there anyone else in your life now?"

She felt the tension in his hands and smiled gently, and her eyes closed into catlike slits. She felt like purring with pleasure. He cared whether there was or not!

"No," she replied, lifting her lips toward his.

His mouth touched hers, and the sweetness of his kiss spilled over and flooded her with longing.

He pulled away suddenly and sank his face into her neck, struggling for control.

"And you," she whispered unsteadily. "Is there anyone in your life?"

She held her breath in agony, but she had to know the

126

truth. The nightmare that had haunted her for so long had been bad enough. If reality turned out to be the same as her nightmare, it would be unbearable.

He lifted his head, and his iron eyes held her fast.

"No. There is no one. No one but you . . ."

And his mouth came down on hers, sealing her question and his answer forever with a searing kiss.

To be kissed by him was to be electrified. The warmth of his lips on hers was like every dream she had ever had of him and more. A current of desire spread until every nerve ending in her body seemed to be switching on, eager to receive its pleasure in turn.

He grasped her head lightly, and she curved into him, wishing that he'd never let her go. His touch told her all she wanted to know. More eloquently than words, it conveyed his eagerness for her.

"Open your mouth," he murmured between kisses.

She relaxed a little and felt his tongue slide between her lips. The kiss deepened and grew as his tongue moved against hers, firmly caressing the warm, moist, inner surfaces and bringing them to an exquisitely sensitive pitch.

Ariel was barely aware that she had released the bedcovers and had shyly placed her hands on his waist. Adam, on the other hand, was immediately aware of her small gesture of surrender. His mouth and body hardened in passionate response against her.

"Ariel," he murmured huskily, trailing hot kisses along her jaw and throat. "I've wanted you for so long." He pulled out the pins in her hair, one by one. "I've dreamed of doing this," he whispered as he loosened it, letting it spill across the pillow.

His mouth was on her neck. Chills of pleasure were rippling downward across her body.

"Ever since that night, I've wanted to see you like this."

And she was as exotic and enticing and beautiful as he had remembered. More so. She was the auburn-haired siren whose call he could not ignore, who'd seemed like some kind of magical soul mate, a woman who'd stepped into his life and stirred up feelings he'd never felt before. A woman who'd left before he could stop her without explanation or farewell, leaving a void of frustration and desire and longing. The long, wavy hair spilling across the bed, the mysterious dark eyes, that air of innocence, the fire, the haunting beauty—all here, all his at last for the taking. . . .

She barely felt the pressure of his fingers as he unbuttoned her shirt. He pushed it off her shoulders, and she arched her back, eager to be closer to him as he kissed the sensitive hollows just below her collarbone. He caressed her waist and hips as he removed her slacks, easing them down over her hips so naturally that Ariel felt as if they had done this a hundred times. With him everything was familiar . . . everything was right.

He pulled her hands to his chest.

"Take off my shirt," he said, less steadily than before.

His shirt dropped from her nerveless fingertips moments later, joining hers on the floor next to the bed.

He loosened her bra, and Ariel sighed as bare flesh at last touched bare flesh. He ran his hands slowly down her sides, lighting fires everywhere he touched, then across her abdomen, in lingering, circular motions.

"You are so beautiful," he murmured, caressing first one breast, then the other.

Ariel, drowning in a sea of sensations, ran her hands shyly over the smooth, hard muscles of his back.

"Yes," he whispered huskily. "Touch me."

And he proceeded to show her how.

With Adam guiding her hands Ariel unzipped and removed his slacks, letting them fall to the growing pile on the floor. Where he touched her, she touched him in return. She didn't know where her pleasure ended and his began. She drew as much delight from his response to her as she did from his caresses and kisses.

He moved his mouth sensuously over her, teeth nipping

erotically, tongue exploring and massaging while she writhed beneath him in sweet agony.

Finally he slipped off her last remaining article of clothing. For the first time Ariel lay naked in the arms of a man. For a split second she felt a stab of hesitation. She pressed her body against him and buried her face in his shoulder. She felt so overwhelmingly vulnerable, so totally at his mercy . . . and so unsure of her own adequacy.

He kissed her ear gently and tenderly pushed her back down onto the bed.

"Tell me if you want me to stop," he told her unevenly. He touched her lips softly, brushing soft kisses on them, teasing . . . brushing . . . teasing again.

Adam ran his fingers through her hair and rubbed his cheek sensuously back and forth across her now-sensitized breasts.

Stop? The word seemed far away and receding fast as his mouth closed over the dark tip of one breast, and his roughened velvet tongue passed in circular motions over its hard, knobby peak.

Ariel moaned in pleasure and clutched him convulsively, entwining her legs in his.

Adam had used the final shreds of his self-control to offer her one last opportunity to refuse him. Now he devoted all of his energies to making love to the woman who had fascinated him for so long. Tomorrow would have to take care of itself.

And, oh, how Ariel felt loved. Each masterful caress, each stroke of his hand, each hot, suctioning kiss spiraled her more deeply into his net of desire. The warm touch of his hand on her hip and on the soft flesh of her thighs . . . the way he pulled her toward him . . . the way he held her, hard and tight and yet as if he were almost trembling. It was all wondrously, ecstatically new. And it was sweetly tender and familiar at the same time.

Inside her, a voice cried out silently, *I love you . . . I love you*. Even though she knew it couldn't be.

He rolled over on top of her, gently forcing her unresisting thighs apart with his knees and cupping her buttocks with his

129

hands. He lay still for a moment, trying to rein in his need for her before it carried him away completely.

There was no doubt about his desire for her, she thought ecstatically as she held him in her trembling arms. You are mine, mine. . . . *Mine,* she thought, delirious with the heat of her own passion and thrilled at the discovery of his.

He buried his face in the softness of her neck and slowly began to move against her, back and forth . . . teasing . . . teasing . . . until she felt herself helplessly, automatically responding, trying to be complete, eager to be one with this man, with this magical, fascinating, known yet not-known man.

He was hard and demanding where she was soft and yielding and warm. And he brought an ache to her loins that became almost unbearable.

"Oh, please," she sobbed, not knowing what to do. "Please . . . please . . ."

Their tongues stroked hot and hard, sucking and pulling in desperation. He pulled her pelvis up and pressed against her in deepening circles of rapture.

Just when Ariel was about to go wild with frustration, Adam groaned and thrust into her. There was a streak of pain, and she dug her nails into his back convulsively. But passion had anesthetized her, and they were both now caught in a tide too strong to resist.

He stroked into her, pulling her buttocks forward toward him until she caught the rhythm and could do it herself. Such sweet pressure . . . so long denied, it broke quickly into something more. The wildness of their kisses was repeated as their bodies lost control. The peak was unbearable and seemed to go on forever until at last Ariel cried out and showers of ecstasy burst from some inner part of her, suffusing her with a deep, fulfilling pleasure as Adam shuddered hard against her and echoed the same release.

They lay together in the darkness, damp and breathing hard and totally drained. At peace for the moment . . . spellbound by an attraction that neither of them fully understood . . .

satiated by the tender and satisfying lovemaking . . . isolated from reality. Just a man and a woman who had found something wonderful.

Wrapped in each other's arms, kissing languorously, they slipped into a peaceful, exhausted sleep.

CHAPTER EIGHT

Unhappily most dreams do come to an end sooner or later. The end came to theirs early the next morning in the form of the shrill ringing of the telephone next to Ariel's bed. After something of a struggle she finally managed to untangle her arms from the sheets and snag the receiver on the sixth ring.

"Hello," she mumbled groggily, eyes still closed and feeling a little overheated for some reason. Maybe she was coming down with a fever.

"Ariel! Are you all right?" came the urgent rejoinder over the wires. It was an all-too-familiar voice.

"Darryl?" Ariel croaked. She cleared her throat and tried again. "Darryl? I'm fine. How are you?" The inane response came out automatically. This was ridiculous. What in the world were they talking about? And what was the suppressed laughter coming from next to her?

She began to toss off the heavy blanket when her mind finally cleared and she woke up enough to remember where she was. And, more importantly, where Adam Locke was.

"Uh, Darryl, I . . . umm," she stammered, tugging the covers up around her bare chest and snuggling down under them for good measure. The heavy blanket moved itself off her hip, apparently seeking a more comfortable position and a good morning stretch. "I'll talk to you later, Darryl. . . ."

"I'm over at the Inn," he went on, as if not hearing her. "I was having a cup of coffee and reading the paper when I heard about the incident last night. Are you sure you're feeling all right?" he asked, deeply concerned.

The incident last night . . . There were incidents and then there were incidents, she thought fatalistically. Some are easier to recover from than others. The previous night—the part that had started and ended in her bedroom—came back in a blinding rush. She saw it like frames in a movie reel running at high speed in full, glorious color.

"I'm feeling just fine," she said in a completely unconvincing, wobbly whisper.

"You don't sound all right," he observed a little reticently. "I'll come over and make you some breakfast," he offered hopefully.

"No," she blurted out, sitting up straight. Desperately she pulled the sheet up around her bare back. "No, don't do that, Darryl. Really. I'm quite all right. And, uh, I've really got to go now. Thanks ever so much for calling."

She was leaning toward the phone, willing Darryl with all her might simply to say good-bye and hang up for once instead of dragging things out.

"You know, when Mother was ill, I learned a good recipe for headaches. I could—"

"No, Darryl. Thank you. I've got to—"

"Could I bring you something?"

"No," she practically shouted, thoroughly alarmed at that possibility. Ariel swallowed hard and cleared her throat, searching desperately for some inner strength in her moment of need. After all, her coach had said it would always be there when she needed it. She fervently hoped that her coach was right.

"No, Darryl," she said more calmly. "Thanks so much for offering, though. I've really got to go now. I'm in something of a hurry. I'm terribly sorry."

"Yes. We could—"

"Bye, Darryl."

"Good-bye, Ariel."

"Good-bye, Ariel" was enough for her. She hung up in

spite of the fact that poor Darryl was still murmuring sympathetically as the receiver clicked.

Oh, Lord, what do I do now? she prayed, frozen in position.

"Are your fingers glued to the phone?" inquired an amused voice from very close behind her ear.

Ariel released it as if it were a hot poker. She curled up on her side, facing the night table, her back to her overnight guest, as close to the edge as she could get without falling on the floor.

Think, Ariel, she told herself. *How do I get out of bed with no clothes on?*

Her houseguest didn't seemed too concerned. He pulled her to him and buried his face in her hair, sighing contentedly. He was as relaxed as she was rigid.

"Good morning," he murmured, kissing the nape of her neck.

That probably was as good a thing to say as any, she decided.

"Good morning," she replied. Now what? Strive for normalcy, she told herself. "Would you like some breakfast?" God, did it sound as awful to him as it did to her? she wondered.

He chuckled and gently nibbled along one bare shoulder.

"What do you have to offer?" he asked.

Ariel couldn't stand it. Double entendres just were not her forte, and she didn't think that her nerves were going to hold up under much more of them. She staggered awkwardly out of bed, tugging the sheet off along with her and winding herself in it as she stumbled away from the bed. She drew herself up regally in the center of the small room, which was now completely drenched in sunlight, thanks to her pale gauze curtains and a blindingly clear fall day. She tried not to think of the image she presented swathed in lilies of the field.

A thoroughly surprised Adam Locke stared at her speechlessly.

"Um . . . about last night," she began, trying to think of it all as a news item that had happened to someone else. This

134

was especially difficult since the other half of the news item's naked body was more visible than not under the goldenrod-yellow blanket that she'd left in her wake.

"Yes?" he said helpfully, still looking mildly astonished. "What about last night?"

She turned her back and waddled across the room, holding the extra sheet like the skirt of a ball gown.

"Well," she mumbled, rummaging through her dresser drawer for some clean clothes. "Um . . . it was very nice of you to put up with everything, under the circumstances, and I'm terribly sorry, but now I think you'd better be going. I really have a lot of things to do this morning."

The immediately noticeable effect of her speech was a little unnerving. Locke roared with laughter. If she'd had the courage to turn and look at him, she probably would have found him doubled up from the sound of it. Naturally she didn't look.

"What are you babbling about, Ariel?" he managed to ask at last, sitting up amid the disheveled remains of the bedding. "Come here."

She tucked her clothes protectively close to her chest and hurried toward the bathroom. That is, she hurried as much as anyone can while tightly wrapped in a sheet.

"Just lock the door on your way out," she suggested breathlessly before shutting the bathroom door. She stared at it for a moment. Then she locked it for good measure. She sighed as she unwound the sheet. She felt almost safe again.

As she turned on the shower she could just barely hear his muffled voice. Fortunately she didn't catch his exact words.

When she opened the door half an hour later, the first thing she noticed was the quiet. She held her breath and practically tiptoed toward the front door, venturing a cautious peek in the kitchen on her way. There was no sign of Locke. She breathed a sigh of relief.

Then she saw the note taped to her front door.

It read: "Gone back to the Inn to change. Will call you at

nine. Stay where you are. And stop thinking until we can talk about it. Adam."

Nine o'clock. That was just minutes away. Then she noticed the small pile of messages lying on the small table next to the door. He had been answering phone calls while she was in the bathroom.

Mrs. Norris had called. And so had Lydia. And David. And Robert Galway.

Ariel's face burned with embarrassment. What must they have thought? Adam Locke answering her phone at eight o'clock in the morning while she was taking a shower!

Then she saw the last note and paled.

Her parents had called.

The notes fell away from her unfeeling fingertips back onto the table. That did it. What in the world would she say to them? Worse yet, what would they say to her? She felt too raw and confused at the moment to face all those people. She was having enough trouble dealing with the events of the past night herself.

Fumbling awkwardly, she finally managed to get her jacket off its hanger in the hall closet and onto herself. The phone rang. As fast as possible, she grabbed her keys and ran out of the cottage. What else could possibly happen? she wondered as she broke into a brisk walk. There surely couldn't be much left!

Adam Locke stood in the doorway to his terrace at the Athena Inn and contemplated the new day. The brilliant colors of fall were just beginning to appear in the trees below, and the day was promising to be a good one. The sky was a clear, pale blue. There was a light, steady breeze. The sun was warm. The air was comfortably cool.

But all he saw was Ariel.

Damn!

From his high-rise view of the surrounding countryside he could just catch a glimpse of Ariel's cottage surrounded by a cluster of trees.

Ariel. He ran his hand through his hair in exasperation and went back inside. He just missed seeing the small figure leave the distant cottage and make its way through the woods.

What in the devil was happening to him? One brisk morning walk, one cold shower, and one view from the terrace later and he was still as turned on as he had been an hour ago when he'd watched her march out of the bedroom in that ridiculous sheet! How could he be staring at her cottage like a lovesick kid and seeing her face wherever he turned? Maybe it was some form of midlife crisis, he thought with unrepressed irritation.

This little venture with Athena was supposed to have helped him resolve this obsession he'd somehow developed for her. Unfortunately things weren't quite working out the way he'd planned. Ariel had gotten under his skin the way no other woman ever had. Something about her grabbed at his heartstrings in the way his first adolescent crushes had. He hadn't felt so peculiar in years, and he devoutly hoped to be over it soon. It was disconcerting . . . distracting. Maybe it was some kind of sexual infatuation. He'd heard of men developing things like that.

That was a little hard for him to swallow about himself, though. There was a different quality about his feelings for her. That was the most perplexing part of the whole mess. He truly felt differently about Ariel than he had about other friends or lovers. And he couldn't quite put his finger on what the difference was. Yet. He'd work on it. He'd have to. The frustration was getting worse instead of better, as unbelievable as that was!

What in the devil was that elusive quality she possessed that seemed so devastatingly attractive? He frowned. She was attractive, shapely, intelligent, self-reliant. But then, so were any number of women whom he'd known over the years. None of them had affected him like this!

He paced into the bedroom, picked up his wallet, and stalked into the living room of the suite.

Maybe it was that cool, self-controlled, almost distant exterior of hers. She'd tried to mask her sensuality here in Annapolis, apparently, but he'd seen her hidden fires in Georgetown when they first met, and he had never forgotten. The protective layering of standoffish naïveté that she wore here at Athena, like that air of being a little off-balance that she'd had in Georgetown . . . He thought about it. Yes. That definitely added to the attraction all right.

After last night he didn't know what to think about her. How could she be the two women she seemed to be? One warm and willing and eager . . . the other timid and reserved and frightened? Had the naive, shy image been real all along? Or was it a false facade used to entice him . . . and others?

He jerked his jacket off a plush chair back.

For months he had assumed that once he'd finally had her, everything would return to normal. He'd feel much better, and everything would become very clear. But Ariel was still an enigma to him. That was extremely annoying. Adam Locke was accustomed to having things work out the way he'd planned for them to work out.

Now what did he do?

He had no particular qualms about having an affair with a woman who knew the rules of the game. There had been one or two women in his life, he reminded himself modestly. He was a big boy. He could handle that just fine.

He paced across the room and lifted the phone, rapidly punching out Ariel's telephone number. No answer. Surely she was out of the shower by now, he thought in annoyance. When he called her, he wanted her to be there, damn it! He hung up the phone rather more forcefully than necessary and glared at the unhelpful instrument.

An affair with a woman who knew the rules was definitely okay. On the other hand, he didn't want Ariel hurt. And if she was really just an innocent young girl . . . well, that was something altogether different.

He strode purposefully out of his suite and ran down the stairwell, not wanting to wait for the elevator.

They needed to straighten out a few things, he decided.

Again. But nagging at the back of all his thoughts was a fundamental concern. He didn't understand why she seemed to be going out of her way to divide her life into separate compartments. What was she trying to hide?

Of course, men did that sort of thing all the time, but that was different, he told himself. That was perfectly reasonable. They were hiding affairs from their wives or running with several women at the same time or keeping their business life separate from their family life.

Why would a woman do it? Why would Ariel? And why did she seem determined to deny her attraction for him? That *really* bothered him!

After last night it was bothering him more than ever.

He turned down the path to Ariel's cottage and nodded unsmilingly at a passing engineer.

Damn it all! This was going to take longer than he'd originally thought. He picked up his pace a little. He'd get her worked out of his system one way or another. Even if he had to devote his every waking moment to the effort!

Genevieve Radnor stood patiently in her husband's study and waited for him to signal that it would be all right for her to speak. She'd learned during the first year of their marriage that interrupting him when he was in the middle of a thought was rarely worth the disgruntlement it produced. Since she was a little concerned about the events that had already transpired this morning, she was quite willing to wait for as long as necessary. It gave her some time to decide how to handle the situation. And since the situation involved her daughter, Ariel, she wanted to handle it very well indeed.

The balding, gray-haired man put down his pen and looked up, peering at her over his thirty-year-old tortoise-shell reading glasses.

"Did you get a hold of her?" he asked expectantly, riveting his full attention on her.

"No, but I'm sure that everything is all right, *chéri*," she said soothingly with a slight French accent.

139

Marcus Radnor stood up and placed his fists, knuckles down, on the desk. He leaned forward, glowering in the direction of his patrician spouse, looking quite formidable in spite of his modest stature and rather rumpled appearance.

"Am I to take that to mean that some man answered Ariel's telephone again?" he thundered.

"Non, non, mon cher! Pas du tout!" she hastened to say, graceful hands fluttering in the air for added emphasis.

"Well, then," he grumbled sternly. "What happened?"

Genevieve Radnor nervously smoothed her silken black hair, which was snugly wound in a French twist with not a strand out of place. She couldn't meet her husband's eyes, so she looked a little away from him. She gave a small, very Gallic shrug.

"Perhaps she may have gone out. No one answered," she said helplessly.

Professor Radnor straightened without a word and marched out of his study in a huff, snorting about "perhaps indeed!" on his way to the hall.

Genevieve hurried after him.

"Chéri! Ariel is a grown woman now," she reminded him as gently as she could. "We can't just go to her home, unannounced, behaving like . . . like . . ." She searched for a noninflammatory word to use, looking on in agitation as Marcus Radnor began buttoning his fifteen-year-old London Fog raincoat.

"Like parents?" he supplied gruffly.

He slowly stopped buttoning his coat as he considered what she was trying to say. He wanted to tear something down, but he didn't know what. It was rather how he had felt when Andrew had broken off the engagement and married that other girl.

His wife smiled at him in sympathetic understanding. He was a solitary, devoted man. For almost thirty years she had loved him. Even so, there were times when she despaired that he would see the world as it really was. He seemed to see the past so much more clearly than the present. And the people of the past—he understood them much more than those that surrounded him, especially Ariel.

He still hadn't been quite able to accept the fact that his little girl was no longer a child, that he no longer could protect her from life. She had grown up, and he had to let her go.

She sighed. As a historian, he'd spent all of his adult life working in the past. Would he ever know anything about the present? Or the people in it?

She came closer and gently began unbuttoning his coat.

"Yes, *chéri*, like parents. Like very loving parents." She tried to say it as delicately as possible. "Like parents who are, perhaps, a little bit jealous of the man who answered the phone."

She ended with just the tinest inflection of sympathy and laid her cheek against his for comfort.

"Jealous!" he grumbled, though not quite as forcefully as his wife had feared he would. "That's ridiculous!"

She made soothing, sympathetic noises and helped him off with his coat. She deftly put it away and steered him toward the breakfast nook in the kitchen.

"I'll fix you a nice, warm cup of café au lait," she said brightly.

"But I want to know what's going on down there, Genevieve," he protested, even though he had allowed himself to be detoured for the moment.

"Of course, *mon ami*. And you are right to want to know. But perhaps we should consider the proper time—"

"Proper time!" He snorted, watching her heat some water and pull the milk out of the refrigerator.

Proper time indeed! He wondered despondently who the faceless man was who had answered his daughter's phone that morning and where she was now. In spite of his instinctive desire to protect his little girl, he knew in his heart that his wife was right. Ariel was grown-up now. He couldn't protect her from life forever. Even when he thought he'd found her a safe haven, a steady helpmate, it had turned out all wrong.

But it still hurt to think that she might suffer at the hands of others. He'd seen too many of his students disappointed over the years to believe that she would be spared.

Genevieve Radnor returned with their coffee a very short time later. She smiled reassuringly at her husband, but she, too, was concerned. Ariel was their only child, and they both doted on her terribly. They always had.

When Genevieve had called Ariel the second time, at nine o'clock, there had been no answer at all. Of course, that could mean anything. But she had so wanted to just hear Ariel's voice. The whole thing was quite unsettling. Ariel had had only one boyfriend, one man in her life. And she'd not mentioned anyone in her letters. If she could just keep Marcus from doing anything foolish until she could have a heart-to-heart chat with her longtime friend, Margaret Norris. . . .

"Here you are, *chéri*. Now, may I make a small suggestion?" she said in that wonderful, melodic, slightly accented voice that had so enchanted Marcus Radnor from the very first moment he heard it.

And he did love to be enchanted. Marcus Radnor was no fool. He willingly entered into the little games his wife wanted to play. And, basically he was quite content in his role. He looked in tender amusement at the deceptively reticent woman who was so magnificently skillful in manipulating him out of the problems he regularly, though inadvertently, provoked. She was always so thoroughly gracious about it, too, never claiming any credit for the resolutions, trying to make it seem as if he'd thought of it all himself.

"Of course. What do you suggest?" he asked, confident once again that she would come up with a winning play.

"Well . . ." she began hesitantly, with her habitual flourish of the hand, "perhaps we should plan a small trip for next weekend."

"A trip, eh?"

"*Oui*. A trip."

*   *   *

Had Ariel known that it was her mother calling, not Locke, she might have left with even greater speed than she did. As it was, she just barely managed to push her worries somewhat out of her mind when she reached the gymnasium.

To her surprise it didn't feel quite the same to walk inside the familiar surroundings. That was disappointing. She closed the door behind her, slipped off her shoes and jacket, and tried to feel at home. It was the same and yet not the same.

She started to do some stretching exercises and felt the same stinging sensation she'd felt earlier. Okay, I'm not the same, she admitted unhappily. But it's not the end of the world. I'm not going to stop and dwell on it. She pushed the memory away, but it kept coming back.

Angrily she walked over to the far corner of the mat and walked through one of her old floor routines. Then she went through it at a faster speed, turning the walkovers into somersaults. She was doing a one-handed handstand when she felt a cool breeze and heard the door open. She dropped to her feet and looked up.

The large figure of Jim Reeves was not exactly what she needed to see right now.

He was grinning and clapping enthusiastically.

"Hey, that's great stuff! Don't quit on account of me!"

Ariel smiled wanly. It was hard to respond graciously under the circumstances. Even though the gym was for everyone's use, few employees other than Ariel ever came down here. This morning, of all mornings, she had wanted to be alone. His presence was an intrusion she could really do without.

His gaze slid down, then up, her body, tightly molded under her leotards. It was a thoroughly masculine, admiring look. Since she didn't particularly care for him, however, it made her feel almost unclean to be looked at like that.

"You sure are a strong one . . . especially for such a pretty little girl," he said in his customary friendly, easygoing way.

He slipped out of his coat and walked closer.

143

"I heard that you come down here," he said. "Why don't you show me what you can do? I'm a great audience."

He grinned broadly, holding out his arms expansively as if to show how big and harmless an audience he really was.

"Well . . ." She didn't want an audience. She'd never been too wild about them. Maybe that was why she never succeeded in the really big meets. But where else could she go to try to pull herself together this morning?

"You know," he told her proudly, "I used to wrestle in high school. Played first string on the football team too." He gave her a warm look, accompanied by another admiring assessment of her body. "I guess I always did like contact sports best. . . ."

There was something suggestive in his voice and his eyes. Ariel had the feeling that most of Jim's contact sports were played someplace other than on a field.

Ariel grimly chalked up her hands and reached for the parallel bars. That piece of equipment was farthest way from him. At least it was until she started working on it. It didn't take him long at all to get to it.

"Say, I heard you got conked on the head last night," he said, sounding both concerned and curious. "Are you okay?"

"Yes."

Her hands slipped a little.

"What happened?"

She almost lost her grip on the handstand. She held it long enough to answer him.

"I have no idea. A burglary attempt, I guess."

"Hm. Do they know who did it?"

She forced herself to keep going, in spite of the difficulty in concentrating she was having.

"No."

He was silent while she worked through most of the remainder of the routine. Near the end, however, he spoke again.

"Say, since I never got that dance the other night, how about going out to dinner with me tonight?" he asked casually.

Ariel was straddling the bars and swinging into a shoulder stand when he asked. The thought of going out with him was so unappealing, she barely made it up.

"Uh . . . I don't think—"

"Aw, come on, Ariel. I'm a nice guy," he said, teasing her and reaching out and snagging her ankle playfully.

Ariel hadn't been crazy about talking while doing a routine, but she'd hoped if she kept working out, he'd give up and go away. He was the type who enjoyed being the center of a woman's attention, not a sitter on the sidelines. She'd never dreamed he'd try to pull her off the equipment! As a result she completely lost her balance and could do nothing to save herself when he pulled her down into her arms.

Which was the scene that greeted Adam Locke when he pushed open the gymnasium door.

"Put me down!" Ariel said angrily as she tried to get her feet low enough to touch the floor and push her hands against Reeves's broad, hefty chest.

The sound of another person entering the building caused them both to look toward the door. The forbidding look on Adam Locke's granite features turned them both to stone.

"Put me down," Ariel hissed, squirming as hard as she could as the blood drained from her face.

"By all means," Locke said in dangerously congenial tones, "please do put her down. I have a few things to discuss with Ms. Radnor, and I'm sure that she'd rather not have to listen to what I have to say while hoisted up in the air like that."

Locke was crossing the room in an unhurried manner, unbuttoning his jacket and raising an eyebrow just enough to give a sardonic cast to his face.

Reeves let Ariel slide to the floor.

"About tonight . . ," he said, a little less confidently than before, half looking at Ariel and half looking at the fast-approaching Locke.

Adam's eyes narrowed dangerously.

Ariel didn't know where to turn or what to say. She'd been

145

completely shocked to see Adam walk through the door. She was deathly afraid of being alone with him again. Much as it revolted her to think it, it was possible that Jim Reeves might offer a certain amount of protection for her at the moment. The only problem with that, of course, was that she wasn't sure she could stomach paying Reeves's price. And at this point she wasn't even certain what his price might turn out to be.

Locke realized that she was hesitating and wondered with more than a little impatience why. After thinking about it, it suddenly dawned on him that she was toying with using Reeves to avoid him. Damn it all! He'd get her to stand and face him whether she liked it or not!

"Ariel's going to be working for me. All day. This evening as well." He smiled as he smoothly put an end to her escape. The smile did not, however, reach his eyes.

Ariel shot him a look of amazement mixed with rebellion.

"Did you forget?" he inquired blandly, and his hard eyes bore into hers like blue steel.

"I . . ." She'd started to say that she didn't recall, had made other plans and couldn't possibly change them now, but Reeves had already correctly sized up the situation and was ambling toward the door.

"That's okay," the mailman said genially, bending to pick up his jacket from the gymnasium floor. "Some other time. See you later. Watch that head, kid."

He winked at Ariel and nodded at Locke. Then he stepped out of the gym and left them alone. The last thing Ariel heard was the sound of his whistling as it faded away in the distance.

Locke stopped a few feet away from her. Ariel could not bring herself to look directly at him. She felt so exposed, so embarrassed . . . so naked before him. She'd never felt quite so miserable in her life.

"Didn't you see my note?" he asked casually, loosening the hand that had clenched only a moment earlier. Something about her drained off his anger and made him want to comfort

146

her instead. She looked so vulnerable and alone standing there, as if she were afraid even to look at him.

"Yes," she said, as strongly as she could. It still sounded pretty shaky, she thought.

"Then why didn't you stay in your cottage?" he asked with a sigh of exasperation. He was still angry, but he didn't know why he was angry or what there was to be angry about at this point. Maybe he was angry because she'd run away from him. Again. It was a damned annoying habit she had! He wondered if she ran away from all men like this or if it was something about him that made her take off with such remarkable regularity.

Then again, maybe he was angry that she looked so damned unhappy. He was beginning to feel pretty miserable, himself, just looking at her.

Or maybe he was angry at having found her in the arms of another man. The thought made a flame of fresh anger flare through him. Yes, he was angry about that all right, he admitted. Well, after all, he'd just left her bed. It was natural to be annoyed, under the circumstances, he told himself, conveniently forgetting some other times when it hadn't bothered him in the least.

And he was angry at himself, he realized. That was a little harder to come to grips with. He was beginning to feel guilty about Ariel. Maybe she was suffering because of what had happened between them last night. He told himself she was as responsible as he was for what had happened, but he felt guilty and responsible all the same. Damn it all! If she just didn't look so blasted miserable! He couldn't stand to see her look like that. It twisted something very tender in the vicinity of his heart.

He stepped closer, to within an arm's length of her. He saw her stiffen. He made no move to try to touch her.

"Ariel," he said softly, "why did you leave?"

Why did he have to speak to her like that? she wondered, anguished at the tenderness in his compelling, commanding voice.

147

"I . . . I just didn't want to talk to you," she said, as firmly as she could. She felt trapped and exposed. Now he wanted to talk about it, for pity's sake!

Like a cornered animal, she felt herself growing angry. She knew it was a form of self-defense, but she couldn't help the way she felt. She was well aware that lots of people handled things like this with no problem at all. And she was quite painfully aware that she wasn't one of them. And she was angry that Locke was going to see it and most probably laugh about it, shake his head and pat her on the back, telling her something like, "Don't worry about it. Everything will seem better in the morning. . . ."

"Now, would you mind if I got back to my workout?" she snapped, turning back to the parallel bars.

His hands clamped down on her shoulders, and he pulled her back against his chest. She could feel his body through his coat, pressed against her shoulders, her back, her buttocks, the backs of her thighs. And she could sense the coiled tension in him, in all of him, not just the powerful hands that had stayed her flight.

"Yes, I would mind," he ground out. "I would mind very much indeed. You're coming with me. We're going to have a long talk. And when we come back this evening, we're both going to feel much better than we do right now," he added, each word harder and more succinct than the last.

"I don't want to go anywhere with you," she argued angrily, wriggling to get away from him.

He turned her around and pulled her hard up against him, one arm belting her waist while the other pulled her head toward his. His eyes locked with hers. Anger, frustration, confusion, desire . . . they chased one another and mixed and roiled until their mouths fused.

Ariel didn't know if she raised her lips to his or if he lowered his mouth to hers. Maybe it was a little of both. But the hungry, passionate contact took them both by surprise. His lips were hard and warm and tender and demanding and took from her as much as he gave. She moaned and wrapped

148

her arms around his neck, lost in delight, lost in him, lost to herself.

He was breathing unsteadily when he finally broke off the kiss and rested his head against hers.

"Please, Ariel," he whispered against her lips. "Come with me. There are some places I want to show you. Some people I want you to meet." He kissed her again, deeply. "And I can't stand the thought of not being able to kiss you again like this."

Ariel rested her cheek against his. When she was in his arms, it was easier to say yes. She closed her eyes and tried to shut off her mind.

"Stop thinking, sweetheart," he murmured as his tongue traced an erotic line on the lobe of her ear. "Please, come with me. I promise you'll feel better."

"All right," she whispered.

CHAPTER NINE

Ariel had to admit it. She did feel a little better.

Somehow that kiss had broken the ice between them, and Adam was careful to keep nurturing the thaw along. With little conversation he managed to escort her from the gym to his car, detouring by her cottage just long enough for her to change into some clothes a little more suitable for sailing. He stayed very close to her this time, touching her constantly in light, but very comforting, ways: holding her hand, grasping her elbow, lightly encircling her shoulder or waist. It kept them connected. It kept her from freezing up again.

And it didn't exactly hurt Adam any, either.

Locke owned the kind of car that she'd more or less envisioned that he would. She spotted it the moment they set foot on the Athena parking lot. It was a pine-green Jaguar XJ6. Like its owner, it managed to look both elegant and sporty at the same time.

She squeezed her eyes shut for a split second as he helped her into the front seat. Stop thinking. Stop thinking! *For today . . . for just this once I want to stop thinking and be the person I really am inside, not the image I'm supposed to be.*

"Ready?" he asked with an encouraging grin as he locked the doors and turned on the powerful engine.

He covered her slender hand with his and squeezed it gently. Ariel felt a little safer. In fact, she was beginning to feel a little safer every time he touched her. When he touched her, she wanted to be closer to him, to cuddle up against him and feel safe and sheltered in his arms. *Just don't let me go*, she asked silently. *Just don't let go. . . .*

"Ready," she replied, even though it took an effort to make herself say it. Once the words were out, though, she almost did feel ready. Maybe it was like learning a new routine, she mused. You have to see it in your mind first, will yourself to do it, believe that you can—and then you can.

Maybe that was it. *Well, Ariel*, she told herself, *you can't be a kid forever*. She turned her hand palm up and clasped his fingers in hers as Locke edged the car smoothly out of the lot and onto the road toward Annapolis.

David Carrollton watched with intent curiosity as the powerful, green Jag disappeared over the crest of the hill, heading toward the bridge that crossed the Severn less than a mile away. So, Ariel was spending time with Locke. Maybe that would give him the excuse he was looking for. . . .

Carrollton turned on his heel and headed for his own car, a much-repaired, twenty-year-old Volvo. First he had an appointment to keep, but after that . . .

He smiled automatically at Robert Galway, who was just driving into the lot. Then he stepped on the gas and sped down the road away from Athena.

Robert Galway wasted no time in walking across the Athena estate to Dr. Norris's home. Margaret Norris, who had been told to expect him, ushered the chief security officer into her husband's study immediately.

Norris looked up and frowned.

"Well?" he asked peremptorily, as soon as his wife had left them alone.

"It looks like it was an inside job," Galway said. "We've got no fingerprints. No physical evidence of any consequence. No eyewitness description. Nothing to help identify the perpetrator."

"Nothing!" Norris shouted angrily, slapping down hard on the large, mahogany desk at his side the journal that he'd been reading. "Damnation! How in the hell are we going to find out who did it, then? Or what in name of all that's holy is going on?"

It infuriated Dr. Norris to think that one of his employees was spying or stealing from him. It inflamed him even more to think that he appeared to have no way of putting a stop to it or finding out who was doing it.

"Do you have any suggestions?" he asked challengingly, venting some of his frustration on his nearby subordinate.

Galway wisely ignored his employer's temporary ire. He was in his late fifties and had seen enough of life to recognize that Norris's anger wasn't really directed at him. He just happened to be a convenient target for it. Besides, he was pretty well disgusted himself right now too. After all, it was his security that had been breached. Galway wanted to nab the culprit just as badly as his boss did. And he'd been thinking about how to do that for several hours now.

"As a matter of fact, I do have some ideas," he replied calmly.

Norris paced around his desk and indicated for Galway to have a seat.

"Well, let's hear it!"

Walter Lewis recognized the sound of Locke's engine before he saw the car. The soft crunch of the gravel-top road under smoothly executed turns told him that Adam was driving it.

He grunted and ran the blade of his knife one more time over the belly of the piece of wood in his left hand. When he heard the car pull up and the motor cut off, he just kept on with what he was doing. Doors opened and slammed shut. When he heard footsteps on the wooden planking leading up to his small house, he lifted his graying head.

"Waalll, morning, Adam," he drawled, as a slow grin spread across his weather-beaten face. "Good to see ya. And who's this pretty lady you brung with ya?"

Walter Lewis's pale blue eyes were kindly and sage. He

took in the sight of Adam Locke holding a young woman by the hand and politely decided not to tease him about it. They looked to him as if they were in deep water and had barely gotten their sea legs. And the way they were holding on to each other . . . it was like it was a sort of lifeline helping them keep from being washed overboard.

He studied the girl for a minute. Then he shrewdly took a good close look at Adam. Yep. There was definitely something going on here, he decided. Something mighty interesting. Mighty interesting.

Adam had said hello and made introductions while his old friend and Ariel looked at one another. Adam squeezed her hand a little tighter, and Ariel managed to smile graciously and say hello.

"The *Catarina*'s all ready fer ya," Walter said, putting down the duck decoy he'd been whittling.

The old man got up and walked with them down to the small boat slip nearby. He asked about Ariel's family, and showed a genuine interest in her line of work. He gave Adam his opinion of the weather forecast for the day and a couple of changes in channel markers that were being made.

By the time they were ready to get on board the boat, Ariel felt like she was Walter's friend too. He was a warm, down-to-earth man with just enough formality in his ways to make him a real gentleman in spite of the faded overalls he wore and his river man's appearance and speech.

The *Catarina* was ready and waiting for them, snugly moored alongside Walter's small dock. Adam had called earlier in the week and told him that he wanted to take the *Catarina* out sometime. That was no problem. It had given Walter something to do, as a matter of fact. He enjoyed checking her over, tightening things up, mending a few tears, touching her fine wood surface.

Adam grinned at the gnarled old man standing with his hands stuffed into the pockets of his faded bib overalls.

"Walter and I are co-owners of the *Catarina*, but I'm afraid he does most of the work on her, don't you, partner?"

Walter eyed him and nodded.

"But, then, I get to keep her all the time," he pointed out genially. Adam had manufactured endless excuses to put money into Walter's boat slip and into repairs of the old skipjack. Now he'd be able to keep his own boat, a possession he'd cherished for a lifetime.

"Walter here is my oldest friend," Adam said to Ariel. He turned to Walter for confirmation. "Isn't that so, Walter?"

Walter harumphed and pulled the dinghy around and out of the way, giving the *Catarina* plenty of room to move away.

"Meanin' I'm older than most of the others?" Walter growled, although the gleam in his eyes severely undermined his attempt to appear intimidating and offended.

"That, too, I guess." Adam laughed as he placed the food and drink he'd picked up on the way into the *Catarina*.

"Yep," Walter said. "S'pose I must be at that."

"Walter taught me everything I know about sailing too," Adam noted, looking back at Ariel. God, how the sun glinted on her hair like red gold. He looked quickly toward Walter to quell the desire to pull her into his arms and kiss her, to smell the sweet scent of her hair in his nostrils again.

Walter grimaced at Adam's remark.

"Don't blame me if you can't get her home in one piece, boy," he cracked, shaking his head. "You ever sailed before, Ariel?"

He eyed her intently.

"A little."

"Can ya swim good?"

Ariel laughed. And Locke felt it like a caress deep in his chest. He looked at her in fascination. He hoped she would keep laughing like that.

"I'm passable," she answered, amused at the way Walter teased Adam. The fact that he included her in it made her feel like she was . . . family.

"That's good," said the old man with a reluctant satisfaction. "I jes hope that Adam here don't try to make you show just how passable!"

154

Adam laughed and stepped into the center of the cockpit. He held out his hand to Ariel.

"Come on! Let's get going before he scares you off with some really farfetched tales! Walter entertains himself in the off-season by spinning yarns. I'd hate to be the victim of one!" His fingers closed over hers as she stepped into the boat with him. "Don't believe half of what he tells you. He's spent so many years on the rivers around here that his brain's been waterlogged!"

Walter laughed and tossed Adam the bowline. Ariel caught the stern line as Adam hoisted the sail and readied the *Catarina* to get under way.

"Talk to you when we get back tonight!" Adam shouted as they pulled away.

Walter gave a wave of his hand and watched them go.

The *Catarina* was a graceful, Bermuda-rigged sloop and the perfect length for a two-man crew. The rich, natural hues of her fine wood build glowed beneath their protective sealant on the foredeck as her white-painted hull cut through the cold, dark waters lapping at her bow.

At first they were kept pretty busy. Ariel mostly ducked as the boom swung around or followed Locke's occasional instruction. He took the tiller and mainsheet, trimming and easing as he felt out the wind and the current. Ariel sat a little farther forward and soon found herself responsible for the jib. A light, steady breeze filled the sails, both blindingly white except for the vivid red of a stylized lock imprinted on the mainsail's head.

The breeze carried the briny smell of the sea, which was close at hand. It ruffled their hair and brushed a light spray of water over the gunwales from time to time. Overhead, a gull cried and chased and flapped, diving to pluck a quick-finned morsel from the river for his lunch.

Adam pointed out some landmarks as they worked their way up the shoreline.

"If we'd headed downriver, we could have seen the city

docks or even sailed out into the Chesapeake if you wanted to,'' he explained, trimming the mainsail a bit with a twist of his wrist.

Annapolis had a well-deserved reputation for its restored waterfront area. Teeming with boats during much of the year, it was a popular place to visit, and handsome indeed to see from the water. He would have enjoyed showing it to Ariel. Maybe he would sometime.

He wasn't particularly eager to sail out on the bay, however, and hadn't been for years. As a matter of fact, Locke avoided the Chesapeake as much as possible, sailing on it primarily to get to one of its tributaries, happy to be off of it as soon as possible.

Ariel said she didn't mind and was enjoying the direction they were taking.

"We're heading upriver, right?'' she inquired, certain that they were.

"Yes. I thought you might enjoy seeing what Athena looks like from the water,'' he replied. ''And, besides, it's a little quieter upriver.''

Which meant that he'd have time to talk to her, he unnecessarily reminded himself. Otherwise he'd be more tied up with navigation on the more crowded waterway near the city.

Upriver was indeed quieter. And very beautiful. There were occasional boat slips and homes nestled near the water's edge. Some were elegant and stately. Others were rustic and simple. The richly forested banks and hills crowned them all with democratic abandon. The shores were generally high, opening every so often into a charming, snug little creek just begging to be explored.

They were within sight of Athena's cliffs when they spotted a ketch anchored not too far from the banks below. A small dinghy was secured alongside, and unseen hands were furling the boat's mainsail. With the sail down they could just make out two figures as they disappeared below deck.

"Anyone you know?'' Ariel asked, mainly because Adam

156

had been hailed by three of the four other boats they'd passed.

He studied the craft as they glided by at a good clip. He'd raised the centerboard and was sailing a close reach. It was a glorious feeling, slicing through the water like that, but he had to pay close attention to what he was doing. A slight shift in the wind could make a big difference in a hurry.

He shook his head.

"Nope. Don't recognize it. Maybe it's the same one we saw up there"—he nodded in the direction of the cliff top—"from the terrace Friday night. Might be an off-season vacationer taking a close look at some of the snug little creeks and coves around here."

Which reminded him of what a snug little cove Ariel was and how he wanted to find someplace soon to anchor awhile so that he could have that nice long talk with her that he'd planned on. Among other things.

Adam found what he was looking for not much later when he located an inlet that had somehow managed to remain untouched by boat-loving homeowners.

After they were safely anchored and the sails furled, Adam unlatched the insulated carrying case that contained their food.

"*Voilà*," he said cheerfully as he handed her two large mugs and placed a fair-size metal plate on her knees. "It's heavier than a paper one," he explained as she looked at it in surprise. "Doesn't blow away as easily."

He poured hot tea from one thermos and hot soup from another, then did the same thing for himself, handing them each large beef sandwiches and fresh apples as well. He looked at her expectantly.

"Okay?" he asked hopefully.

Ariel couldn't help it. She had to laugh.

"Are you kidding? It's much better than okay and you know it. I'm used to being handed cold drinks in a can and nondescript munchies from a bag. This is great."

And it *was* great too. The hot chowder warmed her up and

157

the hearty sandwich tasted delicious. They ate in companionable silence, Adam finishing before Ariel.

"Have you been here before?" Ariel inquired after a while, feeling a new attack of shyness. They were so alone, and there was something intimidating to her now about the prolonged silence between them.

He smiled reminiscently and stretched out, lacing his fingers behind his head.

"Yeah. This is one of my favorite spots."

Ariel had to agree with his choice. It could easily become one of hers, too. It made her feel good to think that he'd chosen to share it with her. She decided she didn't want to know if he brought many people here or anyplace along the river, for that matter. She'd close her mind to that possibility and think of it as theirs.

"When I was a kid," he went on, "I used to sail up here a lot during the summers. It was my place to escape to, I guess." He gazed fondly at the shoreline, his eyes skimming the banks and trees like they were old friends. "Of course, the whole river is much more built-up now," he told her, shrugging philosphically. "I imagine one of these days even this place will be changed."

Changed.

The word reminded her of what she'd been trying to forget. She'd pretty much succeeded for a while. But the memory of the preceding night came back unexpectedly as the word sank in.

Ariel put her plate and mugs back into the carrying case with Adam's.

"Yes," she murmured, bowing her head to hide her face from him for a moment. She couldn't stop the burning in her cheeks, but maybe it would fade in a minute. "I guess change is just to be always expected."

She felt his fingertips under her chin, tilting her face upward until he could see her clearly. There was no escaping his penetrating, quiet scrutiny. And he read the ambivalence, the lost look in her eyes.

"Is that part of our problem, Ariel?" he asked seriously. "Change?"

Our problem. He had said *our* problem. For some reason it made her relax a little bit to hear him put it that way. He wasn't blaming her, telling her she should try harder, that she was the problem.

"I don't know," she said in all honesty. She tried to give him a small smile. It was unconvincing. "Maybe I'm just a little behind the times," she added lamely.

Adam shoved a few things toward the bow end of the cockpit and pulled her over next to him. He put his arm around her shoulders and pulled her head down into the curve of his neck. Ariel sighed and slipped her arm cautiously behind his back.

His *ummm* of satisfaction gave her the courage to curl the other arm over his waist. He covered her hand at his waist with his and pulled her close. She snuggled contentedly against his warm, relaxed body. The fact that they were both warmly dressed in heavy cotton slacks, sweaters, and Windbreakers barely mattered. Her nerves were energized by his closeness as much as they would have been in shorts or cutoffs.

Locke had already decided that it was easier for them to talk when they were physically close to each other. He wasn't sure why that was. And he hadn't any idea how he knew that. But he knew he was sure.

"Now," he said quietly, "we need to talk about a few things."

Ariel wasn't convinced of that, but she didn't want to spoil the tender feeling of closeness between them by arguing about it. She just prayed that talking wouldn't ruin their lovely afternoon.

"I want you to tell me what happened this morning," he said, gazing down at the top of her head as she snuggled against him like a rabbit. "Why did you take off and leave me like that?"

She knew exactly what he was referring to. If there could

have been any doubt, his low, compelling, hushed tone of voice would have made it abundantly clear to a village idiot!

"I . . . was embarrassed," she admitted. "I didn't know what to do . . . or what to say."

More vividly than she wanted to, she recalled exactly how awful she had felt waking up next to him like that. But, strangely enough, admitting it out loud to him was making her feel as if a small weight were being lifted from her shoulders.

Maybe it would help to talk things out. It was something that she didn't have a lot of practice at. She and Andrew had certainly not had the occasion for any truly intimate discussions. Until the end. That wasn't much of a help to her now.

And she and her parents had certainly never talked about anything remotely like this.

She felt his body next to hers and drew comfort from his nearness. She was certainly willing to give it a try. Yes, indeed. She'd certainly try. . . .

Adam stroked her hair thoughtfully, letting his fingertips slide slowly over the neatly coiled silk. He wanted to just come out and ask her if he had been the first, but he didn't want to sound crude or make her feel any worse than she already obviously did. He searched for a way.

"Not used to waking up with a man in your bed, huh?" he teased gently in a warm, tender voice that melted her heart.

That had to be the understatement of the year, she thought, stifling the sudden urge to laugh and cry at the same time.

"No, I guess I'm not."

"Did you ever wake up with Andrew beside you?" he asked calmly, though he didn't feel so calm at all inside.

He felt her stiffen, but he kept on holding her and stroking her tenderly, and gradually she relaxed against him again.

"No," she whispered. "It wasn't like that between us."

He was surprised how glad he was to hear that. He gave into the impulse to place a soft kiss on her cheek, then settled them back into their previous position and asked another question.

"Tell me about you and Andrew." He knew he'd never liked that name. "After knowing each other as long as you had, why wasn't it like that between you?"

He consciously chose to use her words, hoping to ease her into an explanation. But for the life of him he couldn't conceive of knowing her for years as this guy obviously had and not going to bed with her. It was beyond his ken. But he was sincerely grateful that it hadn't been beyond old Andrew's!

"I don't know," she replied slowly. "We just never . . . maybe there was never any real . . . fire there between us."

She had always known, deep down, that that was true, but this was the first time that she'd ever actually admitted it to herself or anyone else. Saying the words gave it a sort of reality and a finality, and it gave her a surprising sensation of relief. Saying it hadn't been so bad after all, she discovered. Adam wasn't laughing at her. She was still herself. She drew in a fortifying breath and told him the rest.

"Andrew and I were friends. Good friends. If our families and friends hadn't been so shocked and upset at our breaking off the engagement, or if I'd taken it better than I did, we'd probably still be friends."

Locke knew he didn't like that idea at all, but he knew better than to blurt out his disagreement and kept his editorial observation to himself for once.

"He felt awful about it, in spite of the fact that he was wildly in love with the girl he left me for. He never wanted to hurt me. Even then I knew that."

The more she talked about it to Adam's interested though somewhat enigmatic face, the easier it was to say more. So she kept on.

"Andrew Moorland is a very nice guy." She smiled fondly as she remembered what carefree fun they'd had together as teenagers, before life overtook them. "You'd probably like him yourself," she said, not realizing how wrong she was in thinking that.

Locke hadn't been able to see her smile, but he'd heard it in her voice, and jealousy assailed him.

"I seriously doubt it," he muttered tightly. His retort was so swallowed by his annoyance that Ariel heard it more like a grunt, but she caught his meaning all the same and hugged him for it before she realized what she was doing.

It was sweet—no, exhilarating—to feel he might be just a little annoyed about her involvement with Andrew.

"In a way we might have been better matched as brother and sister than as . . . fiancés."

Ariel stumbled over the word *fiancés* because she'd first intended to say *lovers* instead. Just before the word left her mouth she caught it, unable to say it to Adam's face.

"Or as lovers," he added softly, saying it for her.

Lovers. She heard the word reverberate silently in her head as she said it in the privacy of her own unvoiced thoughts. You are my lover now. And I am yours. That's what it's all about.

Her face warmed with embarrassment, and her body began to tingle. But the tingling came from remembering—and wanting him to touch her like that again, the way he had last night. That wicked thought only served to make her blush more, and it tied her tongue to boot.

"Go on," he encouraged her, giving her shoulder a reassuring squeeze. "How did you get together to begin with, and why did you stay together for so long if there wasn't any . . . fire?"

She sure as hell couldn't say something like that about their relationship, he thought as he remembered in detail the fires she'd ignited in him every time they met. And so damned effortlessly too!

Ariel shrugged, frowned a little, and then shook her head slightly from side to side.

"I don't know. I guess we liked each other well enough when we first met in high school. We were living in the same small town, going to the same small high school . . . in an environment where everyone knew everyone else. If you did something you were ashamed of, it was almost always going to end up as public gossip and common knowledge. There was no room for making any mistakes. Then, too, our families knew each other well, and we had the same friends. It was just so easy to keep it up. Just the same way so many of the adults kept up their marriages out of convenience more so than anything else. It would have been so much work, so disrupting to everyone, if we'd broken up. At least that's the way it seemed the few times our relationship ever seemed strained. After a while everyone thought of us as a couple. People were always asking me how Andrew was and vice versa. Maybe that held us together for all those years. I don't know. Maybe it was easier that way. After all, we were pouring all of our energies into our careers then, too, remember.''

''Hmmm.'' Adam gave her conclusions some thought. ''I've known plenty of people, men especially, who've poured a lot of themselves into their education and later into their work. But generally that doesn't completely rule out the possibility of an active sex life along the way.''

Ariel squirmed uncomfortably at that, but he held her in place.

''No, I guess not,'' she replied sharply. His somewhat doubtful response had come too close to her own secret fear. There had been something wrong with her, and that was the problem. Irrationally the thought grabbed hold of her again and wouldn't let go.

''I guess it all gets back to me, then.'' she said forcefully. ''I just didn't have what it takes to turn a man on. Andrew was a dear to put up with me as long as he did, and when he finally found a woman who has what it takes, he did develop a sex life, as you put it.''

She ended angrily, hating Locke for saying what he had and furious with herself for being such a failure and not having the vaguest idea of how to fix the problem, terrified that she never would.

Her anguished fury blinded her, and she was startled by Locke's lightning reaction to her outburst. Before she realized what he had done, she found herself hauled over on top of him with his arms clamped tightly around her as slate-blue eyes bore into her with unyielding intensity.

"Stop putting yourself down like that, damn it all," he ground out between half clenched teeth. He hadn't meant to touch a nerve like that and was mostly furious with himself for having done so. He had never been the type to berate himself over such *faux pas* in the past and, true to form, reacted by venting his ire on someone else. In this case the object of his affection and concern, Ariel. "That's the most ridiculous thing I've ever heard you say!"

"Is that so?" she snapped, trying to pull away from him without the slightest success at all.

Locke wrapped his legs around hers for good measure, completely immobilizing her. And thoroughly arousing her temper.

"Well, then, what's your theory about my unfortunate love life?" she jeered, blazing at being unable to free herself, hurling words at him for lack of anything more forceful.

"My *theory*," he said pointedly, and a little loudly considering that they were nose-to-nose and he really had no need to shout, "is that you two just weren't destined to fall in love, damn it!"

His choice of words was so unexpected that her mouth fell open and she froze in his arms with surprise.

Destiny wasn't one of the more popular things to apply to one's life and its ups and downs these days. It was such a nice, old-fashioned, downright *romantic* word. Hearing Locke apply it to her like that made him seem rather touching. It was so . . . endearing, really. It threw her quite off-balance.

"And," he went on, very forcefully, "I think that you both used the convenience of a steady relationship to protect yourselves from getting involved in other, more serious, more challenging relationships with people!"

He was practically glaring at her.

"What others?" she asked in genuine surprise.

"If you'd stopped hiding behind each other all those years, you'd have been forced to risk more of yourselves . . . give more. Other people have first loves like you did. Some of them last, but most of them don't. You two outgrew each other but were reluctant to admit it and go on to the next stage."

He'd talked himself back into a calmer state, especially since he'd finally realized that she wasn't fighting anymore; she was listening to him.

Gull cries broke the silence. Ariel stared into his hard, yet uneasy, eyes. To give more . . . It had struck a chord in her. She and Andrew had never really given much to each other. Oh, there had been camaraderie, a steady correspondence, an attractive date on important occasions always at the ready, and a friendly fitting into each other's family and circle of acquaintances.

But she knew that she'd never given to Andrew what she'd given to Adam. In all those years . . . Nor had Andrew shown any indication that he wanted to give her more. She felt closer, more vulnerable with Adam. How could that be? she wondered in confusion.

She could not recall Andrew ever expressing any frustration, disappointment, or dissatisfaction with what she now was beginning to recognize as the superficiality of their relationship. It had been superficial physically. And emotionally as well. Only the nice, polite, cheerful feelings had been expressed between them.

She hadn't recognized it before, because she'd had no basis of comparison. And her family had encouraged her to keep looking at things the way she had.

But Ariel recognized it now because she was staring into the face of the man that had stirred her own physical and emotional needs and had tempted her into expressing them.

"Like Cory must have stirred Andrew's and set him free . . ." she murmured, not realizing at first that she'd spoken the thought out loud.

"Cory?" Adam echoed huskily as he felt himself helplessly falling into the haunting depths of her bewitching brown eyes, so open now with the pupils dilated, so dark and mysterious, so vulnerable yet enticing.

She felt wrapped up in the man and shared the thought with him before she could think not to.

"Cory must have touched Andrew like . . ." But she trailed off as she stared into the shifting emotions in his own mesmerizing eyes.

But he read what she was thinking as clearly as if it had been printed for him to see. He finished the sentence for her, in a voice now roughening.

"Like I touched you?"

He loosened his grip on her unresisting body and grasped her well-shaped head in two eager hands. His fingers sank into her scalp as he pulled her down to him.

"Like this?" he muttered hoarsely against her lips just before he fused his mouth to hers in a blistering kiss.

A tide of pleasure and relief poured down through him as their lips met hungrily and he proceeded to kiss her with urgent thoroughness. He could feel the slender strength of her through the layers of clothing and burned to be closer still. As his tongue lingeringly caressed the interior of her sweet mouth, his mind was gradually being engulfed by his desire to make love to her.

Before his rational powers drowned entirely, he managed to tear his mouth away from hers. He stifled a gasp and pressed his lips against the cool, satiny skin of her neck, swearing softly.

"Forget every word I said," he muttered in a thick, unsteady voice. "Your ex-fiancé must have been deaf, dumb, blind, and lacking in every tactile sensation to have spent that many years with you without either making love to you or going stark raving mad."

Ariel lay trembling on top of him, exquisitely aware of every inch of her body and his. Her lips were throbbing a little. From being kissed? Or from yearning to be kissed some more? Maybe both. She felt sort of like she had the night she first met him. Wildly adventurous, eager to live, a little scared, yet even getting a thrill out of being a little frightened for some perverse reason.

And, wonder of wonders, she was sure she could attract a man, a real man, an attractive and successful man, just like other women could. And she also knew that that didn't really matter at all. Lydia had been right. It was *this* man that she'd wanted to attract, not just anyone.

She knew beyond any doubt that the triumphant joy that had surged through her was rooted in that. She pulled his dark head close to her, letting her fingers luxuriate in the feel of his soft hair.

She was giddy and glad and joyous and terrified because it was Adam who wanted her in spite of everything. Even though he knew much more about her than he had before, he wanted her. He really wanted *her*. It wasn't just the teasing seductress poured into an elegant dress at a Carnaval party that he was attracted to. It was the reticent translator too.

Ariel smiled and started to laugh happily.

Adam looked up and was stunned at the radiant beauty he beheld in her face. The beauty had always been there. The radiance had not. It was as if some inner warmth had finally been allowed to shine through.

"You are really something," he murmured in soft admiration, placing his hands on her rib cage and hoisting her up a little, needing to control her like that, needing to get a clearer view of this beautiful woman.

His hands felt hard, even through the layers of clothing. But it was a good feeling to Ariel, and she smiled down at him, lost in him, wanting to feel like this forever.

He let her down, lowering her until she lay again on his chest. He needed to touch more than Ariel bundled up. He needed to feel the soft warmth of her against him again, like a thirsty man yearns for the cool wetness of a drink to assuage the ache of his tongue. He slipped his hands under her coat and sweater and shirt. He didn't stop searching until he reached bare skin.

With a sigh he turned his mouth again to hers.

"You sure know how to light my fires. Every last one of them," he muttered, underlining his declaration with a kiss.

He pushed her thighs apart, until he was intimately pressed against her in spite of their clothing. He rocked against her once and slid his hands down into her slacks, caressing the slope of her bottom.

"And you light mine, Adam Locke," she said softly, gazing down at his handsome face with a mixture of gratitude, the beginnings of trust and more than a little desire.

Her admission startled him for a moment. When he realized what she'd admitted, he folded her tightly against him. Neither of them had much of an interest in talking again for quite a while after that.

CHAPTER TEN

Walter was leaning against one of the big, rough-hewn timbers that supported the front porch of his house when he caught sight of the *Catarina* in the middle of the afternoon.

"Hmph," he grunted. "Still don't like to be on the water late in the afternoon, do ya, son?"

He turned to go inside and put on the fire under the kettle on the old gas stove.

"Guess I can't rightly blame ye, though. If it'd happened to me, I imagine I'd still be avoidin' that too."

By the direction from which they were coming he knew that Adam hadn't sailed onto the bay, either. That was where the tragedy had taken place, years ago.

"Must be." He squinted his eyes and pursed his well-creased lips, rubbing a twisted hand thoughtfully over his whiskery chin. "Must be close to twenty-five years since that storm . . . since the *Felice* went down."

But that unforeseen disaster had permanently torn the souls of a boy and his young sister, leaving them bereft and throwing them alone into life years before they were ready for it.

Walter pulled out his coffeepot and set out some cups and saucers. They were heavy, dime-store china. Their simple blue-and-white pattern bore the chips and stains of years of use. It was the only set of china that Walter owned. The only one he ever had. His wife had bought it the first year of their marriage.

"Clara," he mumbled softly to his wife, whose gentle

memory had never left him, though she'd passed away years ago. "You and I must've looked like that when we was courtin'. Ain't it nice that young Adam finally got himself a girl? Hope he's lucky enough to keep her for a wife. Like I was lucky to keep you."

He screwed up his face, trying hard to push back the nearly unbearable sadness that came to him.

"Clara . . . Clara . . ." he said mournfully, shuffling slowly back out onto the porch. It was cool and damp there, caught in the afternoon shadows. "If only you were here and we was young again. There's so much good livin' to do and not nearly 'nough time fer it."

He rubbed a shirt-sleeved arm across his eyes and snuffled some. Feeling self-conscious, he drew himself up straighter and made an effort to pull himself back together.

"Welcome back, chil'ren," he said roughly, though they were nowhere close to the dock yet and couldn't possibly have heard him.

Ignoring the distance, he waved his arms. Ariel waved back.

"Welcome back," he repeated, closer to a shout.

He limped down to the dock and waited for them there. The way he saw it, closer was always better.

"Good sailin'?" he said a little while later as he helped them dock and unload the *Catarina*.

"Great sailing!" Adam replied enthusiastically, grinning broadly as they walked back up the planking to Walter's home.

"Hm. Still don't look like ya got yer sea legs yet, though," Walter muttered, wryly chuckling under his breath as he looked over the couple walking a few feet ahead of him, hand in hand.

He decided that this trip must have aged them considerably, too, since neither of them apparently heard what he'd said. They were going deaf early in life. Since they'd missed his observation, Walter decided to spare them repeating it. He contented himself with grinning at their backs.

"Come on in. Coffee's hot. Got some tea bags here, too, if you'd ruther. Got time fer a game of checkers b'fore you go, Adam?"

"I wouldn't miss it, Walter. Thanks." replied Adam, holding the door for them all and clapping Walter on the shoulder as the old man went inside. "Where's the board?"

The afternoon drifted pleasantly by. Ariel gradually began to get to know a little more about Adam, piecing together a few facts and using her intuition to fill in some gaps here and there. It didn't take long for her to realize that Walter was almost like a grandfather to Adam.

Walter was a man of few words but of great depth of feeling. His wife's faded picture still graced the main wall in his living room. Adam and Walter's occasional references to her kindheartedness and ever-ready feasts made her seem like she was still with them, might even appear in the room at any moment.

There was no mention made of Adam's parents or grandparents. Nor of any blood relations at all until Walter made a casual reference toward the end of the visit.

"How's that lively little sister of yours doin'?" he asked as he jumped the next to last of Adam's kings.

"As lively as ever. I guess you remember that she's been living in Boston for several years now. She stayed on after she graduated from college. Liked it quite a lot. But the firm she's been working for finally made her an offer she couldn't refuse and she's being transferred to their Washington branch. As a matter of fact, she should have gotten into town last week some time if things worked out the way she was planning," Adam explained, returning the favor and jumping one of Walter's checkers.

"They gen'lly do," Walter observed with a grin.

Adam chuckled and nodded his head in agreement.

"That they do," he agreed as Walter cornered his last man. "Looks like you've got me, Walter," he said magnanimously, rising to his feet. He looked at his watch. "I think

Ariel and I had better be going, Walter. Could I show her your boat on our way out?''

It was clear that nothing would have pleased the old man more. He grinned proudly and ushered them into the covered dry-dock and boat house that was attached to one side of his home, saying, yep, of course Ariel could see his boat. No one could have missed Walter's deeply ingrained pride in either.

"This is the *Eastwind*," he waid gruffly, introducing them to his aged skipjack. "I'm doin' a little sandin' and paintin', like I do every winter. After I finish with her I'll do the *Catarina*."

Walter had earned a good living as a young man working the *Eastwind*. He'd used the skipjack for oyster dredging, like so many others in the bay area. Well into adulthood it had supported him and his wife.

"She's small for a skipjack," he pointed out, like an auctioneer going over a fine point for an interested buyer. "Thirty feet long and fourteen feet wide. But she was a good working boat. If you wanted to work her, she still would be. Or you could live on her, I guess, like some folks like to nowadays."

She had the traditional, shallow-vee bottom, single aftraking mast, leg-o'-mutton sloop, and clipper bow of her breed. And unlike some of the newer ones made of man-made materials like fiberglass, the *Eastwind* was made of wood.

"She even won me a couple of races," Walter recalled proudly.

Ariel looked at the aging wood and realized how much work—and how much love and craftsmanship—was going into the *Eastwind* year after year to keep her in good condition.

"I spent many a happy day with Walter working on that boat," Adam said, reminiscing and draping an arm casually over Ariel's shoulders.

And now you're repaying it by helping Walter keep her, aren't you? she asked herself. Adam was a loyal surrogate grandson to this worn old waterman, just as Walter had been the patient and kindly adoptive grandparent to Adam all these years.

As they got into Adam's car and waved good-bye Ariel wondered just how wrong she had been in her first impression of Adam. He certainly wasn't fitting into the unflattering stereotype she had first assigned to him. There was more to the man. Much more.

Adam offered her another source of insight later that afternoon. He glanced at her he turned up the gravelly country road.

"Could I talk you into dinner too?" he asked in a hopeful, teasing voice.

She laughed at his uncharacteristic hesitance.

"Sure," she answered, still smiling as his hopeful expression disintegrated into a grin of accomplishment.

For dinner he took her to a local bar-and-grill-style restaurant called The Anchor's Point. Its owner, Marge Calloway, was another old friend of Adam's, as it turned out.

Marge was as loquacious as Walter had been laconic. She folded Adam into her arms with a chubby-armed bear hug and cry of welcome. She kissed him roundly on the cheek and beamed at Ariel as he turned to introduce them to each other.

"Very glad to meet you, Ariel!" she said warmly, linking her arms through theirs and strolling cheerily through the restaurant to a large, empty table in the corner. "You just make yourselves at home now. I'll be right back."

Marge's food was tasty, simple, down-home cooking. There was lots of fresh seafood on the menu, of course, the standard bay area offering of crabs and oysters, rockfish, flounder, and bluefish. And you could have them almost any way you wanted: steamed, broiled, deep fried, sauteed, raw, in soups and chowders, in salads or by themselves. And then, of course, there were home fries and hush puppies, corn bread and biscuits, ham and steak, and homemade pies and custards for dessert.

It was little wonder that The Anchor's Point was a favorite

of tourists. Its food was delicious, and the price was always right. But it was popular with the local people as well.

By the time their sizzling steaks and cold beer had been served, it was crowded with friends and neighbors, catching up on the latest gossip and filling up with gusto on Marge's good food. There were quite a few local fishermen, apparently intent on trying to outdo one another in impromptu tall tales. And a surprising number of patrons said hello to Adam, stopping at their table for friendly chats.

They were half finished eating their meal when Marge returned for a few minutes, just to make sure that everything was okay. When Marge hurried back to the front in order to seat two new customers, Ariel turned to Adam in mild surprise.

"A lot of these people seem to know you rather well," she observed, unconsciously letting go a little more of her original stereotype of him as she did so.

"Yes," he agreed, taking a long swallow of his beer. "Many of them have been more like family than friends over the years, I guess."

Marge's buxom, ruddy-complexioned figure reappeared at their table.

"Have you noticed my artwork?" she asked Ariel eagerly, with a suspicious gleam in her twinkling green eyes.

Locke looked a little uncomfortable at that and finished off his beer in a hurry.

Ariel had indeed noticed it. And she had admired it quite a bit. Original pastel drawings were hung on all of the walls. There must have been close to forty or fifty original works of art tastefully arranged in clusters of two to five . . . all apparently sketched locally, if their subject matter was any indication.

Some of them were clearly identifiable as local subjects. There was the portrait of Marge's restaurant, a skipjack on the water, the Annapolis city dock, scenes of crabbing or fishing, blue herons in flight, snow geese in a field, waterfowl in their habitats . . .

And then there were the wonderfully sensitive renderings

of people. The portraits were of working people, mostly on their jobs, or close-ups of their faces. There were men on their boats and women in front of shops. More often than not, they were portraits of ruddy, wholesome, weather-beaten people smiling out into life from their paper and frame home.

"Yes, I have," Ariel replied. "They're wonderful." Her eyes had been roaming the walls as they spoke, and suddenly she noticed a portrait that she hadn't seen earlier. "Isn't that a picture of Walter over there?" she asked in surprise.

Marge chortled at Adam's succinct reply that it was. She clapped him fondly on the back, ignoring his slight embarrassment.

"You didn't tell her, did you, Adam?" She smiled broadly as he shrugged off the question. "Adam drew all of these. He's quite an artist, you know."

"No, I didn't know," murmured Ariel in amazement as she turned to stare at Adam. Why in the world did he seem embarrassed about it too?

"Why, when he was growing up," Marge rolled on, oblivious to the undercurrents between her two patrons, "we all figured that he'd either be an ornithologist specializing in Chesapeake Bay waterfowl or he'd be an artist. A portrait painter, something like that."

You could have knocked Ariel over with a feather. The image of Adam as a cutthroat businessman was forever laid to rest. So he had an artistic side, she thought, wondering how he managed to keep it alive now that he was running a business.

"But that uncle of yours got you on the straight and narrow, I guess, didn't he?" she teased fondly.

"It wasn't just *his* thinking, Marge," Adam pointed out good-naturedly. After all, he knew when he was licked. There was no point in trying to avoid the subject now. With her customary bluntness Marge had opened it up enough to run a truck through it.

"I never could figure out how I would be able to support myself by sketching people or wildlife," he reminded her.

175

"On the other hand, sketching buildings—now that's something someone'll cheerfully fork over some cash for."

Marge laughed and chatted awhile longer. As they were leaving, she pointed out another sketch to Ariel. It was hung behind the register with a special light on it. Ariel admired it uninterrupted for a moment while Locke tried to pay the bill and Marge tried to shove the money back into his wallet.

"That's a sketch Adam did of his folks," she said. This time there was a tender cast to her face and a gentleness in her voice that hadn't been there earlier.

They were a handsome young couple. They were standing arm in arm in front of a sailboat, smiling happily. Ariel had the feeling that they were looking right at her and smiling at her. It was as if it wasn't a sketch at all but a window, and they were on the other side, looking in.

"Feels like they're smiling right at you, doesn't it?" Marge said, trying again to push Adam's outstretched handful of money away. "I don't know how he did it, but everyone feels it," she continued as Ariel nodded her head in agreement. "I guess he wanted them to look at him one last time, and he caught the feeling for us all. We sure all appreciated it. We loved his folks, too, around here. It sure did hurt when we lost them like that."

Adam didn't feel like discussing his family tragedy in front of a restaurant cash register, even if it was Marge's. He slapped the bills down on the counter top and held them in place with his hand.

"Marge, if you won't let me pay when I come here, I'm not going to eat your food anymore," Adam argued in frustrated annoyance.

"Nonsense!" she bellowed merrily.

They were like the irresistible force and the immovable object. Ultimately, by some miracle, they arrived at a compromise. Adam paid half the regular price.

"You come back soon, honey," Marge called out as they got into the car.

Adam grinned at her and waved.

It was dark now. And time to go home.

The drive back went quickly. Too quickly. The closer they got, the harder it was to accept that their day of escape was rapidly coming to a close.

Adam had to resist the urge to slow down. At the same time he was becoming increasingly uncomfortable. He knew it was just a matter of time before Ariel voiced the question that had hung unspoken between them since leaving The Anchor's Point. He wasn't certain that he was ready to confront that question yet. He was caught in a current of conflicting feelings as they followed the cliff edge on the road back to Athena. He wanted to sort out his own feelings before things went much further between them.

"This is like home for you around here, isn't it, Adam?" Ariel ventured softly.

He had to admire her approach. It was very tactful but left no room for him to change the subject easily.

"Yes, it is," he admitted.

The countryside had been doused in nightfall. There were just a few lights still visible through the trees behind them . . . a last remnant of Annapolis and its immediate environs. The soft whir of the engine and the pressing *whoosh* of the tires on the pavement were the only sounds to penetrate the awkward silence that fell between them.

Adam hesitated. He wanted to tell her yet he didn't.

He had wanted to change her mind about him at first, after her accusations on the terrace. It had bothered him unreasonably that she had thought he wasn't her "type" and that they were from "different worlds." It had annoyed and frustrated him that she seemed to be repelled by his connections with some of Washington's movers and shakers. He was used to women being attracted by that. He didn't quite know what to do about a woman who found it intimidating or suspect.

He had wanted her to be willing to be with him, to be comfortable in his presence, to talk to him. Instinctively he had exposed some of his private life to her. He'd shared aspects of his personal life that very few people knew about.

177

Of course, she had no way of knowing just how much he was opening up to her or how much more than most she now knew about him. Even so, now he was beginning to feel a little uneasy about it all. He'd let down some of his protective camouflage. If she still chose to play hot and cold with him for some reason now, it would be harder to take.

He never gave any thought to whether that made much sense in the larger scheme of things. After all, he had come here planning to get her out of his system. Why was he going to all this trouble? Surely there were less risky ways of going about that. But he had forgotten his original intent for the moment. And he was beginning to feel caught in his own snare instead. He felt exposed, vulnerable. It had been bad enough driving himself nuts for six months trying to decide whether to go after her or not. He wanted to be careful not to dig himself any deeper into that hole than he already was. He was used to being in control of his life and everything in it. Damn it all, he needed to regain the feeling that he was in control of things where Ariel was concerned.

Sometime during the day that feeling had slipped away. He wanted it back!

As it turned out, things still didn't go the way he would have liked, in spite of his new surge of determination that they would.

Ariel cleared her throat and looked at his profile in the darkened car. The fact that they were in shadows and could not see each other too well made it easier to ask.

"Your parents," she began hesitantly. "Would you mind talking about what happened to them?"

Damn! If she just hadn't asked it like that . . . hesitantly, as if she felt it was his private business and she regretted trespassing or stirring up any unhappy memories or inadvertently stumbling over something he might prefer not to discuss. What could he say to that?

He sighed and resigned himself to the inevitable. He might as well tell her the whole story and get it over with.

Of course, after opening up that much of himself to her, it

178

would give him the right to ask her some things, he thought, searching for a way to balance out their relative knowledge of one another a little bit. He was sure there would be at least a hundred things he could think up to ask her about her life.

That cheered him up a little and he relaxed.

"No. I don't mind," he said. By now he really didn't mind too much. As a matter of fact, once he'd decided on it, he found he was almost looking forward to her knowing. "When my sister and I were small, my folks used to come down here for long summer weekends to sail. That was their ketch in the picture at Marge's.

"We had a great time, the four of us. Those trips to Annapolis gave us time to be together. And that was rare for us. My father was a self-made man and ran his own company. He was a workaholic and spent eighty hours a week at his job. But when he brought us down here, he never gave it a backward glance. He was all ours."

"He and my mother used to like to sail in the afternoons. I don't know why. Maybe it was sailing in the sunset. Maybe it was his contrariness . . . going out when most everyone else was coming in. Anyway, one afternoon he left my sister and me with Walter. He and my mother went out on the boat. We were helping Walter fix some of his crabbing nets. We were outside when the storm came up."

How could it still seem so real after all these years? he wondered grimly.

"It was one of those freak, late-afternoon thunderstorms that they have around here every once in a while. I've never seen the sky get so black so quick. We ran down to the dock."

Two small children crying out. Walter running ahead of them as fast as he could. Calling out ahead of them to some men in uniforms. So much turmoil. The ear-shattering booms of thunder and angry waves breaking against the wharf . . . He still heard it with the ear and mind of the boy he had been . . . even now, years later.

"Walter notified the coast guard. But . . . it was too late."

179

Why did you have to go out. damn it! he cried out silently, angrily. just as he had then. All these years he'd been calling out that angry, desperate question. There never was an answer. He knew there never would be. That only made it ache worse.

"They never had a chance out there," he went on in a grim voice. "The bay was just too rough, the wind too strong, the waves too hard and high for a two-person crew on a boat like that. The *Felice* went down." The stab went through his heart. It was an old, familiar pain in an old, familiar wound. It had dulled with the passage of time, but it still hurt. "My folks . . . went down with her."

He had spoken with the even voice of a man who had his emotions under careful control. Ariel hurt for him. And she hurt for the boy he had been and the suffering he'd had to bear for so long. She reached out and tentatively placed her hand on his shoulder, unsure whether her gesture would be welcome or not. She knew he hadn't been exactly eager to tell her about this at first.

"I'm sorry," she said softly.

He shrugged, trying to be indifferent about it without a lot of success.

"It was a long time ago," he said, as if closing the discussion.

A long time ago, maybe. But it had left its mark on his life forever. He'd been catapulted into being "the little man of the family" for his younger sister. He'd been forced to choose his work because it would be lucrative. He'd had to be tough and successful because there were no parents to fall back on if things didn't go well.

"I'm still sorry," she repeated softly.

He covered her hand with his, pulling it down to rest on the top of his thigh, unexpectedly grateful to have her close to him and sounding like she really meant that.

"We went to live with my father's brother in Georgetown after that," he went on, suddenly wanting her to know the rest. "My uncle took over Dad's business. It swallowed up

180

his life just like it had my father's. Fortunately, for my sister and me, he kept our cottage outside of Annapolis and allowed us to come down for the summers.''

"That's how you kept in contact with Walter and Marge and the others over the years,'' Ariel correctly surmised.

"Yeah. Those people are as much family to me as my uncle is.''

He was relieved to see the entrance to the Athena Corporation parking lot about then. The feel of Ariel's hand on his thigh was turning his thoughts rapidly elsewhere. And if he'd been ambivalent about undertaking their conversation, he was absolutely torn apart about what to do when he took her home.

"I want to stop by the Inn first. Why don't you come with me?'' he suggested, steering her firmly by the elbow in the direction of the steps that led from the parking lot up to the Inn's main entrance.

Ariel agreed without any argument. She wanted to be with him; she wasn't ready to say good-bye to him. Being with him a little longer, on any excuse, was more important to her now than worrying what the desk clerk might say.

She wandered around his living room and worktables while Adam showered and changed into fresh clothes. His architectural drawings were taking shape now. There were a variety of designs and floor plans scattered around on the floor and tabletops. They offered only a limited opportunity for the artist in him to come out, she thought, wishing that people paid lots of cash for sensitive portraits as well as handsome buildings.

"Come on,'' he ordered as he joined her in record time a little bit later on, his hair still a little damp near his collar. "I'll take you home now.''

It seemed to Ariel that the walk to her cottage took forever. They walked side by side, not quite touching. It made her excruciatingly aware of how much she wished they were. The new distance between them, which she would have welcomed the day before, was now only a source of surprise and distress. She'd gotten used to touching him.

Don't be ridiculous, she told herself as they marched briskly down the hill. Don't turn into a clinging vine now! He probably is getting tired of so much togetherness. Maybe he's eager for the day to be over with. He probably wouldn't mind a break from you after so long. Give the man a break, for heaven's sake!

Adam's thoughts had turned heavenward as well. He was hoping to high heaven that he'd have a break . . . a break from the unrelenting need to put his hands on her. He was beginning to wonder if the term "midlife crisis" wasn't understating his problem a little. Maybe what he had was some kind of acute psychological breakdown. All he could think of was lying next to her in the boat and how good it had felt. Every inch of his body hungered for her.

He was certainly reluctant to touch her, but it was because he wasn't sure what he'd end up doing next. He was afraid of what touching her might ignite in him. No. He'd keep to himself for a while and try to cool off.

They stood awkwardly on her doorstep, both hesitating, but for different reasons. Ariel wasn't sure whether she should smile like she was feeling just fine, tell him what a great day it had been and that she'd see him at work tomorrow or whether she should invite him inside. She ached to ask him in, but the words were stuck in her throat. If she asked him, would he think that she wanted him to make love to her? Soft coral colors darkened her cheekbones.

Well, she did want that. And he probably was aware of that by now, anyway. She could hardly stop thinking about it. She wanted to be folded in his arms and be lost in his desire for her again. Maybe if she extended just a slight overture . . .

Ariel pushed open the door and stepped inside. She held it for him and stared across the chasm separating them. He was frowning a little and staring gloomily back at her.

"Come in," she said with slightly forced cheeriness, hardly able to believe that she'd actually managed to do it.

I made the first move for once, she thought a little proudly. She blinked as she suddenly remembered that night months ago in Georgetown when she'd given him a come-hither look. Well, maybe not quite the first. There had been that one other time.

She forced a smile and went into the kitchen to make them some hot cocoa. Adam certainly brought out the initiative in her, she thought.

While Ariel got cleaned up and changed clothes Adam made himself at home in her living room. He looked over the bookshelf next to her couch and out of curiosity pulled out her high school yearbook. When he located her photo, he half smiled. She hadn't changed a whole lot. Her face was a little fuller, more mature now. But her demure, carefully turned-out style of dressing was quite similar.

He looked around the simply, tastefully furnished living room. It was comfortable and homey. He grinned at that. He never would have expected her to have a homey-looking cottage after having seen her office! The sterility, the cool and untouchable quality of that place had been something of a shock to him. After their first meeting in Georgetown and all those months of fantasizing about her, he'd been expecting her to have the office decor of a flamenco dancer and the personal surroundings of a pasha's favorite dancing girl!

He closed his eyes and tried to recall what her bedroom looked like. The colors were light and airy . . . lemons and pale golds, coral shades mixed with dark pinks and creams, like a young girl's bedroom.

He remembered the two small figurines on her dresser. They were Hummel casts of young girls, portraits of dewy, innocent youth.

Just like Ariel, he thought. She was a woman who had forced herself to fit into a role that didn't do her justice anymore. It was a role that she'd outgrown, but she couldn't admit it to herself. Maybe she hadn't realized that it was even happening, he mused.

And yet something still troubled him about her. He wanted

to believe that he was right and understood her now. He didn't mind admitting that he was wrong about her in the first place. After all, she'd been wrong about him too. It happens.

But was he entirely wrong? There was still that man she had been staying with in Washington, the man who'd answered the door the morning after she'd run away. When Adam had gone to the effort to track her down, the friend had answered the door and blown away his dream of finding her. The friend was listed as C. Laslow on his apartment mailbox. Ariel called Laslow Candy, and referred to Laslow as a "she." Out of embarrassment? What was she trying to hide?

It was possible that the Laslow who'd answered to that name when Locke knocked on his door was not the Candy that Ariel kept referring to, he reluctantly forced himself to admit. At the time he had been so startled, it hadn't occurred to him that there could be an innocent explanation. It had been obvious. Ariel had stayed at a man's apartment. But now . . . maybe the guy was married to this Candy . . . or . . .

Adam clenched his teeth in frustration and tried to decide how to ferret out the truth about that. If he asked her straight out, he'd have no way of knowing if she were lying or telling the truth. He'd have to accept whatever she told him as true. Lord knew he wanted to believe that she was telling him the truth.

But Adam Locke hadn't become a successful Washington businessman by believing that people always told you the truth. He'd been skeptical and cynical about people and their motives for too many years to suddenly change his ideas where Ariel was concerned.

Damn it all! How could he find out?

"Would you like some more cocoa?"

Ariel's soft voice broke through his preoccupation.

"No, thanks."

She was barefoot and standing in front of him in a pair of clean twill slacks the color of her hair. He stared at her and felt his mouth go dry. She'd let it loose . . . it was hanging

184

free, curling in waves around her, a rich, auburn cloud floating down her shoulder blades and over the cream-colored shirt, open for the first time in his memory down to the soft, swelling cleft of her breasts. It instantly brought back the image of her in her bed the night before . . . lying under him in the half hidden darkness while their hot, damp bodies fused in an agony of delight.

Adam snapped to his feet and marched straight for the door. He had to get out of here before he made a complete fool of himself. She'd think he couldn't keep his hands off her. He swore silently and put his hand on the doorknob of her closet door, intending to get his coat and leave at once. Maybe by tomorrow he'd have cooled off enough to see her again. Maybe he'd have gotten hold of himself again. Maybe he'd be able to think straight by then or at least just think at all!

He felt her arms go around his waist as she pressed herself shyly against his back. The feel of her soft cheek against his shoulder blade caused desire to shoot through him.

"Thank you, Adam. I've had a wonderful time. I'll remember it always," she said softly, trembling a little, wanting desperately for him to put his arms around her and kiss her, unable to do anything more about it.

Adam closed his eyes in a final losing effort to leave. Slowly his hand slipped from the doorknob. He turned to face her. His body burned at every point of contact with hers. He sank his hands hungrily into her lush hair, letting it cascade through his fingers as he pulled her close and lifted her chin to face him.

"Ariel," he murmured, saying with her name all he could not bring himself to say just yet. Anguish and desire, fascination and obsession, conquest and surrender, doubt and faith . . . they were all there in his anguished moan as her name fell from his lips.

Their mouths met and melted into eager abandon. All day their bodies had been teased and frustrated. Hours of constant touching and caressing, of seeing one another and wanting

185

one another, of falling more and more under the captivating spell that seemed to bind them.

He swung her up into his arms and carried her into the bedroom, not breaking the passionate kiss. Clothes dropped in soft swishes to the floor. There was a gentle creak as they lay down together, enfolded in each other's arms as their bodies touched the bed.

The sweet torment of his kiss only made her crave more, and she half sobbed when he broke away to place hot, damp kisses on her throat. She ran her hands over his shoulders and back, smiling with a primitive surge of joy as his harsh intake of breath told her just how much he delighted in her touch. His hands roamed over her breasts and belly, sending a warm shower through her every nerve ending. His mouth followed in their wake, sharpening the pleasure even more.

She wanted to do the same for him, and he helped show her how, encouraging her with his groans of pleasure as she shyly touched him as he was touching her. Ariel had never felt so alive. To be in his arms, to feel his hands running over her like this, so eagerly, so tenderly . . . to hear his ragged breathing testify to his need for her . . . She wanted it to go on forever. She wanted to be with him forever.

He entered her slowly, wrapping his arms tightly around her hips and holding them both rigidly still in his steely embrace.

"Don't move," he whispered harshly.

It was so exquisite, she'd do whatever he said. She gave him her unconditional trust then without thinking. If it could just be like this between them forever. . . .

He couldn't control the waves of pleasure that were pounding through him. With a helpless moan he surged against her. Again. And again. And she responded, helplessly holding him close in her loving arms as his mouth came down hot and hard on hers.

He swallowed a primitive cry as they both began to drown in the rhythm of ecstasy and need that was breaking over them now like a powerful storm, pounding them into one another until the fury was exquisitely, breathtakingly spent in a final, shattering burst.

Peace gently washed over them. And they were one.

CHAPTER ELEVEN

She was neither awake nor asleep. Drifting in the drowsy, clouded world that lies somewhere between the two, Ariel gradually discerned that a kiss was being tenderly pressed just beneath her ear. And two strong arms were holding her, pulling her back snugly against the warm, hard front of a man's body. They were lying on their sides in the darkness, neither wanting to disturb the sense of security that nestled with them.

Locke ran his hand lovingly over her breast, cupping it as he nuzzled her neck affectionately.

"It will be light soon," he whispered huskily.

She laid her hands on top of his, not wanting him to go yet.

"I don't want to go," he sighed as he buried his face in her hair and held her tightly.

They lay quietly together, holding each other, knowing that their time alone together would soon come to an end. He pulled her over to face him and kissed her, almost chastely, then traced the curve of her cheek with his fingertip as he looked down at her. If he didn't watch out, he wouldn't be able to leave, he realized.

He gave her a smile and reluctantly got out of bed. He was amused to see that Ariel was still a little shy of him. She was looking away from him while he got dressed. When he'd finished, he leaned over her, placing a hand palm-down on either side of her shoulders on the bed.

"Go back to sleep," he told her softly. "I'll call you at

work later on this morning.'' He leaned down to give her a soft, reassuring kiss on the lips. "Can you have lunch with me?''

She was so happy that he asked, she forgot to try to be nonchalant about it. She threw her arms around his neck and kissed him full on the mouth. When she fell back onto the bed, he was grinning down at her and beginning to look a little flushed.

"I take it that means yes?'' he said, and chuckled softly.

"That means yes,'' she confirmed, laughing up at him with stars in her eyes.

He couldn't help himself. When she looked at him like that, he just couldn't walk away from her without just one more kiss. That kiss melted into another, deeper, soul-wrenching kiss that he just managed to tear himself away from before he began stripping off his clothes and climbing into bed with her again.

Adam shook his head as he rolled off Ariel, still feeling the imprint of her body against his, even through the covers.

"If I don't get out of here now, I never will,'' he said raggedly as he sat up and, for the second time, got off Ariel's bed. "See you soon, sweetheart,'' he called out softly as he hesitated at her bedroom doorway. "Go back to sleep.''

And then he was gone.

"See you soon, Adam,'' Ariel murmured after he had left.

She lay in her bed, every inch of her body vibrating with the desire to be in his arms again. She'd never felt so wide-awake or so vibrantly alive before. She broke into a smile, then started laughing for the joy of it.

Go to sleep! There was no way she could do that now! Not the way she felt!

Ariel closed her eyes dreamily and hugged herself tight.

He'd called her sweetheart. . . .

A slender beam of light winked once in the misty early-morning darkness. The man who had been sitting in the small dinghy beached on the riverbank saw it at once and stepped out of the boat. He moved into the damp, chilly shadows, toward the source of the light.

"Over here," he whispered tensely, trying to attract the attention of the unseen person who had just signaled to him.

A figure stpped cautiously out of the sloping woods, carefully approaching the small craft and the man who had been in it.

"Well? What is it?" bit out the man who had come from the cold waters. "After what happened on Saturday night I thought we'd agreed not to meet again for a while . . . to let things cool down first."

He was impatient to be gone from this place. It was too close for comfort. Someone might stumble onto them, and then . . . He looked around nervously. It was still dark, more than an hour or so before dawn. No one was out now. They were alone.

"You're sure you weren't followed?" he asked the figure that had emerged so stealthily from the shadows. His voice was sharp with anxiety and an ingrained presumption of authority.

"I'm sure," growled the person who had signaled him from the woods. "Couldn't be helped. The Athena security honcho is snooping around, doing some background checks, maybe even a little wire-tapping and surveillance. It'll be too risky for me to call you for a while. If you want to get in touch with me, you'll have to use the boat . . . like we planned."

"All right. Are you going to need any help?"

There was a decisive snort from the forest prowler.

"No. It's a piece of cake. There'll even be someone around to take the fall for me when it's all over."

"Good. Just make sure that there are no more slipups."

"There won't be."

"If she'd seen you—"

"She didn't," retorted the figure locked in shadows, angry at the underlying insinuation. "I know what I'm doing."

The specter that had emerged from the woods moved a half

step closer to the man issuing the orders. No arm reached out; no weapon was displayed. But an underlying menace radiated from him and poisoned the air.

"Just make sure that the rest of my money is where it's supposed to be two weeks from today," the silken-voiced figure reminded the nervous man.

The man from the dinghy backed a step closer toward his craft. It was too late now to wonder if he'd made the right choice.

"You deliver your end of the deal, I'll deliver mine," he snapped defensively, furious at being threatened by this nobody.

The shadowy object of his ire slapped a slender steel flashlight repeatedly against the palm of one unseen hand.

"I'll deliver, all right. Don't you worry about that. I'll deliver."

The slight rustling of newly fallen leaves signaled that the meeting's convenor had departed, sidling back up the cliffside without further explanation.

River water lapped softly at the sides of the dinghy. The oars dipped carefully, then were pulled back. Again. Again. Until it reached the mother boat moored near the channel.

When Lydia hurried into Ariel's office first thing Monday morning, she thought for a minute that she'd taken a wrong turn somewhere along the way and landed in the wrong place by mistake.

"Ariel?" she asked in surprise as she stared at the figure bending in front of the coffee machine and rummaging through drawers in a futile search for something.

"Hi, Lydia! Sit down. Be right with you," Ariel called over her shoulder.

The office was a mess. Files were open. The desk had been pushed to a new location. And Ariel looked like she'd been wrestling with her dictionaries instead of calmly sitting and translating as she always had done before.

Lydia dropped into a chair, and her mouth fell open when

Ariel straightened up, giving her friend her first clear view of her.

"What have you done to your hair?" Lydia gasped in surprise.

"My hair?" Ariel repeated blankly. Then she remembered. She brushed a hand self-consciously over the rich auburn waves that were gathered softly at the nape of her neck by a dark red velvet ribbon. Ariel mumbled something about not doing anything in particular with it, avoiding Lydia's eyes like the plague.

"Yes, you have!" Lydia declared protestingly. She stared in pensive fascination at her friend, then suddenly pointed a finger at her. "You've let it down! I've never seen it like that before, Ariel. It's great!"

Lydia's obvious enthusiasm for her new and adventurous hairstyle soothed Ariel's embarrassment.

"What in the world are you looking for, anyway?" Lydia questioned, waving a hand at the room in general. "Gosh! I never thought I'd see your office look this way, Ariel!" Lydia stiffled a giggle. "This looks more like mine than yours!"

"Don't be silly," Ariel said dismissingly. "Your office and Dr. Norris's affairs are always in apple-pie order and you know it!"

"Well, yes, I suppose so," Lydia conceded. Then she amended her concession with, "But this sure could be a twin for my cottage!"

Ariel laughed. She couldn't deny that. "Would you like some coffee?" she asked, finally remembering to offer it. She'd misplaced something and had been flustered to discover it gone. Locating the document had temporarily taken precedence over etiquette and manners. However, Ariel was too polite to forget herself indefinitely.

"Sure," said Lydia cheerfully.

Ariel handed her a Styrofoam cup of coffee with cream and sugar. That was when Lydia noticed what Ariel was drinking out of: the ceramic mug that had decorated the desk, so virginally untouched since its arrival months ago.

Lydia practically choked in her hurry to swallow the mouthful of coffee she'd taken.

"Deflowering your mug?" she teased, then stared in genuine surprise as Ariel blushed and looked at her in confusion.

Something was going on here. But what? Lydia smiled at Ariel comfortingly.

"I always liked your coffee mug, Ariel," Lydia reminded her, wondering what they were really talking about at this point. Never mind. She would find out soon.

Ariel cleared her throat.

"Well, it *is* for drinking coffee," Ariel needlessly pointed out. "I just thought that it was about time it was put to the use it was intended for. . . ."

Ariel blushed harder. Of all the stupid, inane, inconsequential remarks she'd made in her life, this conversation was likely to win honors as the worst!

"By the way," Lydia inquired, concern written all over her, "are you all right? I mean after what happened here Saturday night?" She leaned forward sympathetically.

"Oh, yes," Ariel answered, trying to shrug it off. She really wasn't too eager to think about it, to be honest. The feeling of being at the mercy of a stranger, the blackness engulfing her . . .

"David told me what happened," Lydia explained. "He was on his way into town and just happened to be passing your building as the doctor was leaving. We called to see if you needed any help, but Adam said he had everything under control."

So it was Adam now, Ariel thought, immediately berating herself for being unreasonably touchy about Lydia's use of Adam's first name. After all, most people around here were on a first-name basis with everyone else. Why shouldn't Lydia call him by his first name? Besides, Lydia was her friend, for crying out loud!

Ariel smothered the irrational twinge of jealousy, but it took an effort.

"That's why Dr. Norris cancelled this morning's staff breakfast," Lydia explained in a low voice. "He didn't want to face any questions just yet. It's all anyone talked about around here all day yesterday."

"Have they discovered who broke in?" Ariel asked.

"No. Not yet," Lydia replied softly. She knew from the strained look on Ariel's face that it wasn't the answer she wanted to hear.

Ariel's heart sank. She didn't like feeling that someone was out there, someone she would not know if she saw him, someone who wanted something in her office. A shiver of apprehension snaked down her back. She forced herself to shake it off. Worrying about it certainly wasn't going to change anything.

"What *are* you looking for, anyway?" Lydia repeated her question, this time with a mixture of amusement and exasperation.

Ariel had begun looking through her desk drawers. From the look of them it wasn't the first time.

"A report." Ariel sighed. "Darn it all! I was sure that I'd left it on my desk Saturday before I went home." She looked despondently over the mess surrounding her. "I guess I was mistaken."

Lydia frowned slightly.

"Ariel, do you suppose—"

Lydia's supposing was interrupted by the ringing of Ariel's telephone. Ariel lifted the receiver to her ear.

Automatically she said, "Hello."

"Good morning," said a dearly familiar male voice, bringing Ariel's heartbeat to a temporary halt, fuzzing her thoughts and shooting a hot current of longing straight through her like an arrow.

Lydia watched in mild astonishment as her cool and unflappable friend wilted in her chair. To her amazement Ariel's eyes seemed to glaze and go out of focus and she began absentmindedly curling the beige-colored telephone cord around one index finger.

"Good morning," Ariel replied in a voice a little huskier than usual.

Lydia bit her lower lip a little to keep from gaping too much. Was this starry-eyed, breathless girl the cool, efficient, don't-you-lay-a-hand-on-me young woman she'd known all these months? At the moment it would have been easier for Lydia to believe that aliens from outer space had replaced the real Ariel with a clone! And the Ariel clone was certainly enraptured about something—or someone!

Lydia's ever-ready grin began teasing the corners of her mouth as everything finally started to click into place.

"All right," Ariel was saying softly. "I'll be there at twelve-thirty." She blushed slightly and turned her head away from Lydia's steady, goggle-eyed scrutiny. "See you later."

Ariel replaced the receiver. It clicked softly into place.

"Was that Adam?" Lydia ventured casually, although she'd somehow slid to the front of her seat and was leaning forward when she asked.

"Yes." Oh, yes, that was Adam. Ariel started rummaging for a paper clip to avoid looking at Lydia just yet. She knew she'd given herself away.

When she finally steeled herself enough to look up, she found her friend Lydia grinning like a cat burglar who'd just broken the combinations to every safe in Monte Carlo. That did it! Ariel looked at her a little defensively.

"Yes. As a matter of fact, it was Adam," she said, this time tilting her chin defiantly.

Lydia hopped to her feet and practically leapt the short distance to Ariel's desk. She threw her arms around Ariel and gave her a quick hug, just barely holding back the laughter that threatened to overwhelm her. Her Cheshire-cat grin was a dead giveaway of that.

"Well, is there anything wrong with my seeing him while he's working here?" Ariel asked challengingly.

Lydia shook her head and started backing toward the door, her eyes as big as saucers and twinkling unrepentantly.

"No, no! There's not a thing wrong with it. In fact, I think it's terrific, Ariel! I think it's just terrific!"

Ariel heard the underlying laughter and sighed. She knew she'd given herself away. And she'd probably fare no better with any of the other people around here. It would be just a matter of time before they realized that she and Adam were . . . involved. Of course, she could always comfort herself with the thought that no one would actually know just quite *how* involved unless she or Adam spelled it out, which wouldn't happen in any event, she was sure.

Even so, she really didn't know what to say or how to act. She and Adam weren't exactly a couple, but they weren't just acquaintances, either. She was uncomfortable. It was an in-between kind of relationship, and Ariel had no experience with that type. She'd hardly dated anyone except Andrew and was used to being thought of as a single woman or as an engaged woman . . . not as a woman involved in an unde-fined relationship with a man.

She mentally gave herself a kick. She'd better get used to it very quickly. Otherwise she'd never keep from acting like a complete idiot every time she heard his voice or remembered his touch in someone's presence. She couldn't spend the next two weeks melting into the furnishings several times a day!

Lydia didn't seem overly concerned about Ariel's new problem. She was laughing, very pleased, downright amused by it, as a matter of fact.

"Good luck, Ariel!" she called out encouragingly. "Have a good lunch!"

Lydia's cheery closing comment stayed with Ariel long after Lydia had gone. With a friend like Lydia, maybe it wouldn't take too long to get the hang of it, Ariel thought hopefully.

Locke watched from his terrace as Ariel crossed the court-yard and quickly climbed the steps at the front of the Athena

Inn. His gaze lingered over the shapely calves of her legs, about the only part of her besides her head not covered by clothes. He'd seen her nod and give a friendly hello to people as she passed them. It reminded him that she was well known and well liked here. And well respected.

And beautiful and sexy as hell, he thought with a sigh of frustration as his undisciplined thoughts began to run amok again. He ran his hands through his hair, wishing he could get as good a grip on the wildly galloping thoughts churning beneath.

He strode into the suite and latched the terrace's sliding doors after him. He could just envision her flustered smile as she scurried by the desk clerk about now on her way to the elevator. Like she had the first time. Poor kid.

That brought a slight frown to his face.

Damn it all! He didn't want her embarrassed! And he didn't want her flustered or guilty about seeing him. He most emphatically did not want her to become a hot topic for gossip and speculation around here.

A strong desire to protect her welled up in him, and he paced the room, trying to shake off some of the tension that had come along with it. What could he do?

He didn't want anyone or anything to hurt her. Himself included. That, of course, presented him squarely with a problem he'd been trying to avoid like the plague.

His original intention had been to meet her again and do anything necessary to work her out of his system. At least, that's what he'd been telling himself with great authority for some time now. It wasn't exactly working out that way, in any event, he had to admit.

If he went through with that plan and left her when the project was finished, would she be hurt? He was sure of it, even if she was still something of a mystery to him and he didn't know everything about her yet. He knew enough to know that it would hurt her. And he did not want that. Not one bit did he want that.

And he was beginning to admit that he wouldn't be too

happy about leaving her now, either. He stared irritably at the door to the suite, wondering why it was taking her so long to get upstairs. He paced around the room once, like a caged lion. All right, so he'd be feeling pretty damned miserable himself if he just walked out on her in two weeks. He'd never had masochistic tendencies, and he certainly wasn't about to begin developing any now!

So where did that leave him? he asked himself. Things weren't going quite as he'd planned. All right. He could deal with that. The more he saw of her, the more he wanted to see her again. All right. He could probably survive that too. The more he made love to her, the more captivated he was by her. It was like falling into an endless abyss of desire. He had no idea if there was a way out at some point. The only way he would find out would be to keep seeing her and see what happened.

Damn it all, it was like some kind of enchantment. And the worst part was that he was enjoying it more than he'd ever enjoyed anything in his entire life!

He couldn't imagine going back to his life as it had been before, without Ariel. All those tomorrows had her face in them.

That image stopped him dead in his tracks. All those tomorrows. Their tomorrows.

The timid knock at the door won him from his startled preoccupation. He knew it was Ariel. If he hadn't been expecting her, anyway, he would have known from that shy touch—just like the shy touch on his body. He flung open the door, wanting to see her as soon as possible. He was not disappointed.

"Ariel," he said roughly, pulling her inside and shutting and locking the door after them.

She had been breathless before, partly because she was excited about seeing him and partly from the speed with which she'd gotten from her office to his. When he pulled her through the door and hauled her up against his chest and stared down at her like he was doing now, she practically forgot to breathe at all.

Ariel opened her mouth to say hello, but before she could utter a word, his mouth closed over hers and all thoughts of conversation instantly vanished. The rest of her felt like it was dissolving as well when he pulled her hungrily into his arms a second later. She was transformed into a glowing, tingling, eager lover before either of them realized what was happening.

Adam staggered back a step, shutting his eyes to block her out. He could still see her. And, worse yet, he could still feel her without even touching her! A pained expression was stamped on his handsome features.

"I really meant for us just to have lunch," he said apologetically, trying hard to cool down and stick to his original plan.

Ariel couldn't quite comprehend what he was saying. The words had reached her, but something was interfering with her ability to understand him. She'd been enveloped in a golden cloud, but it was beginning to feel cold now that he'd moved away from her and was starting to talk.

She stepped forward and looped her arms around his neck. Ahhh, she knew that was better. . . .

Adam's still overheated temperature soared. He placed his hand firmly on her hips in order to push her away, but before he could do a thing, Ariel pressed forward and he could feel the delightfully erotic sensation of her soft breasts pressing against his chest.

He stifled a groan and cleared his throat in an effort to clear his head.

"I had them send up some food for us," he explained, his voice as rough as sandpaper.

She gazed into his darkening eyes in mesmerized fascination while the sound of his husky voice lulled her into a deepening lethargy. She succumbed to the desire to run her fingers up along the back of his neck, unaware that she was sending hot flashes coursing down Adam's shoulders and back in the process. The innocently seductive look on her smiling face hit him like a blow to his midsection, showering sparks down deep inside. In spite of her own rather dazed condition, Ariel blushed as the sparks ignited another, very noticeable, reaction in him.

His mind got busy telling his hands to push her away, *right now*, for God's sake. It shouted at him to talk to her about the weather, to chat about work, to have lunch with her, for crying out loud. After all, that was why he'd invited her up here, wasn't it? *Wasn't it?*

His rational self never had a prayer. It didn't have the slightest effect on anything that Locke could notice. Not that he could notice much of anything at this point. All of his ability to notice had been absorbed by Ariel; the feel of her in his arms, the scent of her hair and skin, the sound of her soft breathing, the memory of her nearness this morning before dawn. He sank willingly into the abyss that swallowed him and told his mind to go take a flying leap.

His willful hands pulled her hips toward him, easing a little the aching meteor shower that was swirling hotly in his belly. Confident feet backed them both toward the couch, avoiding the chair, until he toppled them back onto its soft contours, pulling Ariel down on top of him. Rebellious hands reacquainted themselves urgently with the beautiful slopes and curves of her tightly compact body. He sighed into her neck, delirious with the nearness of her and loving every exquisite minute of it.

They forgot about lunch. And everything else.

He loosened her clothes, pulling and tugging them gently apart while still managing to kiss her until she felt her body reach the melting point and turn into liquid fire. Their clothes rapidly acquired a rummage-sale look, scattered half on or half off their bodies, depending on how one looked at it. They groped and twisted and writhed together, oblivious to the fact that they hadn't gotten around to removing all of their clothing.

Adam pulled her on top of him, and within moments that

somehow seemed like forever, they stumbled into the welcome, convulsive release from that wondrously exhilarating torment neither of them wanted ever to fully escape.

They were both breathing like sprinters as they lay in each other's arms a few minutes later. Neither was quite sure of what was happening to them. Both hoped that whatever it was, it wouldn't stop.

"Do you want some lunch now?" he said a little while later, teasing her.

Ariel rolled down between Adam and the sofa back and started to laugh.

"Lunch!" she exclaimed as he caressed her well-disheveled body and smiled at her. "You mean there's more?"

He growled at her warningly and gave her a thoroughly hungry kiss for punishment.

"So you think you can tease me and get away with it, do you?" he said, trying for a threatening look.

It didn't quite make the grade, mainly because his eyes kept drifting down admiringly over her bare breasts and stomach. He looked up at her unrepentantly.

"All right," he conceded with a grin. "So you can tease me."

In between leisurely kisses and more teasing conversation they somehow managed to pull their clothing back together and sit up to eat lunch.

They were side by side, close together on the couch, finishing their coffee when Ariel sensed a changed in his mood. He'd grown a little quieter. Even without looking at him she knew his face would be somber.

"Ariel," he said, sounding serious.

He tucked a silken strand of hair behind her ear, stalling for time.

"We need to talk."

Something about the way he said that made her both afraid and hopeful at the same time. *Come on, Ariel, act like a big girl now*, she told herself.

He looked moodily at his hands, trying to select the right words the first time.

"This fascination we seem to have for each other . . ." he began, putting an arm around her shoulder and drawing her close. "It's strong stuff," he said huskily. He gave her a reassuring kiss on the cheek. "As a matter of fact, it's so strong when we're together that I forget everything but the need to touch you, to be close to you. But I don't want you hurt as a result of this," he added, pulling her face up to his and kissing her tenderly on the lips.

When he'd reluctantly released her lips, she opened her eyes and looked up at him. She could see that he wanted to say something more, and yet he didn't want to. She tried to tell herself that it didn't matter to her that he was ambivalent. But it didn't work.

She kissed him softly on the cheek.

"It's all right, Adam," she told him softly. "There are no strings between us. I know that. We never made any promises to each other. There are none for you to keep."

He fell back against the sofa and closed his eyes in frustration. Damn it all! Why couldn't everything be clear? Right now! He wanted to say that he loved her. But that was absolutely crazy! His mind kept telling him it was crazy. And his mind ought to know. Besides, once he'd told her that, he couldn't very well take it back later if he woke up from this dream and realized that he'd made a mistake. Maybe this was some rare form of temporary insanity he was suffering from. If he could just keep from doing any permanent damage to anyone while the disease ran its course, maybe things would work out all right in the end, he told himself.

Adam felt Ariel curl up next to him and begin gently massaging the tight muscles across his neck and shoulders.

"It's all right, Adam," she said soothingly.

He opened his eyes and looked into her smiling face. Gratitude welled up in him for her generous sympathy. It was especially kind of her to offer it now, he thought. She proba-

202

bly needed some sympathy and reassurance pretty badly herself right now.

He pulled her into his arms and held her close, nestling her head in his neck with one loving hand.

"There's something else," he said softly, his lips brushing a feathery kiss against her ear. "I haven't done anything to prevent your getting pregnant."

And boy, didn't he feel like an idiot now having to mention that to her? After all, she'd been so inexperienced. He should have taken care of that. And yet, when he was with her, he wanted her so much, it was easy to tell himself that it probably wouldn't matter. It was just this once, just a small risk.

"I assume that you haven't, either," he murmured gently.

She managed to shake her head no and kept her face in the comforting shelter of his neck. At the moment the idea of being pregnant with Adam's child was very appealing. Quite startlingly so. It made her warm with happiness, as a matter of fact.

"We'd better do something about it from now on, sweetheart," he murmured, planting another kiss on her cheek.

Which meant that there was to be a "from now on," Ariel thought with elation. Even if it wasn't forever. He was saying he would he hers for a while. She hugged him fiercely. While he was hers she would not spoil it by thinking about endings. She would live every day, one day at a time, not thinking about the morrow.

It was then that Adam faced the fact that if she became pregnant, he wouldn't be the least bit upset about it. As a matter of fact, the only feeling he could imagine having under those circumstances was a kind of overwhelmingly proud, protective joy.

He ran a hand slowly, possessively down her back.

"I'll take care of it, Adam," she whispered unsteadily.

They held each other close, each lost in private thoughts that were running along remarkably parallel lines.

CHAPTER TWELVE

Adam did not get his wish.

The story about Ariel getting hit on the head Saturday night in her office was bumped from its number-one position on the gossip charts, all right. It fell from that distinction by Monday evening. It was immediately replaced, however, by the Ariel-and-Adam-seem-to-be-getting-it-on piece, one of the juiciest tidbits that employees of the Athena Corporation had had to chew on in quite a long while.

The employees of a think tank are not stupid, however. Everyone prudently avoided letting Adam or Ariel know about their own popularity. This wise decision undoubtedly stemmed from a deeply rooted belief that their faces might be violently rearranged if Locke got wind of the conversational drift.

In that they were absolutely correct.

Adam and Ariel remained contentedly unaware of their best-selling status in the gossip ratings. This was mainly because they felt as if they occupied a separate universe from everyone else.

Adam could certainly believe that he had been mysteriously catapulted into another universe. He sure wouldn't have been caught dead sneaking discreetly out of a woman's home before dawn every day in the universe he'd grown up in! Nor would he have had this much difficulty in concentrating on his work in the old one . . . or be closeting himself with this ravishing woman at every opportunity like some sex-crazed adolescent!

No. The parallel universe theory made about as much sense to Adam Locke as any of his other theories did right now.

On Monday Ariel was struck by how oppressively sterile and colorless her office looked. All afternoon she kept wondering how she could have stood it all these months. It felt like it belonged to a stranger.

On Tuesday she set out to rectify that.

Late in the afternoon she went into Annapolis to do some errands. She parked on one of the winding, colonial streets and visited several small stores in the heart of the downtown area not too far from the public dock. It was bustling with shoppers and people doing some sight-seeing in the historic community. The steep steps and high dome of the state capitol building were barely visible from the street she was on, but there wasn't much activity there at this time of year. Just an occasional amateur photographer or two taking snapshots.

As evening was darkening the city Ariel made her last purchases. Looking into the window of a small boutique on Duke of Gloucester Street, she debated whether to resist the impulse to go in. Her car was just a little farther on. She could put the things in it and be home in no time.

She noticed the gaslight outside the boutique begin to glow. Evening was darkening the city.

She gazed in fascination at the radiant colors of the clothes on the store mannequin and saw her own reflection in the glass beside it. She was pale and subdued in comparison. Just like her office, she thought. A rueful smile came unbidden to her lips. She certainly didn't feel pale and subdued. She felt vibrant and brilliantly alive. And she needed some plumage to match, she realized, wanting to laugh.

"Could I help you with something?" inquired a saleswoman as soon as Ariel entered the shop.

She smiled encouragingly at Ariel and held the door open for her, inviting her inside with a subtle tilt of her head.

Ariel felt her last drop of hesitancy dissolve. She smiled

back and walked inside, shifting the packages to a more comfortable position in her arms as she did so.

"Yes," Ariel replied. "I think you could."

Wednesday afternoon found Dr. Norris standing in his office with his hands resting back to front on top of each other on the small of his back. He rocked onto his heels, then back onto the balls of his feet. The PERT chart spread across the cork-paneled wall that he was facing should have made him smile. All of the Athena projects were on schedule. Some of them were even ahead of schedule. PERT was a great system for letting you know things like that.

The environmental impact assessment project that Athena was conducting for the Appalachian Regional Commission would be finished this week. The final report was being typed up now. He'd already reviewed the draft. It was outstanding. He knew that the commissioners would be very pleased.

The first phase of a three-part analysis of policy development and decision making that was being performed for the Maryland State House of Delegates was being delivered today. There would undoubtedly be some negotiations with the delegates before proceeding to the second phase, but he'd already had some very positive feedback from the chairman of their oversight committee on the content of the report. The final phase would produce some controversy, he was sure. The delegates would want to set up a format for presenting the findings that would minimize that. That's the way it usually went with projects with strong political implications. He was very proud of the way the project team was approaching the whole thing. They had designed an excellent, state-of-the-art framework for analysis. The results should be about as bulletproof as they could get. Yes. That project would be highly respected in quite a few circles when it was finished.

And then there were the numerous engineering projects that were in various stages of development. The problems that were cropping up in them were the normal, garden-variety glitches that were routinely experienced in that line of work.

He rocked back onto his heels again, slapping the back of his hand against the worn, brown wool suiting that covered his lower back.

There was only one thing that was concerning him. It was a problem that did not appear on the maze of PERT chart lines, squares, and triangles spread across his wall.

Who had broken into Ariel's office? And why?

The buzzer on his desk sounded harshly. He marched over to it and punched down the intercom button.

"Yes?" he said gruffly.

"Robert Galway is here to see you, sir," Lydia said in her usual, calm, cheery voice.

"Send him right in, Lydia," Dr. Norris commanded.

Now maybe he could chart a timetable of events to predict the resolution of that one offensive problem that gnawed at him day and night. He wanted the end in sight on that one. And he wanted it now.

David Carrollton was less sanguine than Dr. Norris about the rate of progress of his particular project. Things kept turning out differently than he expected in his computer simulations. And he couldn't figure out why. He put in all the figures himself. But the models always varied slightly from the way he'd thought they'd look.

"Gail," he shouted in the direction of a tall brunette across the room from him, hoping that his voice was loud enough to carry over the noise of the high-speed printer that was furiously pulling paper through its tractor feed midway between them. "When will the run be finished?"

She glanced at her watch.

"About two more minutes, David," she shouted back.

He paced back and forth, decided that he was getting nowhere fast, and draped one hip over a nearby desk, lighting there for the duration.

As soon as the printer stopped he leapt to his feet and covered the room in three long strides. He bent over the neatly folded pile of paper and plucked it deftly from its cardboard box on the floor.

"You really are in a hurry today!" she said, teasing him laughingly.

Gail Marlow was one of Athena's two full-time computer technicians. She and her co-worker were responsible for keeping their hardware and software up and running twenty-four hours a day. That was no small feat considering what heavy use the equipment was put to around there.

She was also a very attractive young woman.

David gave her a rather forced grin. He liked Gail well enough. He'd taken her out a few times. Recently he'd been trying to decide whether or not to get more involved with her, as a matter of fact. Kissing her was turning out to be one of his great current interests in life, he recalled with a soft pang of pleasure. He had the feeling that pretty soon, kissing would not be enough.

David straightened up and carried the mass of papers that formed the data base for his report on Locke's project toward the computer room door.

He knew what was bothering him. Athena was such a small place. He wasn't sure that he wished to be cast in the role of a "love-'em-and-leave-'em" lady killer here. He'd had that distinction before, when he was in college. And he was afraid that might happen again, with Gail. He was concerned that their relationship would never be much more than a little friendship and a heavy dose of sexual attraction. She was such a lighthearted girl; she never seemed to take anything very seriously. Except the damn machinery, he reminded himself with an unexpected sense of annoyance.

He forcibly pushed all those complicating thoughts firmly from his mind. That he could not deal with right now. He had more pressing concerns to deal with. All of them revolving around Locke's project.

"Yeah. I guess I am in a hurry," he shot back agreeably, managing a friendlier grin this time. "Catch you later, Gail."

She watched his lean, rangy figure disappear down the

hall. A wistful, almost sad look settled in her eyes as soon as he turned his back to her. As usual she was careful not to let David see it. After all, he wanted to keep things light between them. That was only too obvious. Well, she was doing her darnedest to keep it that way.

She turned back to take another look at the defective board she'd removed from one of the computers. Work didn't seem to be as satisfying as it used to be, though. Not nearly as satisfying.

Robert Galway was leaving Dr. Norris's office just as Lydia buzzed him again on the intercom.

"I'm sorry to bother you, Dr. Norris," she said apologetically.

"That's all right, Lydia," her boss assured her. "What is it?"

"Professor Radnor is on the line. He'd like a word with you."

His gaze shifted to the button on his phone that was flashing its clear, white light intermittently.

"I'll take it," he said.

He depressed the button, cutting off his secretary and picking up the outside call.

"Marcus! How are you?" he exclaimed warmly.

It had been a while since he had talked to his old friend. Too long, for that matter, in more ways than one.

Ariel was sitting in front of the computer terminal in Locke's suite, staring at the amber monitor and trying to figure out why the listing she was searching the files for refused to appear on the screen. She was positive that she had seen it the other day when she'd gone through the index. Now . . . Well, she was beginning to think that it might have been a figment of her imagination.

And such figments were notoriously hard to retrieve from something as lacking as imagination as a computer, she thought in exasperation.

She closed her eyes and leaned back in the chair, pinching the bridge of her nose just between her eyes, then pressing down a little. The pressure helped relieve the tension a little.

Then the phone rang.

Relieved at having another excuse not to search for the title for a while, she answered the phone

"Hello, Mr. Locke's office," she said in a businesslike fashion.

There was half a moment of silence, as if the person on the other end had been startled by Ariel's response. Then the caller spoke. And Ariel's stomach squeezed a little in uneasy surprise. It was a woman.

"Hello. May I speak with Adam, please?" she asked. Her voice was well modulated, if a trifle distant-sounding.

"I'm sorry. He's not in at the moment. May I have him call you?" Ariel inquired as coolly and calmly as possible in spite of the fact that her imagination was beginning to tease her unmercifully. All sorts of possibilities were coming to mind regarding the caller's role in Adam's life. Ariel reminded herself that he'd told her there wasn't anyone else. But . . .

The caller apparently needed to think Ariel's question over a bit because she didn't answer at once.

"No," she said finally. "I'll be between phones as soon as I hang this one up, I'm afraid."

She sounded as if she were thinking out loud. The muffled sounds in the background made Ariel wonder where the woman was calling from. It sounded like someplace public and bustling with activity. There was a kind of hollow reverberation to the noise that made it seem like a large, empty building and the barely audible sound of a loudspeaker, like the scheduling announcer at a train station. The noise was too muted for Ariel to be sure.

"Just tell him that Catherine called," she said finally. "And that I'll call him again when I can."

"All right." Ariel agreed, jotting down the message.

"Thank you. Good-bye."

"Good-bye," Ariel said quietly.

She heard the click at the other end and replaced the receiver on its cradle.

Now, who was Catherine? she wondered darkly. And what was she to Adam? An old girlfriend perhaps? Ariel stared despondently at the note in front of her. The name she had written stared back at her in unresponsive silence.

She put the note down next to the phone with his other messages and told herself not to be silly. This was probably nothing. There was no reason to react like this, she thought, feeling a pang of sadness.

She, after all, had no particular right to be possessive or jealous of him. She herself had pointed out to him that there were no promises between them . . . no obligations . . . no commitments.

She had the almost irresistible urge to wad up the message in her fist and throw it into the wastepaper basket. With great effort she managed to resist the temptation. Answering the phone, however, had spoiled the tender atmosphere she had experienced earlier in Locke's suite.

Ariel grabbed her purse and coat and left. Maybe she could find some work to do in her office until quitting time. Anything would do at this point. Anything at all.

Meanwhile Jeanne Wells, the newest typist in the corporation's word-processing center, was turning into a nervous wreck.

"Barbara," she hissed, leaning toward the woman working at the station next to her. "Do you have any of my diskettes, by any chance?"

Barbara Hawkins, an unperturbable mother of five teenage girls, looked sympathetically at the frantic-looking young woman at her side. Patiently she began searching her own diskette files for the missing item.

"I don't see any," said the almost grandmotherly-looking Mrs. Hawkins. Nevertheless she began methodically looking through the materials spread across her work area.

211

"I'm sorry, Jeanne, but I'm afraid not. What was it?" she said in her usual kindly, supportive way.

Jeanne's thin body crumpled back against her typing chair, and a pained expression flitted across her face.

"It was a report that one of David Carrollton's engineers gave me this morning. He wants it tomorrow afternoon."

"Can't you use the handwritten original and transcribe it again onto another diskette?" suggested Mrs. Hawkins, not particularly worried about the problem. It wouldn't be the first time that a computer diskette had been misplaced around here before its contents could be printed out.

Jeanne looked even more woebegone than ever.

"No," she wailed softly, trying not to attract the notice of their supervisor. "I can't find *it*, either," she whispered mournfully.

"And you didn't print the report yet?" asked the older colleague, afraid now to hear the answer.

"No," said Jeanne, depressed and scared.

Jeanne had only worked for Athena for a few weeks. It was still her probationary employment period. She needed to do well in order to be granted permanent employment status, and she desperately needed the job. She had two small children to support. This job was the first that she'd found that paid enough for her to accomplish that small, but very significant, feat. But the Athena Corporation had a reputation for high standards. If she was seen as sloppy or unreliable, she'd be dismissed. Of that Jeanne had no doubt.

"Oh, Barbara! I'm afraid to tell that engineer that I lost his report! What if he didn't make a copy of his longhand draft?" Jeanne was truly horrified at that awful prospect. "What can I do?"

"Now, now," her friend said soothingly. "It's got to be here somewhere. Diskettes don't just roll out the door! Let's take another look," she suggested brightly, then added, "Don't worry, Jeanne. Even if we can't find it, everyone understands that these things happen occasionally."

Mrs. Hawkins wasn't really all that certain that their supervisor or anyone else at Athena would end up taking that understanding a posture in a situation like this. However, she wanted to be optimistic for poor Jeanne's sake. The child looked scared to death.

Jeanne Wells *was* scared to death. If it was just this problem, she might have managed to react with a mild case of the jitters and a strong layering of anxiety. She knew that her skills were excellent. That would probably help balance the scales in her favor in the event of an incident like this. That is, if there had been only one incident.

But this wasn't the only incident. She kept losing things, important things. There had been two of Ariel's translations, one of Darryl's summaries of indices of scientific research dealing with toxic fumes, and now an entire technical report!

This had never happened to her before. She was beginning to wonder if she was having blackouts or something.

Fortunately, and to her utter astonishment, the other three documents had eventually turned up again. She desperately hoped that her string of good luck would hold for just one more time . . . If she could just locate that report.

"Hello, pretty lady!"

Jim Reeves bent over her and grinned warmly into her worried features. He pulled her around to look up at him, his grin fading into mild concern.

"Say! You look like you're ready to call it a day, Jeannie!"

No one called her Jeannie except her mother. It sounded so silly coming from a big blond bear like Jim Reeves that she had to half smile and shake her head.

"I'm looking for something, Jim. I'm afraid I'll have to stick around until I can find it."

He looked at her with a kind of casual, sympathic regard.

"Whatever it is, it doesn't walk, right?" he argued with a devil-may-care glint in his eyes.

"No, but—"

He pulled her up and stuffed her into her thin cloth coat, draping her handbag over her slim shoulder.

"Then it's not goin' anywhere tonight, is it?" he pointed out with a triumphant grin.

He pulled the last stack of mail from her "out" box and shoved his last delivery of the day into her "in" box. It was so bulky, some things were spread over the top of her desk.

"He's right," Barbara Hawkins chimed in. "We'll look again tomorrow morning, Jeanne. Sometimes you see things when you start fresh like that. When you're tired, you can't see them even if you're staring straight at them sometimes."

"Yeah! That's the truth!" Jim agreed enthusiastically.

"Come on, Jeannie. I'll give you a ride home."

Jeanne let herself be talked into going. What Barbara had said was true, she thought. After all, she'd found the other things the day after she'd misplaced each of them. With almost no effort at all, unbelievably. They had been within a foot of where she'd originally thought she'd put them. They would have had to have been invisible for her to have missed seeing them as she had. But somehow she'd missed them. She must be too uptight about this job, she thought. It was affecting her perception. There was no other explanation. Things don't just disappear and reappear like magic.

"Thank, Jim."

He really was a nice guy, she thought. The kids liked him too. Maybe she could invite him to stay for dinner.

On Thursday afternoon Ariel took another telephone call for Adam from the rich- and lovely-sounding Catherine. She told herself not to get upset about it. She got upset about it, anyway. And she became even more upset Friday afternoon when Catherine called again.

On Friday evening things came to a head.

"To us," he said, raising the fine crystal wineglass in a toast and watching the elegant beauty across from him to the same.

Ariel smiled and gently clinked her glass to Adam's.

"To us," she said softly.

They sipped the wine, still gazing into each other's eyes. The two sensations mingled together very well.

Dinner was served by candlelight, another highly compatible combination.

Annapolis was a wonderful city to dine in. It offered a veritable smorgasbord of choices for two people out on the town on a Friday evening. There were an incredible variety of restaurants, cafés, and pubs nestled among the beautifully preserved buildings downtown. The architectural selection alone gave it a unique and charming ambience that would have made the plainest food taste well prepared. Georgian, Federal, Greek Revival, Italianate, Gothic, Romanesque, Queen Anne . . . the styles somehow blended remarkably well. As did the restaurateurs and their establishments.

Locke had passed up some of the better-known places, such as Middleton's Public Tavern and the Treaty of Paris Restaurant in the Maryland Inn. The eighteenth-century inns were certainly elegant enough, but he had wanted more than elegance tonight.

He took Ariel to a small, intimate restaurant nestled at the top of a narrow staircase in a nineteenth-century building on one of the numerous winding side streets, away from the floundering throngs of people. With a self-satisfied flourish he ushered her into Chez Henri. Elegant. Quiet. Exquisitely delicious food. An ambience of warmth and intimacy. Tastefully understated. A very classy place.

They were still luxuriating in the pleasure of being there when they finished their dessert a leisurely two hours later. The candlelight flickered softly as the tuxedo-clad waiter brought them two small liqueur glasses filled with Benedictine.

"I've never even heard of this place," Ariel admitted, still a little overcome by that fact.

Ariel thought that she knew the downtown area pretty well. Every so often she would accompany Dr. Norris to expensive restaurants in Annapolis when they had foreign VIPs they wanted to take someplace special. Even though she hadn't been to them all, she had assumed that she'd at least heard all of the big names in restaurants here.

"Henri doesn't go in too heavily for advertising," Adam muttered reluctantly. As he'd expected she didn't d: it at that.

Ariel raised both eyebrows in amazement.

"How does he stay in business?" she asked in surprise.

"Well, he only serves a few dinners a night," he explained, holding the tiny glass in his fingertips and tilting it slightly, pretending to concentrate on the play of light in the dark amber fires in the Benedictine.

"How can he afford to do that?" she whispered, a little astonished at that tidbit of information.

Afford to do it, he thought. He sighed. Maybe they could have this conversation without raking up old coals. He hoped so. He didn't want to have to go back to square one and win her confidence again if this reminded her of what she seemed to have forgotten in the last few days; that he was not exactly hurting for money, and neither were most of his nearest and dearest.

"Henri runs this restaurant primarily for the fun of it," he said bluntly. "To entertain himself."

"You're kidding!" she exclaimed softly. It must have cost a small fortune to decorate it alone, she thought, admiring again the antique French furnishings and Middle-Eastern rugs. And rent wasn't usually free, she added, wondering what it would be in this neighborhood. To say nothing of the cost of the food, which had been fit for a king. "How can he afford to do it?" she asked again, waiting expectantly for the answer.

Locke shrugged uncomfortably.

"It's a hobby more than anything else. If he breaks even, he's pleased. And so is the IRS. He breaks even often enough to convince them that it's a legitimate, for-profit business enterprise. Then, in bad years, he can write off his red ink as a tax loss."

"Good heavens!" she said, having a hard time getting it all to seem real. The place definitely did not look like it belonged to a failing entrepreneur. It reeked of success. That is, it would have reeked of it if it hadn't had so much class. It was too chic to reek.

"But how could I not have heard of it?" she asked, perplexed by that.

Adam smiled but he looked a little embarrassed, almost as if he was embarrassed to tell her.

"Come on! Give!" she insisted, trying her best to give him a threatening stare.

He finished his liqueur and looked around the room.

"Well, it's only been here for a year or so," he replied, halfheartedly stalling for time.

"That's not a good enough reason," she told him warningly, a mischievous gleam forming in her eyes. "If you don't want to tell me, I could always ask Henri," she pointed out.

He grinned at her. He'd always tried to be gracious in defeat.

"Okay. It's really no big deal," he said, trying to brush it off. "Henri's an old friend of mine. So . . . I'm one of the people who know about Henri's establishment."

He watched her take it in. He could tell the precise moment when the light went on in her head and she understood what he was trying not to say.

"You mean," she said slowly, "that only Henri's friends and acquaintances are invited to dine? They're the only ones who know about it?" She was staring at him in complete surprise.

"Yeah. That's about it," he admitted.

Adam signed a small slip of paper that the waiter had brought to him. Since it bore no resemblance to a credit slip, Ariel decided that it must be an original bill. Henri sent out his own bills.

That was when Ariel began to seriously contemplate just how much the dinner had cost. There had been no prices on the simple menu, and they had had so many delicious dishes.

"I hope Henri's got a lot of friends," she murmured weakly.

"Henri would be hovering over you, kissing your hand and trying to talk you into going home with him instead of me tonight," he added. He grinned roguishly and held one of her hands in both of his, looking at her steadily with a familiar, humorous gleam in his eye. "But I outmaneuvered him. I made sure he was in Quebec before I brought you here. So"—he pressed his lips to the back of her hand—"I have you all to myself. No competition."

She smiled at him and shook her head at his teasing.

"We still have an audience, though," she reminded him with a tilt of her head toward the waiter and the two other tables occupied by Henri's eight other friends who'd come to dine that night.

"Not for long," he promised firmly, pulling her to her feet and steering her in the direction of the door.

He helped her on with her coat, admiring again the sizzling colors of the raw silk sheath she was wearing. The elegant cut brought out her beautiful build and fine bones. The colors were warmer than anything he'd ever seen her wear before. She seemed like a newly metamorphosed butterfly to him.

He pressed a kiss on her cheek, a little in front of her ear.

"You look beautiful," he murmured appreciatively. "Have I mentioned that?"

She smiled up at him and slipped her hand in his, lacing their fingers.

"I think maybe you have." She laughed.

Only about two or three dozen times! But she couldn't hear it enough. Especially when he looked at her like that when he said it! It made her glow, inside and out.

A shadow crossed her face as they descended the narrow stairs. Chez Henri brought back a memory she'd almost managed to forget in the past week. Adam Locke was a well-heeled man with affluent friends. They lived in the fast lane of life.

Ariel wasn't sure she'd ever fit in there. Or that Locke would want her to.

Unfortunately she had the dreadful feeling that one of his

218

wealthy friends was a beautiful, cultivated young woman named Catherine. There wouldn't be much of a problem fitting their lives together, she thought unhappily. Maybe no problem at all.

Adam could feel her drifting away from him all the way back. By the time they had stepped into her cottage he almost wondered if she was going to ask him not to stay with her that night. It would be the first time since he first made love to her if she did.

He watched her hang up their coats and make some tea, trying to guess why she acted so nervously. She'd been a little edgy a couple of times in the past day or so. But that hadn't seemed like much of anything. They'd been having a great time together. In every way, as far as he was concerned.

He paced over to her sofa and sat down, waiting for her to join him so he could ask her to explain. He could still hear her rattling around in the kitchen, so he pulled out an old photo album and casually looked over the snapshots.

Until he turned to a page near the end, that is, he was casual. There, with one arm around Ariel's shoulder and his other arm around a girl on the other side, was C. Laslow, the rugged-looking guy who had answered the door that morning in Washington months ago. He was the "friend" she'd been staying with. The one she kept trying to tell him was a girl named Candy.

Anger strained his cheeks. He had to get to the bottom of that. He couldn't stand the thought of being lied to. But he especially couldn't stand it from Ariel. And he was sick of having it hang like a dark cloud in the back of his mind like this. He couldn't keep it back there forever.

He watched Ariel walk into the living room with their tea on a tray. He knew exactly why he cared so much. He wanted her to be perfect. Except for this one thing, he thought she was. Part of his acute mental illness, no doubt, but that's the way it was, and he'd resigned himself comfortably to that facet of it.

And he was jealous of her, damn it all! More every day. He didn't want men putting their hands on her, and he was very angry that this jerk ever had touched her. To say nothing of how he felt about her spending the night, or several nights, under his roof.

Those were two potent sources of vulnerability he had where she was concerned. He was intelligent enough to recognize that.

With an effort he reminded himself of his earlier concern, the one he'd been killing time leafing through her album and sitting on her couch for. First things first. He'd get to Laslow next, he promised himself.

"Ariel," he began, taking a long, careful look at her. "What's bothering you?"

She was sitting in the chair across from him, but Ariel felt as though they were miles apart. How she longed to be sitting next to him like she had been every night this week, with his arm around her shoulder, laughing and talking, as if they were old, dear friends.

Well, maybe not *exactly* like old friends, she had to admit, recalling how the conversation had always mellowed into caresses, kisses, and progressively more intimate touching until they ended up wrapped in each other's arms in her bed.

Don't think about it, she ordered herself. *You've got to stop dreaming like a kid and find out who this girl is who keeps calling him every day!*

It was driving her to distraction. She'd been able to pretend that she and Adam had their own magic world. But when another woman intruded on it . . . It was just too much. Ariel was incapable of being that much of an ostrich.

Their cups of tea remained untouched on the tray.

"Did you get any interesting phone calls today?" she began, trying to approach her topic obliquely.

He looked at her blankly.

"Phone calls?" he repeated, uncomprehending. "No. The usual things. Since I was tied up in that meeting with the

220

engineering team this afternoon, you know most of them. You took the messages."

He gave her a preplexed look.

"Why? Does that have anything to do with what I just asked?" he inquired, his voice gathering an irritated edge to it.

She forced herself to look directly at him.

"Yes, I guess it does."

"Well?" he prompted, unable to fathom this at all.

"Well, taking those messages for you has reminded me how little we still know about each other, I guess," she said lamely, losing her nerve at the last minute.

She just couldn't ask him. What if he told her that Catherine was the love of his life? Or the woman he took to Vegas with him when he wanted a good time? Or his lover from L.A. who'd be in town for a few days and wanted to get together with him? Then what did she do?

Wondering what was going on could be awful, but knowing might just be infinitely worse, she feared. Who was it who had discovered that ignorance could be bliss? Maybe they had a point.

Ariel sprang out of the chair and settled lightly on his lap a second later. She wrapped her arms around his shoulders, comforting herself with his nearness. She'd go back to pretending that he was all hers.

"I'm sorry, Adam. Maybe staring at the computer monitor all week has melted my brain." She sighed wistfully.

She felt his arms close around her hips and waist. It felt so good. She was beginning to think that she could bear anything in order to keep him close to her like this. She laid her head against his and pressed a soft kiss on his temple.

"Please," she murmured. "Just forget it. It wasn't anything in particular."

He was tempted to forget it, all right. The feel of her body cuddling up against him like this pretty much short-circuited the rational parts of his brain, making thinking almost impossible. But something was bothering him, even more than

221

Ariel was at the moment. She had been pretty upset about something. He didn't want that. He wanted her happy. And he didn't want any more shadows between them.

It had something to do with telephone messages, he thought, as unenlightened as he had been earlier. What in the hell could phone messages contain that would make her act like this?

He was racking his brain just as she began forging a chain of warm, provocative kisses along his cheek and jaw. The mental images were getting foggier and foggier as she neared his lips, practically diappearing in a steamy mist as her mouth closed over his, and her tongue played teasingly with his.

He had responded automatically. His arms tightening, his mouth opening, kissing her, his eyes closing in the birth of ecstasy. Just before everything shut down to enjoy the ride into bliss, he figured it out.

And not a moment too soon, either. Considering the way that she was sliding her hands under his jacket, his intellectual faculties would have been completely shut down in another thirty seconds.

He grabbed her by the forearms and firmly pushed her a little bit away from him.

"It was those phone calls from Catherine, wasn't it?" he demanded, a triumphant gleam in his eyes.

Ariel was off-balance when he asked, although that certainly seemed to describe her at almost anytime she was with Adam. Even so, being physically close to him made her a little more vulnerable to his probing question.

Besides, he'd already guessed, she thought, blushing lightly.

Ariel resigned herself to her fate. She might as well get it over with. Now, apparently, was to be the time.

"Yes," she admitted, sitting there on his knees with as much dignity as she could salvage at the moment. "Who is she?"

CHAPTER THIRTEEN

"Catherine!" he repeated, a slow grin spreading across his face. "Who is Catherine?"

Yes. Yes! Who is Catherine? she thought angrily, not daring to speak for fear of losing control. With that devilish look he was wearing, she might just end up doing something really damaging.

He leaned back against the sofa and released her arms.

"Catherine is an old friend."

Ariel didn't care much for that description. And she didn't care at all for that relaxed, easy-spoken way he was talking about Catherine.

"I've probably known Catherine longer than any other woman," he added thoughtfully, with a suspicious gleam lighting his eyes.

Ariel could practically feel her blood turning green. Was he recalling some special highlights of their long, dear friendship? she wondered, appalled and thoroughly unnerved by the direction of his comments.

"She's very pretty. Well, pretty might not do her justice anymore. She's a very beautiful woman." He paused as if contemplating the assets of this vision of femininity. "She has the smoothest, healthiest-looking skin. I'd say that's her best feature." He paused, looking askance at Ariel. Pleased with the effect, he added, "Her personality could use a little tempering, though. I keep telling her that, but all I get back is a lot of flack!"

He shook his head mournfully.

Ariel liked every word he said less than the one before. It wasn't that she wished any ill for this Venus de Milo. It was just that she would have preferred a little less challenging competition. Or, better still, no competition at all.

"She's very sharp. Graduated from Wellesley . . . been working for a brokerage firm for a few years now. I keep telling her that the only reason she's got so many clients is because they like to come in and look at her. And some of the insiders who've got investment-trend information just can't keep from spilling the beans to her when she bats her eyelashes at them. They just babble like babies. Why, she could probably make a good living from just that alone. She could just start up her own investment newsletter."

Ariel had had more than enough. She started to slide off his lap. With a high roller like Catherine calling him all week, Ariel decided she must have been fortunate to have had as much time with Locke as she had. Frustration at that idea was making her angrier by the second.

She did not want to hear one more word about this brilliant, silk-skinned paragon!

Adam reached out and grabbed her before she could get away, pulling her stiff and resistant frame down onto him.

"What else would you like to know about Catherine?" he asked, congenial to the bone.

He was having a increasingly difficult time keeping a straight face, but somehow he managed.

"Nothing! Nothing at all," she said emphatically, trying awkwardly to disengage herself. "I've heard more than enough."

He looked at her in feigned surprise.

"But you haven't even heard the best part," he protested, clamping her down without any effort whatsoever.

She was beside herself. She hated to be locked physically in place like this. She glared at him in protest, thoroughly affronted by his sudden, totally unforeseen penchant for the sadistic. She'd certainly never noticed that tendency in him before!

Adam assumed a pleasantly thoughtful expression.

"Catherine is the woman who knows me best. We've known each other for years. You could say we've grown up together. We've seen good years and bad . . ."

He ran his hand up to her rigid shoulders and held her lightly.

"I named the *Catarina* after her," he said, a tender smile dawning at the memory.

Ariel wriggled her shoulder and pulled violently away. This was really the last straw! He obviously was thoroughly enjoying teasing her with each successive revelation. And here she was hanging on each dreadful fact and turning a darker shade of green every step of the way!

"Well, isn't that nice," she muttered crossly between clenched teeth, trying harder to free herself when her first efforts proved to be fruitless.

He was really grinning now. She was sure that any minute he would throw back his head and start laughing out loud. How could he laugh at this? And how dare he hold her so tightly.

"You didn't have to add anything. I told you, I'd heard more than enough! Let's talk about something else," she said acidly.

With one small twist of her shoulder and a hard, quick shove, she finally managed to free herself from his grasp. She bounced to her feet. Locke almost simultaneously snapped to his and hauled her back into his arms before she could make good her escape.

"You're jealous!" he exclaimed triumphantly.

She glared at him defiantly. Oh, how she hated that feeling!

"Jealous!" she sputtered, as if nothing could be farther from the truth. "Don't be ridiculous! Why would I be jealous?"

Locke's persistent grip was not helping her sense of humor rejuvenate. Being so physically dominated simply heaped fuel on her angry fires.

"Let me go!" she burst out.

The man had the unmitigated gall to laugh! Ariel stomped her foot on his in fury.

"Ow!" he howled before toppling them both onto the sofa and immobilizing her completely in what Ariel thought had to be some sort of full body-wrestling hold.

"Cut that out!" he ordered sternly, wiggling his injured foot a little to make sure it was on the way to recovery.

They were both a little flushed from the escalating verbal tug-of-war. Being so physically close had the effect of heating their simmering temperatures. Something flickered in Adam's eyes, and he bent his head to place a lingering kiss on her throat.

"Stop that!" she protested a little breathlessly.

His nearness was acting on her like an aphrodisiac, in spite of the fact that she was angry with him. Her breathlessness, however, was not entirely the result of their highly combustible chemistry.

"I can't breathe," she said, gasping.

He lifted his head and chest, propping himself up on his elbows with one swift movement. That relieved her torso of the weight that had been suffocating her. She gulped in air, too happy to be breathing freely again to stay angry or try to argue at the moment.

"You don't really need to worry about Catherine," he said, looking both amused and regretful. "You see," he added, interrupting himself in order to press a warm kiss on her mutinously closed lips, "Catherine is my sister."

If he hadn't been clamping her wrists in his hands and holding them down on the bed, she would have shaken him as hard as she could.

"Your sister!" she exclaimed, trying to get her mind to reorganize its picture of Catherine as rapidly as possible.

He grinned down at her.

"Why did you lead me on like that?" she asked indignantly, trying to wriggle out from under him. How could she

226

have a discussion with the man while he was lying on top of her? she wondered in exasperation.

"Mmmm," Adam moaned appreciatively, burying his face in her soft neck. "That feels so good. Keep wiggling . . . just like that."

Ariel stilled instantly.

"That was a dirty trick," she complained, casting him a censuring look. "Why did you do it?"

"I'm sorry," he said apologetically.

He released her and slid his hands under her back.

"I couldn't help it. It just made me feel good to see you jealous," he admitted softly.

What could she say to that? His admission certainly took the wind out of her sails. She ran her hands slowly over his shoulder blades.

"It did?" she asked, still a little confused by the rapid turn of events.

"Ummm hmmm."

"Oh."

"You *were* jealous, weren't you?"

There was an underlying thread of doubt and a need for reassurance that anyone but Ariel would have missed. But she heard it. And it melted her heart.

"Yes"—she sighed, going down in defeat, this time by her own hand—"I was."

His arms tightened around her, and he rubbed his lips along her collarbone.

"I'm glad," he murmured.

"You don't have to keep rubbing it in, Adam!" she told him, giving his shoulder a halfhearted push. "Hasn't anyone ever told you that's . . ." She searched for a word. She foundered on it awkwardly. "That's unsportsmanlike!"

He laughed and began pulling down the zipper in the back of her dress.

"After what you've put me through, no one in their right mind would think a thing about my lack of sportsmanship!"

Ariel frowned and grabbed his hand as it searched for the shoulder of her dress in order to pull it down.

"What I put you through? What have I put you through?" she asked in confusion.

He looked down at her and was of two minds regarding what to do. It was so easy to get lost in her soft brown eyes. He wanted to stop talking and make love to her now. But she'd given him an opening by asking that question. Maybe it was as good a time as any to try to resolve that last remaining shadow.

Damn it all! She'd better be able to explain this, he thought, practically beginning to hold his breath at what was about to unfold.

Adam rolled onto his side and wedged her in between his body and the back of the sofa. He propped himself up on one elbow and gazed at her enigmatically. For the first time in quite a while his eyes were veiled.

"For one thing . . . you ran away from me the first night we met."

"Yes."

Ariel waited for him to go on. What could this be leading up to? Nothing was coming to mind. She'd just have to wait for him to make it clear.

"You went back to the apartment of the friend you'd been staying with . . ."

"Yes." So? she silently prompted him.

"Tell me about your friend," he suggested.

He phrased it in such a carefully crafted, yet casual, way that for a moment Ariel thought she was being questioned by an attorney. He was laying out a trap of some sort, and she was expected to walk into it, she thought a little nervously.

"Candy?" she asked in surprise. "What's Candy got to do with my putting you through a hard time?"

"I'll explain in a minute," Locke said, effectively cutting off her line of inquiry.

Ariel didn't understand, but she was willing to answer his question. That was primarily because she really did wonder

228

what she had done that could be construed as "putting him through a hard time." That was too fascinating to overlook!

"All right," she agreed. "Well, I met Candy in college. We hit it off right away and became fast friends. I was very involved with gymnastics, and Candy was a ballet student. So, we had a common love of physical movement and exercise that wasn't all that common among the rest of the women students. The last year of school, we were roommates. We spent a lot of time giggling over Candy's endless string of beaus." She tactfully omitted the many different wedding plans they had made for Ariel and Andrew. "We helped each other struggle over career choices, and we swore to keep in touch after graduation. Somehow we've managed to do that even now that we've gone our separate ways."

Ariel stopped to take a breath and see of this was the kind of thing that he wanted to hear. He was still wearing that inscrutable face, but she thought she detected a new, slightly perplexed aura as well.

"Is that what you wanted to know?" she ventured.

He pressed his lips together thoughtfully. Candy was certainly real enough sounding now. He doubted that Ariel could or would make up all that!

Vividly he recalled Laslow's apartment. It was one of three that had been carved out of a stately, three-story house. The imposing structure, constructed of large, sculpted stone blocks, was located off Wisconsin Avenue, not too far from Georgetown. The building, like those adjoining it, had been built in row-house fashion. The grand scale and castlelike architecture reminded passersby that the original owner who'd purchased it in the early part of this century had possessed substantial wealth and status.

How could a former ballet student afford that? And who was the man in her residence? Assuming, of course, that Candy turned out to be real, he reminded himself, although only faintly believing there was a chance that she wasn't.

Maybe the guy was this Candy's boyfriend. That was a very brightening thought.

"Does she have any beaus now?" he asked, barely concealing his hopefulness.

Ariel laughed.

"She doesn't have time for any. All she does is practice, practice, practice, perform, travel . . . and sleep."

"What does she do?" he inquired in surprise.

"She's dancing with the Washington Ballet."

That didn't sound lucrative enough to pay for that apartment. It was in a high-rent district if ever there was one! Locke abandoned the indirect approach.

"Who's the big blond guy living in her apartment?" he asked bluntly.

"Who's the . . . ." Ariel's voice trailed off. She stared at him blankly. "What *are* you talking about?" she interjected testily. "What are *we* talking about? Listen, if you have something to ask me, just ask. Straight out."

His eyebrows lowered threateningly.

"There's a snapshot of you with a big guy and another girl. It's in one of your photograph albums. I want to know what he was doing in Laslow's apartment the morning after you ran away from me in Georgetown."

There was an uncompromising, steely cast to his eyes. His jaw jutted out defensively. He was a man determined to get what he wanted if she'd ever seen one.

"Snapshot?" She sat up and crawled down the sofa to her albums.

"That's the one," he growled as her fingers plucked the album in question from the bookcase.

Ariel crawled back up the sofa and settled in, turning the pages until she reached the photograph he had described.

"Who is he?" Locke demanded, jabbing a finger at the grinning face in the picture.

"That's Charles," she said, as uncomprehending as earlier.

"Who is Charles?" he asked, his voice getting sharper with frustration. She'd better come up with a clear answer soon, before he lost his temper.

"Charles is Candy's brother. Actually it's his apartment.

He owns it. He rents it to his sister." She stared at Locke, trying to fathom why he was upset about this. "Charles is an investment banker, and he dabbles in real estate on the side. When Candy landed the job in Washington, she asked him to help her find a place to live and—"

She was interrupted by the relief-tinged sound of Adam's laughter.

"Her brother!"

Suddenly he stopped laughing and began frowning again.

"What was he doing there bright and early the morning after you ran away from me?" he demanded.

"Why in the world do you want to know that?" she asked, starting to get annoyed at this single-minded pursuit. Why was this topic so fascinating to him, anyway? Then something occurred to her. "How did you know that he was there that morning?"

He looked a little embarrassed, but he gritted his teeth, refusing to be put off the scent when he was so close to the answer to his question.

"What was he doing there?" he asked angrily.

"He came by to visit Candy. He does it all the time," she shot back, a trifle loudly. "Now, would you be so kind as to explain what this inquisition is all about?"

Locke looked like he was going gently into a very pleasant orbit someplace far, far away.

"He was visiting his sister . . ." he murmured. Then, more loudly and focusing on Ariel, he added, "You mean that he doesn't live there?"

"No," she said, making an effort to rein in her growing temper.

"And he wasn't sleeping there when you were?"

"No!" she said indignantly. Was *that* what all of this had been about? She stared at him, flabbergasted.

Adam closed his eyes and laid his head down on a pillow fluffed up against the arm of the sofa. He looked very relieved.

"How did you know about Charles?" she asked suspiciously, pushing his chest a little to get his attention. "Come on. I answered your questions. Now you answer mine!'' she insisted threateningly.

He sighed and looked rather uncomfortable. Finally he answered, keeping his eyes closed.

''I tracked you down and went there the next morning. When I knocked on the door, he answered. The mailbox only had C. Laslow on it, so I assumed that he had been the friend you'd been staying with . . . the one you had to hurry back to that night. It's been driving me nuts for months. It's one of the reasons I didn't look you up sooner. I kept wondering who he was . . . what your relationship was.''

''Why didn't you just ask?'' she cried in frustration.

Ariel didn't know whether to be indignant, flattered, or amused at all of this. Seeing how sheepish, how embarrassed, and how obviously relieved he was decided the question. Flattered, amused, and deeply touched won hands down.

She wrapped her arms around him and snuggled up against him.

''Why didn't you just ask me, Adam?'' She sighed, placing a soft, reassuring kiss on his lips.

He sighed in contented defeat and returned the favor.

''You're an irascible, tantalizing, captivating little witch,'' he muttered. Adam opened his eyes and slowly, with great pleasure, scanned her features. ''I didn't want you to know what a fool I was making of myself,'' he admitted with a wry grin.

''You idiot,'' she murmured tenderly, hugging him with all her strength.

''Mmmmm,'' he mumbled agreeably as he hooked a leg behind hers, drawing her into a more intimate clinch. ''So punish me,'' he suggested.

Ariel laughed and proceeded to do just that.

The punishment was coming along very nicely when the phone interrupted things.

Ariel pulled her hands out from under Adam's shirt and tugged on the sleeves of her dress. Locke remained sprawled over the sofa while she crawled off him and made an uneven path across the small room.

She lifted the receiver on the seventh ring. Whoever it was certainly was determined to talk to her, she thought in dismay.

"Hello?" she answered.

The flat, sustained twang of the dial tone greeted her.

She hung up the instrument, giving it a disgusted look before she turned her back on it.

"Wrong number?" he asked, seeing her expression.

She rejoined him and tried to remember exactly where they'd been before they were so rudely interrupted.

"They didn't say." She sighed as she laid her head on his chest. "They hung up before I got to them."

"Hm."

They searched around and found their places again. Clothes began coming off again as they started searching for a few new places as well. The kisses were becoming urgent, the bodies pretty hot when a knock at the front door intervened in the festivities.

Locke groaned, and Ariel went limp in frustration.

"Who in the hell would be knocking at your door at a quarter to eleven on Friday night?" he asked irritably.

"I have no idea," she said, trying to pull her clothes on in some semblance of the way they'd been originally intended.

She ran an unsteady hand over her hair. The caller pounded on the door.

Ariel opened the door, fully prepared to announce that she was on her way out and couldn't talk right now. Instead she stood there with her mouth half open.

There stood Darryl, looking more embarrassed than she could ever recall having seen him.

"Ummm, ahh . . . I'm really sorry to bother you, Ariel," he said, the words tumbling hesitantly over one another. "I know it's very late and Friday night isn't a good time to, uh, visit, but . . . um . . . I certainly wouldn't have bothered you if it weren't, uh, serious."

His eyes were glued to her face. He had to know that

Locke was there, she realized. He was half lying on her sofa in full view, still looking a little disheveled, even if he had buttoned up his shirt and tucked it in his trousers.

"What is it, Darryl?" she prompted as evenly as she could. Please, Darryl, she prayed, just get to the point.

Darryl shifted awkwardly from one foot to the other.

"Mother's had an unexpected relapse and I'm going up there now to try to see that everything that needs to be taken care of is attended to. I, um, I probably won't be back until late on Monday. That is, of course, assuming that the doctors feel she's stabilized enough and I've been able to arrange for someone to look after the house."

"Yes . . . yes," Ariel said, trying to hold her impatience in check and resist the pull to anger. "But what do you want me for?"

Darryl pulled a set of keys out of his pocket and held them out.

"There's a report that needs to be sent to the word-processing unit first thing Monday morning. I just finished it tonight, before I heard about Mother. Well, I was wondering . . . I wanted to ask you . . . could you . . . would you mind, uh . . . I wouldn't want it to be any trouble, but—"

Ariel snatched the keys from his hand and said, "I'll take it down there first thing Monday morning, Darryl. Don't worry about it. No problem! Have a safe trip."

He looked so sad, she reached out and squeezed his arm.

"I'm sorry about your Mother, Darryl," she said sympathetically. "I hope she's feeling better soon. Call me on Monday if there's anything else I can do." She liked to help out in a crisis, but she hoped he heard the word *Monday* in her offer! "Okay?"

His eyes flitted toward Locke and almost instantly back to her.

"Um . . . I'm really sorry, Ariel."

She started closing the door, giving him an encouraging smile as she waved good-bye.

"No problem, Darryl. Good night."

"Good night." His voice was muffled by the sound of the closing door.

"No problem!" Locke said crossly. "Maybe you don't have a problem, but believe me, *I've* got a problem."

She dropped the keys on the table and started stripping off her dress on her way across the room.

She was standing over him in her slip, and he was reaching up to her when the phone rang again.

Locke swore colorfully and snapped to his feet.

"Don't you dare answer that phone!" he growled as he grabbed his suit jacket and started putting it on.

"Why not?" she asked as he watched him pull her dress over her head and help her get zipped back into it.

"This place is like Grand Central Station!" he said angrily, heading for her bedroom. "We're getting out of here and going someplace where we can have a little privacy for the weekend."

"For the weekend?" she echoed weakly as she trailed after him.

"For the weekend."

He was emphatic.

The phone kept ringing and ringing as he stuffed a few of her clothes into a briefcase. He grabbed her coat, put it on her, and grasped her hand.

"Come on, Ms. Radnor. I've got a little work I'd like you to do for me. And I've got just the place to do it in."

While Adam was driving Ariel away to his private retreat, her parents were driving themselves to distraction.

"She didn't answer the phone!" Marcus Radnor wasn't exactly shouting, but his pitch and tone of voice were more than effective in gaining the undivided attention of his wife.

She shifted her worried gaze from the phone, resting on its cradle, to her husband, who wasn't resting anywhere. He was pacing the floor like an enraged patriarch.

"*Mais, chéri,*" she said in soothing, placating tones. "It *is* Friday night. She may be out with friends this evening." She instinctively added the *s* to friend to divert her husband's single-minded obsession.

"Friends!" He snorted, shooting her a scathing look. "She's probably out with that voice on the phone from last weekend!" he exclaimed, his voice quivering with reproof.

"*Peut-être, chéri, mais il faut comprendre.*"

"There's nothing to understand!" he thundered unreasonably. "If she's dating again, or seeing a man on a regular basis, or, well, inviting him to her home at all hours, why hasn't she mentioned it? Why haven't we heard from her in over a month?"

He gave his wife a censuring look, as if she were somehow partly to blame for all these concerns.

His wife was soft-spoken and gentle-hearted, but she was also possessed of an indomitable will. She merely raised her eyebrows in response to his testy remarks and calmly made her reply.

"Maybe she is not ready to talk to us about it . . . assuming, *chéri*, that there really is something for her to talk about."

He stopped pacing and gave his wife of many years a very indignant look.

"Not ready!" he exclaimed huffily. "What in heaven's name is holding her back, Gen? We're not good enough for him to meet? He's not good enough for us to meet? Those are the usual reasons, aren't they?"

She shrugged off his overreaction with a slightly amused light now glimmering in her eyes. He was certainly taking this hard, she thought. But, *c'est la vie, chéri.* Sooner or later your little girl must grow up.

"Marcus, until we see her, perhaps it would be better not to speculate." she suggested softly.

He stomped into the kitchen, muttering that he still didn't like any of this as he rattled containers in the refrigerator and cabinets. That was always a sign that he was beginning to let go of an issue and move on to other things. Ariel's mother sighed in relief. Sometimes he really could be worse than a small child!

Not that she wasn't a little concerned herself. Ariel usually did keep in closer touch with them than she had recently. And they had written to her earlier in the week, telling her of their plan to drive down to Annapolis for the weekend to visit. Ariel surely should have received the letter by now.

But they hadn't heard from her.

So, they'd started phoning her at home in the evening in the middle of the week. They never got an answer. If they'd realized the same thing would happen this late on a Friday night, they'd have called her at her office. But this had never happened before. They had been unprepared.

Of course, Genevieve was not nearly as alarmed about all of this as her husband was. As a matter of fact, she was rather hoping that Ariel had met a nice young man and was having a lovely time. Still, she had to admit she felt excluded . . . uninformed. It was the first time since Ariel had been born that she had ever felt that way. It wasn't a very comfortable feeling for a mother who had doted on her daughter for so many years.

And then, when they had called twice tonight and received no answer either time, the professor's much-strained patience had finally gone up in flames. She always dreaded that. It was so exhausting trying to calm him down and get him back to his normal, absentminded self.

She joined him in the kitchen for a quiet cup of tea. She watched the soft tinge of color in his cheeks and tactfully began discussing a fund-raising dinner that she'd been asked to help organize the following spring for the faculty. When he was embarrassed, the poor man truly suffered with it. She loved her mate well enough to want to spare him that, at least.

She decided that it was probably just as well that she hadn't shared with him all that Margaret Norris had told her when they'd chatted on the phone midweek. She had the feeling that Marcus still could use a little time to adjust to the idea that there might be a new man in his little girl's life. Well, *chéri*, she thought as he started making a few observations about fund-raising, you have until tomorrow.

For tomorrow they would both see for themselves exactly what was going on down in Annapolis.

As it turned out, the Radnors had a little more time to prepare themselves than they had been planning on. Ariel stayed at Locke's hideaway, conducting their very private business, until Sunday afternoon.

"This really is a lovely cabin," Ariel told him for the third or fourth time in two days.

"And you really are a lovely guest," he said as he rolled her over onto her back and gave her a tender kiss on the mouth.

She returned his kiss warmly, feeling as if she were smiling from head to toe. It had been a thoroughly enchanting, unforgettable weekend. She wasn't looking forward to its rapidly approaching conclusion, so she pushed it temporarily out of her mind.

They'd laughed and played and teased and been together day and night . . . away from all the curious stares and unexpected distractions that seemed to be constantly thwarting them at Athena.

They could lie around, half dressed, never giving it a thought. There would be no one coming to the door here. And he didn't have a phone, so there were no phone calls, either. That had come as a tremendous relief to them when they had arrived after midnight on Friday. They put away a few groceries after coming in, then went straight to bed, free to think only of one another at last.

Saturday afternoon they had gone for a walk. It had been a glorious day. Mild, sunny, and with a cool breeze. Locke's cabin was nestled in a stand of loblolly pine, and the air smelled of the clean, fragrant conifers. The soft matting of fallen pine needles cushioned their tread.

Saturday night they had played cards and made dinner

together, eating half of it in the tasting process. That was just as well since they never really got around to finishing dinner afterward. They were half done when they both looked up into each other's eyes. Without speaking they'd abandoned dinner to attend to more urgent matters.

They'd stayed asleep till noon on Sunday. After brunch they drove to a local store for a newspaper. Reading had been so exhausting, they'd wandered back for an afternoon nap. Then, to no one's great surprise, they discovered that neither one of them was nearly as sleepy as they'd thought. A little while later, however, they most certainly were.

It was late afternoon, almost time to leave, when they finally woke up again.

Locke stirred against her.

"What are you thinking?" he asked in a rough, husky voice.

She wrapped her arms around him and sighed contentedly.

"That this has been wonderful."

"That's funny," he said as he nuzzled her ear affectionately. "That's just what I was thinking."

"Hmmm," he murmured thoughtfully as he trailed one hand over her breast and down to her waist.

Ariel curled a strand of his hair around an index finger and placed an affectionate kiss on his neck.

"Hmm what?" she asked, only mildly curious. She felt too relaxed to be any more attentive.

He turned and looked down into her smiling brown eyes, keeping her pinned to the bed by the weight of his body. A slow, devilish grin eased over his masculine features. He moved both hands down to sensitive areas on her waist, as if testing. Ariel squirmed reflexively, making him grin even more.

"I was just wondering if you were ticklish," he announced, proceeding to try to find out with the vigorous enthusiasm of a schoolboy.

Ariel shrieked and writhed and squealed and protested. She

pushed and twisted and laughed until the tears were rolling down her cheeks.

"Stop it!" she gasped amid a paroxysm of nature's most exquisite form of suffering. "Please . . . please!"

Adam was thoroughly enjoying himself and proceeded to try to find every ticklish spot on her entire body. He grabbed her foot as she tried for a desperate dive for freedom, yanking her back within his delighted reach as she pleaded for mercy and gasped for breath.

Under her arms, in back of her knees, her waist, her hips, her feet and ears . . . She had never guessed how unbelievably ticklish she was.

"Adam!" She choked, her sides aching from it all. "I'll do anything!" she screamed as he discovered a particularly vulnerable point of whose existence she had been blissfully ignorant for more than two and half decades. "Anything!" she shrieked through the uncontrollable laughter.

He bundled her into his arms and kissed her as thoroughly as he had tickled her. When her breathing returned to normal, Adam untangled them both from the bed sheet and traced a leisurely path with his finger from her shoulder to her hip, lingering much longer than necessary at a couple of spots along the way.

He looked up at her, humor lighting his slate-blue eyes.

"Anything, eh?" he echoed reminiscently with a pleased chuckle. "Okay, I'll let you off this time. But just remember, wench, if you welch on your promise, there's plenty more where that came from."

While Ariel was wondering what she was going to have to forfeit in exchange for an end to being tickle-tortured, Adam sprang out of bed and pulled on some clothes. He disappeared into another part of the cabin and reappeared a few minutes later carrying a large sketch pad and a box of pastels.

Ariel sat up and pulled the sheet over her breasts in an unsuccessful attempt to look prim.

"Didn't anyone ever tell you extortion is considered a crime?" she asked severely.

"Nope. Guess they didn't," he replied cheerfully as he pulled an old wooden chair up to the foot of the bed and straddled it.

She watched him arrange the box of pastels on the bed and balance the pad on the back of the chair, looking over it at her when he was ready to proceed.

"You want to know what you're going to do for me?" he asked.

He was the picture of a male in relaxed good humor, she thought. And utterly appealing in every way. She stared at him in appreciative fascination. He'd put on his slacks, but his torso was bare. Ariel wondered why she'd never noticed how attractive a man's chest and shoulders could be. Maybe most weren't, she decided, trying with difficulty to do some critical reflective thinking. But Adam's certainly were. She let herself sink back into the friendly haze that seemed to engulf her every time she was near him. Well, she was getting used to that now. It really was very nice.

"What am I going to do?" she asked hazily, not sounding too worried about it, whatever it was.

"You're going to stay where you are while I sketch you," he explained, selecting a color and holding it poised over the page.

She blinked.

"Like this?" she asked in dismay, looking down toward the bed and her sheet-draped form.

"Like that," he confirmed, beginning to lightly stroke the paper . . . a line here, another line there.

He was looking down at the paper or studying her now. Without engaging her as he usually did he added a very welcome explanation.

"I'll leave out the bed and the bedroom. Just you and the sheet. I promise, Ariel, it'll be very discreet. Besides, it's for my eyes only, sweetheart." He grinned then, but he still didn't look at her eyes. He was too busy with his picture.

"Oh," she said, relieved and still a little nervous. "Okay."

He laughed softly.

"A promise is a promise," he reminded her unsympathetically.

"Yes." She was forced to agree. "I should have known that successful men use all the leverage they can get."

There was no criticism in her statement now. She was genuinely teasing him about it, he realized, both surprised and relieved at how far they'd come on this issue. When he spoke, the words came out without thinking.

"That's how they get rich, sweetheart," he pointed out easily.

And somehow it was as if that had never been an issue for her. It seemed like another lifetime or some other person who had been afraid of that. It didn't bother her anymore.

"I guess it is," she agreed with a smile. "But it doesn't make them lovable."

He looked up at her and their eyes locked.

"Didn't anyone ever tell you that it was as easy to love a rich man as a poor man?" he asked, teasing yet not teasing.

Ariel felt her mouth go dry.

"No," she said slowly. "I guess no one ever did." She hesitated only fractionally before adding, "Is it true . . . what they say?"

He was smiling, but there was a very serious undertone too.

"I certainly hope so," he said sincerely. He tore his eyes away from her with an effort. "This'll just take a couple more minutes. Then I want you to get dressed and let me sketch you some more, if you don't mind."

"I don't mind," she said softly, a warm glow spreading in the region of her heart. "I don't mind at all."

CHAPTER FOURTEEN

"Okay. That's it," Adam announced about an hour later.

Reluctantly he returned the pastels to their box. It had been a spur-of-the-moment idea to sketch her. He didn't know why he hadn't done it earlier, though, now that he thought about it. For months he had sketched her from memory, trying to free himself of her captivating hold. Instead, with every sketch, she had fascinated him more, beckoned to him from the paper like a lorelei.

At the time he hadn't been sure if he'd quite caught her look. He wasn't certain that it was possible to capture on paper that quality of elusive beauty, of surface calm masking an inner warmth and fire, of confidence shackled by doubt.

He looked over the sketches that he'd just finished, undertaking a quick, critical assessment. The dewy innocence was there. And so was that vibrant, exciting aura she possessed. And the delicate yet strong bone structure, the soft, doelike coloring of her eyes and hair.

They were all Ariel . . . the Ariel that others saw and the one that he could see as well. The ice and the fire.

"They're wonderful," Ariel said, very impressed.

She had come to stand behind him and look over his shoulder as he reviewed his work. She put a hand gently on his shoulder. He covered it with one of his.

"I had good material to work with," he said with a shrug of indifference for his own talent and a hug of appreciation for his subject.

He put on the rest of his clothes, and they began to get the cabin straightened up.

Adam was putting the sketches and materials in a closet just off the living room when Ariel noticed a large stack of unframed pictures piled along the back wall. She reached toward the one closest to her and picked it up. It was a watercolor of a section of the Severn River not too far from Athena. Adam had signed his initials and dated it last summer.

"This is beautiful, Adam," she said with great admiration. The play of light along the bank and the exquisitely, clear, bright colors showed the touch of a very skilled and sensitive artist. "Could I see the rest?" she asked hopefully.

Adam muttered something she didn't fully understand, but there was no mistaking his nonverbal communication. He was pulling her out of the closet by her elbow and shutting the door.

"Next time," he said.

That part came through loud and clear.

Adam glanced at the brass ship's clock hung on the knotty-pine wall.

"It's getting late. We'd better get going," he added.

"Okay," she agreed. There wasn't much else she could say under the circumstances. After all, they were his pictures.

But Adam glimpsed her last wistful look at the closed door of the art-filled closet. He pressed his lips together in a thin line. He just didn't want her to see those other sketches. He had to hang on to some shred of his dignity. He'd lost just about all of it, but some was better than none at all, he told himself.

Ariel was surprised, however, when he slipped into the driver's seat next to her as they were ready to leave. He handed her a rolled-up tube of paper. Then he leaned over and pulled her head close and kissed her on the mouth.

"For you," he said as he backed out of the driveway.

She peeked inside and was able to make out just enough to identify it.

244

It was the watercolor sketch of the river that she had admired.

When Ariel stepped into her cottage a little after dusk Sunday evening, she couldn't have been more astonished if the roof had fallen on her.

"Mother. Father."

She stated the obvious in a whisper, frozen to the spot, staring at them in shock as the house keys slid from her nerveless fingers. The blood rushed to her face. She hadn't felt so guilty, so embarrassed, or so caught in the act since she was six years old.

Locke, who had initially stood quietly behind her, deftly caught the keys before they hit the floor. He straightened up and sized up the situation without any need for introductions. The portrait facing him was more eloquent than any words would have been.

A couple old enough to be Ariel's parents and bearing a very strong resemblance to some slightly younger people who'd been in snapshots in her album were sitting on Ariel's sofa and looking as shocked as anyone he'd ever seen. Ariel, likewise, gave every appearance of having been turned to stone from the horror of seeing them here now.

"Professor Radnor? Mrs. Radnor?" he inquired, only slightly inflecting the question. There was no doubt in his mind who they were.

"Yes," said Mrs. Radnor after a slight, confused hesitation. Her husband was still speechless.

Genevieve Radnor's breeding and good manners rose automatically to the extremely awkward occasion. She stood up and walked across the small space separating them. When she was close enough, she extended her slender hand in greeting. Locke's closed over it. They shook hands briefly. The beginning of a smile was conceived in Adam's eyes. Ariel's mother warmed to him immediately. To Ariel's great relief her mother smiled at Adam. Not just out of a sense of politeness, either. She liked him. So far, anyway.

"I am Genevieve Radnor, Ariel's mother." Her eyes never left Adam's face. In spite of her reaching out as she had, she was still having trouble adjusting to everything all at once. She added, a little vaguely, "And this is my husband, Marcus."

She intentionally omitted the fact that Marcus was Ariel's father. Mrs. Radnor realized that the one thing that Marcus did *not* need at the moment was a reminder of his paternal responsibility.

Adam certainly didn't need anyone to paint him a picture. Marcus Radnor's angry red face could only belong to an irate papa. Once again his involvement with Ariel had given him another first. He'd never been on the receiving end of a look like that from a woman's father. Not in his entire life. And now he felt he was a little old for it. For Ariel's sake he decided to approach this as tactfully as possible, however.

"And who are you?" the irate professor bluntly asked, having regained control of his vocal cords.

"Adam Locke," replied the object of his inquiry, not sounding particularly concerned.

Ariel was deeply grateful for Adam's forbearance and moral support. She hadn't been sure how he would react. After all, this was a situation that most men don't have to confront after their early twenties. She had no further time to let her thoughts wander down the path of appreciation. Her father had just started glaring directly on her. Now *she* was in his line of fire.

"And where have you been all weekend?" he demanded, sounding like near kin to a low-flying thundercloud.

When Ariel's father got mad, he didn't bother to beat around the bush. He got right to the point. That was one of the reasons she'd always dreaded scenes with him. They always left her feeling stripped.

For the first time, however, Ariel was not intimidated. If anything she was angry at being treated like a child. This time she refused to be cowed. She had no intention of apologizing for her behavior. She stared straight back at her furious parent without flinching.

"I don't believe that's something you need to know, Father. It's my business, not yours. I'm a big girl now. I have to make my own life."

She was polite but firm. As her father gaped at her in amazement she walked to the closet and hung up her coat.

Her father, having once again lost his vocal cords in shock, watched her take her briefcase into her bedroom and return again. She was behaving as though nothing were wrong, as though this were a perfectly normal weekend in her life! He narrowed his eyes and peered at her more closely. She even looked a little different from the old Ariel, he thought in surprise. More . . . comfortable with herself, less anxious, a little more relaxed, now that she'd adjusted to their presence here.

The aging professor cleared his throat.

"We were worried about you, Ariel," he said gruffly, still sounding upset and more than a little defensive but making a real effort toward rational conversation. "We called last weekend and a man answered the phone." He gave Locke a suspicious glance. "We wrote to you saying that we were coming to visit. We heard nothing from you all week. We called you several evenings in a row. We got no answer." His graying eyebrows lowered dangerously. "And then . . . when we arrive here, we find you gone without a trace!" Her father made an effort this time to rein in his anger. "If it hadn't been for Elliott and Margaret Norris, we'd have called the police and filed a missing persons report!"

Ariel was still trying to get over the fact that they'd planned all this to check on her. There was nothing really new in that, she realized, recalling how they'd kept her under their wings all these years . . . even arranging for her job interview with their old friends, the Norrises. She was also kicking herself for putting off opening her mail all week. The letter was probably there somewhere. She'd had more interesting things to do this week than read letters, however. Another first in her previously well-organized, meticulous life!

247

Her father eyed Locke condemningly, then returned his full, accusing attention to Ariel.

"What do Dr. and Mrs. Norris have to do with this?" Ariel asked, with a sinking feeling that she wasn't going to like the answer.

Ariel's mother smoothly intervened in the increasingly upsetting conversation.

"When we couldn't find you, *chérie*, we spent some time visiting with Margaret and Elliott," she said. "Margaret mentioned that you had been seeing quite a lot of Adam. She thought perhaps you were with him. . . ."

For the first time since Adam's arrival Ariel wondered what people were saying about them. She blushed at the possibilities, but it didn't bother her as much as it would have weeks ago. She realized that it really didn't matter what people said as long as they left them alone.

"Mrs. Norris was right," Ariel said. "That's exactly where I was."

Her parents stared at her as if seeing a stranger for the first time. Her father cleared his throat noisily, once again at a loss for words. Momentarily her admission left him with nothing to say except recriminations and warnings that were obviously now too late. Ariel's mother looked at her daughter and suddenly saw herself as a young woman, miraculously finding the nerve to tell her outraged parents that she intended to marry a young, foreign, nearly penniless college instructor and go with him to live in another country.

At the same moment both of Ariel's parents looked toward the man who had precipitated such disruption in their peaceful little family. He was gazing at their daughter with a very odd look in his eyes. Surprise? Admiration? A touch of something else . . . But when he met their eyes, there was something else there. Both of Ariel's parents saw it clearly. Protectiveness of their daughter.

Genevieve Radnor was trying to remember. There was something about Adam Locke that reminded her of someone

. . . or something. A fragment of a memory teased her, then slipped elusively from her grasp.

"Why don't we all sit down and get acquainted?" suggested Ariel's mother hopefully.

Maman! You are a gracious hostess even in someone else's home, Ariel thought humorously. She turned to Adam. He seemed relaxed enough, although there was a rather enigmatic look in his eyes.

"If you need to be getting back . . ." Ariel said softly to Adam, leaving the rest unspoken. She wanted to give him an opening to go if he wanted to. The last thing she wanted was for him to have to sit through an uncomfortable family squabble with her still-ruffled parents.

To Ariel's surprise he grinned at her and sat down comfortably in a chair.

"I'm in no hurry," he replied easily. "And I'd enjoy the opportunity to get acquainted with your parents."

Ariel dropped into the other chair. Her mother and father settled themselves stoically on the edge of the couch. At first the conversation was a little stilted. Her parents were reluctant to ask what they really wanted to know. They were afraid to hear the answer. It was already all too obvious. All that Ariel could think of to discuss was how ecstatic she'd been since Adam had come back into her life. Now didn't exactly strike her as the right time, place, setting, or audience for that. She confined herself to brief replies to the comments of others and listened attentively.

It was Adam who broke the ice for them all, inquiring about her father's work and her mother's activities.

"I'm active with the local art league," Mrs. Radnor said gratefully, only too pleased to help Adam steer the conversation toward safe topics. If they could find any.

"Are you an artist, Mrs. Radnor?" he asked with polite interest.

She smiled graciously and waved a hand for emphasis.

"Please, you must call me Genevieve, and this is Marcus." She had the feeling her husband would have dragged his feet a bit in extending that courtesy. "And, yes, I am an artist . . . amateur only, you understand. I've been working in oils more than anything else. Recently, though, I started dabbling in watercolors again."

Art kept them all safely occupied for quite a while. When they'd finally exhausted everybody's thoughts on that, silence began to stretch out awkwardly. No one could think of something safe that might hold their interest.

"What have you done all weekend?" Ariel asked at length. It was an obvious choice, although it skated near a rather more colorful topic that her parents had politely sidestepped for the time being. What had Ariel and Adam done all weekend?

"We stayed with Elliott and Margaret Saturday afternoon and had lunch with them on Sunday," Ariel's mother answered. Then her eyes brightened enthusiastically. "Saturday night Marcus and I had dinner in Annapolis. Do you remember my old school friend from Montreal, Marie-Claire Beaudré?"

Ariel didn't see what those two things had in common, but she let that pass for the present.

"Yes, of course, Mother."

Genevieve fluttered her hands extravagantly in the air.

Everyone missed the way Adam's ear had perked up on hearing the names Montreal and Beaudré linked together.

"Her older brother, Henri, has opened a restaurant here in town."

Henri. No, it couldn't be, Ariel thought.

"It's very small, very chic, and the food is the most delicious French cuisine I have ever tasted!" she said with great admiration.

Ariel looked at Adam. He looked like he'd just been hit by a truck. She nearly laughed at the look of amazement on his face. And apparently it was his turn to experience speechlessness. His mouth was half open, but he wasn't saying a thing.

"We were so sad that you could not come," her mother

added, recalling their disappointment. "Perhaps next time. Have you heard of it? It's called Chez Henri."

She was joined by two voices, one feminine and the other masculine, who had simultaneously said "Chez Henri" as well.

Adam shot an astonished look at Ariel.

"We've heard of it," he muttered. "I thought you said we traveled in different circles?" he reminded her in amusement. "I'd better not hear that one again!" he told her with an iron gaze and a spreading grin.

Ariel pulled her eyes away from her teasing lover and back to her confused parents.

"Henri is Henri Beaudré," she explained to herself. "Yes. We've heard of it all right, Mother. You're right. It's very elegant."

That led them to an informative exchange of information about mutual acquaintances in Canada and who liked what in the way of French cooking. By the time Ariel's parents were ready to leave, everyone was feeling a little better about things.

"I still don't know why she couldn't have at least opened her mail," her father grumbled as they drove off. He hated to have to reverse himself entirely in one day. "She used to have such a level head. Looks like it's stuck up in the clouds now!"

His wife laughed.

"Marcus!" she exclaimed, "I just realized who Adam reminded me of when he was standing behind Ariel and you were growling and snapping at him like a dog who wanted his favorite bone back!"

"He reminds me of you," she said fondly, giving his arm a reassuring squeeze. "Remember when we told my parents that we were driving to the United States to get married and live? You stood next to me with that same look of determination, *chéri*."

"Don't be ridiculous, Genevieve!" he blustered, adding

251

that if they were to get home in one piece, she should refrain from any further conversation.

She merely laughed warmly.

"*C'est ça, chéri! C'est ça.*"

It was still dark on Monday morning when Adam was awakened by the jarring sound of a ringing telephone. He reached out, fumbling blindly over the night table until his fingers closed over the unwelcome instrument.

"Hello," he mumbled, his eyes still closed.

"Adam?" asked a familiar feminine voice. "This is Catherine."

Locke slowly opened his eyes and searched for his watch.

"Why in the hell are you calling me at"—he squinted to make out the face of the watch—"at six in the morning?"

He'd only just fallen into bed an hour earlier and was sincerely wishing now that he was still in Ariel's instead.

"I'm sorry, Adam, but you're a hard man to reach these days." She laughed. "I've called during the day several times and left word with your secretary, but I'm never in when you call back."

"She's not my secretary," he said growling warningly.

Catherine hesitated. No. She'd follow up on that later. Better give him the information quickly before he got mad and hung up on her. Little sisters had such little status in their older brothers' eyes, she thought in amusement.

"Okay. And I've called on the weekend and in the evening, but I never seem to catch you at home. Anyway, this may be important, so I tried a dawn attack as my last-ditch effort."

Her brother turned on the lamp next to the bed and sat up.

"This *may* be important?" he said incredulously. "Let me tell you . . . it better had be! Out with it, Cat. I want to go back to sleep. I'm bushed."

That didn't sound like the energetic brother she'd known and loved for years. Her curiosity began to simmer a little more.

"Well," she began. "I was having lunch with a client in New York earlier in the week. I called you from Penn Station before I caught the train to Boston, trying to tell you right away."

"Cat!" he roared threateningly.

"Remember a few years ago, you testified against Grant Forrestman when he was accused of fraud and violating safe building codes?"

"Yes."

"Well, my client works for an underwriter who says that Forrestman is trying to get some backers for a new business that he wants to raise from the ashes of the old one."

"After he was found guilty and his company bankrupted?" asked her brother in surprise.

Catherine laughed humorlessly.

"You know as well as I do that people will put money into anything if they think it might be profitable," she reminded him.

"True enough," he agreed. "But why do I need this urgent piece of news?"

"Because Forrestman is having trouble raising enough money. There are a couple of big investors who want to find a vehicle for some of their cash assets. They are apparently considering sinking some funds into resurrecting Forrestman's business. He was fairly successful at turning over tidy profits to his shareholders every year, if you recall. In spite of everything, that lure is hard for an investor to completely disregard, Adam."

"All right. But I still don't see what that has to do with me, Catherine."

"They're still a little nervous about his brush with the law. If he can clear his name, they'll give him the cash."

"How in the hell is he going to do that?" asked Adam. "He lost in the appeals court, and his lawyer advised against pursuing the case further!"

"True," said his sister. "But all he apparently needs to do

is to persuade the potential investors that he was given a bum rap . . . not prove it in a court of law."

"Catherine," he said tiredly. "I still don't see what that has to do with me."

"I hope it had nothing at all to do with you, but . . . well, apparently Forrestman told the potential backers that you lied in court . . . that you'd framed him in order to put him out of business. He claimed you did it to destroy your chief competition and that you destroyed the evidence that would have permitted him to prove it legally."

"That's ridiculous!" Adam exclaimed angrily. "Anybody who knows me, or knows Forrestman, for that matter, wouldn't believe that for a minute!"

Cat sighed. "No. Probably not. But I never trusted Forrestman, Adam. You never have, either. I'm afraid he's planning some sort of revenge against you as the vehicle for resurrecting his own scattered fortunes. My client told me that those investors are giving Forrestman until the end of the year to document his accusations in some tangible way. If he can sway them, he'll get the money he needs. That's pretty strong motivation for him to do something effective, Adam."

Locke ran a hand through his rumpled hair.

"Yeah. I guess it is," he reluctantly agreed.

"Just . . . keep your eyes open, big brother," she advised softly.

"Okay, Baby Blues," he said with a laugh, using her childhood nickname.

"By the way," Catherine said, changing the subject before he had the chance to hang up. "Who *was* that woman taking your messages last week, Adam?"

"Ariel. Ariel Radnor."

There was a pause.

"That's all?" she asked incredulously. "That's all you're going to tell me?" She sensed that there was more to this. There was a funny change in his voice when he referred to this mystery lady. And he'd been acting kind of odd for months now, she recalled.

"That's all for now, pest!" he retaliated, laughing. "Maybe I can introduce you to her in the near future. If you're a good girl, that is! I'll be wrapping up here pretty soon and coming back to Washington."

That wasn't exactly a happy thought for him. It reminded him that he would soon be separated again from Ariel. Unless he could figure out some way to avoid it.

"You know, Adam, no one could ever ask for a better big brother," she said softly. "Whoever she is, I hope she's making you happy."

"Hey! What is this? An X-ray telephone?" he protested with more laughter.

"No," she answered, a smile in her voice. "You've always been transparent to me, big brother."

"It's a good thing you're not in the employ of my competition!" he observed, expelling a defeated breath. "And, yes, she's making me very happy," he admitted. "There. Satisfied? Just remember what curiosity can do to little cats!"

"All right. All right! Sorry I woke you up, Adam. You go back to sleep. Let's just hope it's my overactive imagination. But . . . I thought it was better to let you know. At least he can't blind-side you if there's something to this."

"Thanks, Cat. I owe you one."

He hung up the phone, thinking it was a pretty useful thing to have a sister in high finance sometimes.

He lay in the darkness staring at the ceiling.

Grant Forrestman.

It was funny Catherine should be worried and call about that now. There had been some peculiar things happening on this project. Missing notes. Things not turning out exactly the way people had expected . . . as though someone were manipulating or interfering with the work. . . .

He laced his fingers behind his head.

Galway had better be on the right track. If Forrestman *was* involved, things could get pretty rough. He wasn't a man known for using kid gloves.

* * *

255

The Monday morning staff breakfast featured an overview of new projects that Athena employees would be working on during the upcoming month. It rated a big yawn of indifference from most of those in attendance. Again there was no mention made of Ariel's assailant or any problems with Athena's security system.

There was some mumbling among the crowd about the administration's deafening silence on both of those counts, but no one raised the issue for public discussion. There had been no new incidents and no one else had been hurt.

Time was dulling the memory of that mishap. Soon it would be forgotten.

"Hi, Ariel!" said a hale and hearty-looking Jim Reeves.

He had threaded his way through the crowd to her side, catching up to her by the time she'd reached the bottom of the steps outside the Inn. He had seen her bid farewell to Locke inside the dining hall. The opportunity to walk her to her office was too tantalizing to pass up.

Ariel was definitely not eager for company. Especially not Jim Reeves's company.

"Hi, Jim," she said, picking up her pace a little.

He began to walk faster as well.

He seemed oblivious to her lack of enthusiasm for his company. Lack of practice, no doubt, Ariel thought cattily. Like a night-prowling tom, Reeves thought women would be delighted to have his company. Every last one of them!

Reeves talked a steady stream of weekend sports figures to Ariel all the way to the door of her office. While she searched her purse for her keys he leaned against the wall next to her and nodded at passersby.

"See you later, Jim," she said, relieved to be leaving him.

To her surprise he didn't continue on his way. Instead he hung around her door, chatting easily and meaninglessly with employees on their way to work. Especially the women.

Quite a few seemed pleased, if not downright flattered, by his attention. For the life of her Ariel couldn't figure out why.

Personally she found nothing pleasing or attractive about Jim Reeves or his attentions.

It was the darkness of the adjoining rooms, visible through the glass half wall that ran along one side of her office that finally jogged Ariel's memory.

"Darryl!" she exclaimed, searching her purse again.

"Did you say something?" Reeves asked, sticking his head through her door. Seconds later the rest of him wandered in as well.

Ariel was beginning to worry. Where were the keys to Darryl's office? The connecting door between them was all that stood between Ariel and the report that she had promised to deliver for him this morning.

"I can't find the keys to the library," she explained, not paying much attention to him.

The jangle of keys caught her attention. Her fingers stopped somewhere in the middle of her purse, and she looked at Reeves. He was grinning and walking toward the connecting door.

"Here you go," he said proudly as he slipped a key into the lock and opened the door.

She stared in surprise.

"Passkey," he explained with a bored shrug.

Ariel got the report and returned to her office.

"Say, your office really looks great, Ariel," Reeves observed as he strolled around it, touching a plant here, picking up a new knickknack there.

"Thanks," she murmured, not really paying any attention to him.

Something in the title of Darryl's report had caught her eye. She began leafing slowly through the pages, scanning the entries.

"Is that going to word processing?" he asked casually, coming to a halt beside her desk. He sat down on the corner.

"Yes," she replied absently as she turned another page.

There was something about this compilation of titles of

research publications that bothered her. She couldn't quite put her finger on it. But it was there. Somewhere.

"I'm going by there on my way to the mail room," he mentioned in an offhand way. "Want me to drop it off for you?"

"No," she murmured. She began searching the Rolodex on her desk. "That's okay, Jim. Thanks just the same."

She didn't notice the hardening of his eyes at her resistance. Reeves didn't like to be turned down. Especially by a woman.

"Sure thing." He ambled toward the door. "Catch you later, Ariel."

She was already dialing the phone number of a friend of hers at the Library of Congress and didn't see him go.

"Have you found out who did it?" Locke asked bluntly.

He was standing in front of Dr. Norris's desk, next to a noticeably silent Robert Galway. He waited impatiently for an answer.

The director motioned for the two men to be seated.

"No, but we've narrowed the field of suspects considerably," replied Dr. Norris. "And we have a plan for flushing out the guilty party."

Locke nodded his head in approval. Norris turned his attention to his security chief.

"Robert, tell Adam what we know, what we've guessed, and what we're going to do."

Galway acknowledged the directive with a grunt and a brief nod of his head.

"After the incident in Ariel's office I conducted a thorough check of the premises. There was no forced entry. Not in her office. Not anywhere in the corporate compound. After the police investigation produced no useful physical evidence, we decided to conduct a private inquiry on our own."

He omitted that the "private inquiry" had been vigorously encouraged by one of Athena's corporate clients, a small business that was a front for a national intelligence agency.

258

Its parent organization wanted to make absolutely certain that the work being done for it was in no way being compromised. The only good news that Dr. Norris had heard thus far was that that particular project appeared to have absolutely no connection to Ariel's mishap.

"I hired a private investigation firm," Galway was saying, "to help us out at that point. Internally we performed a quick, in-depth assessment to identify all of the employees who could have had access to Ariel's office . . . who has a set of keys. We screened that list and handed it over to the firm, asking them to compile background information on those for whom we had only sketchy information about their past employment or personal history. After assessing the reports we asked the firm to follow three leading contenders and provide us with a profile of their current activities and life-styles."

Galway pulled a small notebook from his pocket and consulted it briefly before continuing.

"We unearthed some very disturbing facts about two of these individuals. Disturbing enough to qualify as strong motivation for breaking and entering. Facts which lead us, at this point, to suspect that one of them is the person responsible for the attempted theft or sabotage that occurred in Ariel's office."

"Who are they?" Locke demanded.

"David Carrollton and Darryl Fontaine."

"See you later, Lydia," David Carrollton said, giving his sister a tight smile.

Lydia watched her brother walk into Ariel's office, hesitating fractionally. She really needed to get to her office. Things were piling up there. But she was worried about her brother. He'd become so strained-looking recently.

"Lydia, go to work!" she muttered to herself. "You can sit down and have a heart-to-heart talk with your enigmatic brother at dinner tonight!"

And when he got to her cottage, she was determined to find out what was bothering him.

*　　*　　*

"Here's your rose, Ariel. Sorry I'm late with it today."

Ariel looked up from Darryl's report and smiled warmly. She'd begun to worry about her friend recently. His appearance this morning was not reassuring. What was the matter? she wondered.

"It's never too late," she said reassuringly, smiling at him gratefully.

She put the bud in the slender vase on her desk just as Locke appeared in her doorway. She was turned away from him and didn't notice his arrival. When he saw the scene unfolding in her office, he stayed where he was, not announcing his presence.

So that was the source of that damned flower, he thought irritably. It wasn't the plaid-suited bozo from the library. It was the debonair playboy from engineering.

When Ariel bent over the debonair playboy, gave him a hug and a kiss on the cheek, Locke felt the urge to yank them apart and hit something.

They were speaking in low voices, almost in whispers to his oversensitive thinking. Locke thought that Carrollton looked drawn and tired. After what Galway had told him he didn't wonder why. He thought he already could guess.

He thought that if he had to watch this any longer, he'd make a fool of himself. He was furious at Ariel for her attentions to Carrollton. He turned sharply on his heel and walked away without a backward glance.

The terrace of the ballroom was a good place to be alone on a Monday morning. Locke walked to the railing and gazed out onto the river below, trying to discipline his jealous thoughts. He had an avalanche of work to do today. And more tomorrow. He simply could not let seeing Ariel with Carrollton blow his concentration.

His eyes drifted over the scene below.

The ketch was there again. Whoever was sailing her certainly liked to anchor at that spot. It was turning out to be a lengthy vacation apparently.

Locke frowned.

Under the circumstances he found that rather peculiar. Athena already had more than its share of unexplained circumstances. That ketch's repeated visits could just be coincidence, of course, he told himself. On the other hand . . .

He strode inside and pushed down the call button for the elevator. When he got to his suite, he called his old friend at the Anchor's Point, a veritable central processing unit of local gossip.

"Marge," he said a few minutes later when he had gotten through to her on the phone. "I want to ask you a favor. . . ."

When Ariel finally got to the word-processing unit to drop off Darryl's report, she found another unexpected crisis.

Gail Marlow was working on Jeanne Wells's workstation, apparently trying to adjust a recalcitrant part of its internal workings. Jeanne looked as if she'd lost her best friend. Barbara Hawkins, everyone's permanent mother figure, looked like she was at her wits' end.

"Jeanne," Ariel said softly, joining the unhappy trio, "what's the matter?"

Jeanne looked up at Ariel's sympathetic face with bleak, despairing eyes. She saw the report in Ariel's hand, and something snapped in her. She put her hands over her face and began to cry.

Monday was a bumpy day. The evening wasn't much smoother.

Adam picked Ariel up at her cottage as they had arranged. Without much trouble she sensed that Locke was preoccupied. He noticed the same thing about her. They rode in awkward silence, both aching for the way things had been between them before.

It took a while for them to let go of the day's worries and find each other. They had gone back to Marge's, which helped. It held warm memories. By a small miracle they began to relax and enjoy the evening.

"It'll take me a while to get that information you wanted, Adam," Marge said before they began their usual argument over the bill for the meal. "But I'll let you know as soon as I've got it."

"Thanks, Marge," he said.

He saw Ariel's questioning look, but he offered no answer.

That week produced one strained, awkward day after another.

On Tuesday Darryl was back at his desk. Ariel had never seen him look so defeated. She was so worried about him that she called Adam Tuesday afternoon and told him she'd be a little late for their dinner date that night. She didn't tell him why. She didn't have time; he had to go into a meeting before she had the chance to explain.

She was having a long, anguishing conversation with Darryl at his desk in the library after work. Locke was heading back to the Inn and looked in to see how she was coming along. He had assumed that work was the cause of their dinner's postponement. When he saw the real cause, his face hardened. She preferred Darryl's company to his, perhaps? he thought unreasonably. The worst thing was, he knew his reaction was unreasonable, but he couldn't help feeling that way.

A jealous voice asked him silently, *How much do you really know about her? How much of what you think you know is a product of your obsession for her?*

He wrestled against the awful thoughts, but they wouldn't let go. They refused to disappear. He felt as if he were being torn apart. The sooner this weekend came and went, the better. Everyone would have their answers by Sunday night if things went as Galway had planned. He could hardly wait for it to be over with. The week was crawling by, and he felt like his future was suspended over an abyss of unknown threats until this mess was resolved.

Damn it all! he thought angrily. Galway's plan had better work.

He gave Ariel a last, almost anguished look. You'd better not be involved in this, my love, not even a little bit . . . not even to the extent of giving aid and comfort to the enemy.

The walk back to the Inn seemed longer and lonelier than ever before.

CHAPTER FIFTEEN

On Friday night they fixed a simple dinner at Ariel's cottage. They struggled to find the easiest words all evening. The conversation kept awkwardly sidestepping the fundamental problem.

"Adam, what's the matter?" Ariel asked when she finally couldn't stand it any longer. "Have I said something or done something that upset you?"

She was standing in the living room, looking at his back as he stared sightlessly out of the window. Unconsciously she clasped her hands tightly in front of her, waiting in dread to hear his reply.

He sighed and ran his hands through his hair. What could he say? The information that Galway and Norris had given him was confidential. He'd agreed to keep silent about everything until their investigation had been successfully concluded. He couldn't tell her that he was upset because she was obviously a very close confidante and friend of the two prime suspects in the case!

Besides, at this point he wasn't certain himself anymore what was really bothering him. He just couldn't bring himself to believe that Ariel was involved in this mess, whatever it was. And he'd made a disturbing discovery about himself this week. Even if Ariel were involved in some way, he would still be in love with her.

He expelled a sigh of frustration. Sunday couldn't get here fast enough for him.

"No. It's nothing you've said or done," he said quietly.

He felt her slip her arms around his waist and lay her cheek on his back. He covered her hands warmly with his.

"I have to go to Washington tomorrow morning," he said.

He could feel her stiffen almost imperceptibly. Silently he swore that when this was all over, he'd explain to her. He couldn't tell her before. Galway had insisted that for the trap to work, Locke's departure had to appear sudden and unforeseen. Leaving valuable project materials in his suite at the Inn was the bait for their elusive fish.

He hoped that Galway was correct. For the life of him he couldn't see why an original report on obscure Eastern European building projects would attract their mysterious villain. All the evidence of tampering, what little there was, pointed to that, however, according to Robert.

Adam refused to waste any more of his precious time tonight thinking about that problem.

He turned to face Ariel and pulled her into his arms. He rested his head against hers, holding her tightly. Damn. He really didn't want to go.

A new thought streaked through his darkened world like a ray of light. He bent his lips to her ear.

"Can you come with me?" he asked softly.

He thought for a minute that she was going to say yes. She looked up at him, a smile lighting her face. Then the light faded. With a sinking heart he knew what she was going to say.

"I wish I could," she said unhappily. "But I can't. Dr. Norris just asked me to come to his house tomorrow at noon and spend the afternoon, possibly the evening, with him. He's having the senior executive of a Colombian import-export firm come to lunch, then stay for 'an extended period of contract negotiation and discussion of mutual interests.' Those are his words, not mine!" she said, defending herself from his raised-eyebrows look of surprise. "He wanted me there in case there were any rough spots due to language difficulties. He's never met the man before and isn't sure how good his English is. Dr. Norris has no doubt about how poor his Spanish is, though," she added wryly.

She rested her chin against Locke's and rubbed her nose fondly against his.

"With you gone," she said teasingly, "I may be so despondent that I'll have trouble speaking in any language at all."

"Is that so?" he murmured huskily, brushing a kiss against her tantalizing lips.

She closed her eyes to hide the sadness from him, but he heard it in her voice when she spoke.

"Yes. It's so," she whispered.

His mouth touched hers and they closed out the world and all its problems. Together they swirled into the warmth and comfort of a lovers' embrace.

Much later, their bodies still entwined as they lay in her bed, Locke pulled her close.

"When I get back on Sunday, we'll have to talk, Ariel," he said sleepily.

Ariel was so sleepy herself, the best she could do was mumble "Mmmm hmmm." She was half asleep, too tired to wonder what he meant by that. Later it would occur to her that it could be taken in two very different ways.

Under different circumstances Ariel would have enjoyed the luncheon at Dr. Norris's house. His guest was a charming man in a fascinating line of work in an interesting part of the world. The luncheon that Mrs. Norris had served them had been wonderful to both the eye and the palate. Her guests' empty plates were mute testament to that. Except for Ariel's, that is. Because for her the circumstances hadn't changed since Locke had driven away that morning.

Ariel was not enjoying it at all. It was like slow torture to have to sit there and feign smiles when she really wanted to curl up and ache from missing him.

She was beginning to wonder despairingly whether you

could have withdrawal symptoms when your love was taken away. She missed him more than she'd thought possible.

To add to her misery she had the almost uncontrollable urge to tell Adam how much she loved him! Why she should want so desperately to do something so foolhardy, she could not fathom. Maybe foolhardiness was part of being in love, she mused.

She'd become so swallowed up in her little dark cloud that she didn't hear the comment that Dr. Norris directed toward her. He was smiling at her in amused indulgence when he repeated it a little louder this time.

"Ariel?"

She blinked, embarrassment washing over her as she realized that everyone was looking at her in amusement. Now she'd done it!

"I'm sorry, Dr. Norris," she said, sincerely apologetic.

"That's all right. You looked like you were miles away," he said, very entertained and pleased by her transformation since Locke had arrived. "About thirty-five miles, to be precise, I'd say."

The distance from Annapolis to Georgetown.

Color suffused her cheeks.

Their foreign guest looked a little baffled, not being that conversant with the local geography or the local gossip.

"Ariel's friend is in Georgetown," Norris explained vaguely to his new associate.

He turned to Ariel.

"My dear, you're certainly welcome to stay if you like," he said kindly, "but I don't think that we'll be needing your professional services. So, if you wish to leave, feel free to go whenever you like."

Ariel tried not to look too happy. The fact that she was gone before her good-byes had evaporated from the air gave them all a subtle hint, however.

She was home in no time at all. Along the way a very appealing idea had sprung to life, adding wings to her feet.

She dropped her things on a chair and dialed the phone. No answer. Well, he was probably at his office.

She dropped the receiver back on its cradle but refused to abandon her plan. After all, Adam *had* invited her to go with him. If she were to pop up like a surprise on his doorstep, surely he would be as happy as she, wouldn't he? They'd been so close . . . and he'd been to edgy as she'd been as the week came to a close. And he *had* said that he wanted to talk to her on Sunday.

She kept talking herself into what she so very much wanted to do. She quickly and haphazardly packed a few things in her overnight case.

She called again just before she was ready to leave. Still no answer. He wasn't home. She dialed information for his business listing. When she called it, there was no answer there, either.

Well, no matter, I'll announce myself when I get there, she told herself encouragingly.

It was just that she so very much wanted to see him again. Their fairy tale was getting dangerously close to the ending. But she couldn't tell whether the ending was going to be the one she wanted.

She hopped in her car and took the road that led to Washington. And to Adam.

It was Saturday night in Georgetown. Traffic crawled. Crowds glutted the sidewalks. Neon lights and honky-tonk. Elegant boutiques and limousines. Restaurants and bars and street-corner cafés. There was something for everyone in Georgetown on Saturday night.

Ariel threaded her way through the main drag until she reached the tiny, brick-paved side street she was seeking. Her car bumped slowly over the uneven surface between the expensive houses lining either side. Even at night the Georgian and Federal architecture was still impressive and serene.

And then she saw Locke's house. She parked her small

268

compact on the street, gunning her own psychological engines a little to help get her inside.

"No cold feet!" she told herself sternly, marching herself up the hard stone of the three front steps. She lifted the heavy brass lion's-head knocker and clapped it against the door.

Nothing.

She clapped again.

Still no response, even though the lights were on in the living room. She could see them through the windows.

One more time. Nothing.

It was chilly. Standing outside was pointing that out to her. A couple passing by eyed her curiously. She smiled at them awkwardly. She couldn't just stand here.

She hadn't seen Adam's car anywhere when she arrived. Maybe he'd gone out for something. She eyed her own car thoughtfully. She could always sit in it until he came back . . . or to grab a bite to eat and come back later.

She knocked one last time. Giving up, she'd started down the steps when one last possibility came to mind. Maybe he was home but couldn't hear her. He could be in the back or in the basement or taking a shower. No harm in trying. She tried the door handle. It turned.

Tentatively she stepped inside.

"Adam?" she called out softly. "Adam, are you home? It's me . . . Ariel."

Silence answered her.

She closed the door and looked around. It had been a long time since she'd been here. It hadn't changed a bit. From the plush wall-to-wall carpeting to the antique chandelier hanging in the library off to her left, it was all the same.

She saw Adam's coat draped carelessly over one of the sections of the dark gray sofa. He was here, then, she decided. A warm rush of happiness and excitement at her surprise visit shot through her. Maybe he was asleep. The stair and hallway outside the bedrooms were dark and silent.

She noticed that the door leading to the lower lever was

269

ajar and that a ray of light was lancing across the floor. Maybe he was downstairs.

She opened the door and descended the stairs. The thick runner tacked to the staircase muffled the sound of her shoes. She hadn't come down here the last time. She was surprised at what she found. So surprised, she stopped before she reached the bottom step in order to gaze admiringly around the room.

It was an artist's studio. Paints, brushes, pallettes, a worktable, and a couple of easels were arranged in a corner near a large sink. Art hung on the walls . . . all over them. There were pieces from near the ceiling to close to the floor. Landscapes. Still lifes. Portraits. Oils. Watercolors, Pastels. Pen and ink.

She leaned over to get a closer look at the signatures of some of the works near her. A. L.

Adam Locke. He'd created his own personal gallery. They were all good, too. Very good.

She heard the door open.

Adam walked through from the adjoining room. He was holding a bottle of wine in one hand and the door open for someone else with his other. And he was laughing.

"Well, he *did*," protested a smooth and sensuous-sounding feminine voice.

Ariel's stomach clenched. No. This couldn't be happening. Not again.

Raquel Dos Santos walked into the room, laughing too.

She was elegantly casual in a designer dress that hung from her well-shaped body as if it had been cut for her own personal mannequin.

A cold, sick sensation closed over Ariel. She looked away. She couldn't stand to see them. She had to get a grip on herself. She chose the wrong way to look. Her eyes fell on an object that made her feel even worse.

There, leaning against the wall next to the door to the wine cellar, was a portrait done in oils and framed in an intricately carved walnut frame. It was the portrait of a woman with

270

raven hair and dark eyes, dressed in a softly clinging wine-red gown. Its neckline plunged between her half revealed, softly swelling breasts. Her hair was slightly mussed. Her wet, red lips had a pouty look. She radiated sensuality. Her beckoning eyes would have pulled any living man into her arms that night.

It was a portrait of Raquel.

Ariel didn't need to see the initials to know who had painted it.

Only a lover could have painted a woman like that.

Ariel's world began to crack. The pain of its shattering was almost more than she could bear. She ricocheted away from the couple, still unaware of her presence at the opposite end of the room.

"Thank you, Adam," said Raquel huskily, embracing Adam. He was obviously in a celebratory mood and made no effort to move away. "It's so good to be with you again. It's been such a long time."

She kissed him on the mouth.

Ariel felt as if she'd been slapped by a bear. The claw marks hurt from her face to her stomach. Grief and outrage exploded beneath her icy horror. She choked back a sob—half of betrayal, half of fury.

Two heads snapped around in her direction.

"Ariel!" Adam exclaimed in astonishment. If it weren't so awful, his face would have been comical to behold.

"Sorry," Ariel replied acidly. Fury had overwhelmed all her other conflicting emotions. "I obviously don't learn from my mistakes. Believe me, I have learned it this time."

She whirled and fled up the stairs. Feelings blinded her. She never saw the door as she slammed it open, flying down the steps to her car.

Locke, temporarily frozen in shock, freed himself from Raquel's arms.

"Here," he said, shoving the bottle of champagne into her unready hands. She still looked completely stunned.

"I've got to go," he muttered.

"Bye," she called out, shrewdly guessing the root of the problem as he took the steps two at a time. "Good luck!"

He quickly crossed the threshold of his front door, the door still open after Ariel's stormy departure. He saw the lights of her car. She was half out of the space, ready to pull into the street.

"Ariel!" he cried, his hands slamming the back of the car's roof.

Ariel stepped on the gas. The car shot down the street, slamming mercilessly on every brick.

Locke swore and watched helplessly as she took the corner and disappeared from sight.

The people next door had been getting into their car. They paused with one foot in and one foot out, staring curiously at their normally cool, suave, bachelor neighbor as he ranted and raved at the night. He looked like he was ready to kill.

"Catherine!" he shouted angrily. "I want my car back!"

Ariel made it halfway to Annapolis on fury alone. It was really too bad that she needed to burn the gas. Blinding fires of outrage kept her foot to the floor down Route 50; it was a miracle that she wasn't ticketed every mile of the way by the normally attentive Maryland State Police. Luckily she wasn't ticketed and didn't wrap herself around any telephone poles, either.

She found that her fires had pretty much burned out by the time she reached the bridge over the Severn River. That was really too bad. That was when she could have especially used them.

She made the mistake of looking at the river as she crossed it. The memories came flooding back. Tender looks . . . loving kisses . . . laughter and hopes that were not going to be fulfilled. Regrets for what could have been . . .

The tears were blurring her vision as she turned up the road to Athena.

"I loved you!" She sobbed, hating herself for having made

272

such a fool of herself. For the second time! With the same unbearably attractive and captivating man!

What was the matter with her? she wondered wildly. How could she have let herself in for this? How could she have been so stupid? So naive? She not only let herself have an affair with him, she let herself fall in love with him!

She hated him for that. But worst of all, she still loved him.

She jerked the car into park and got out, forgetting her bag in the backseat. The darkness didn't help any more than her tears did in steering a steady course. She stumbled all the way to her cottage.

The minute she stepped inside, she knew it had been a mistake. Everywhere she looked she faced reminders of him. Eating dinner in the kitchen the night he'd first come home with her . . . facing her parents together in the living room . . . fleeing into the bathroom wrapped in a sheet the morning after they'd first—

She closed her eyes. She couldn't go into her bedroom and try to go to sleep. It held more than she could face. She fervently vowed never to enter that room again.

The phone rang. Ariel picked it up.

"Hello," she said, her voice still husky from crying.

"Ariel!" Adam shouted urgently. "Listen to me—"

She dropped the receiver back on its cradle. She felt numb. *How could you do this to me?* she cried in silent suffering. *How could you make love to me, care for me, or at least seem to, and then . . .*

The phone was ringing again.

Ariel knew who it was. He never let go. She couldn't bear to hear an apology, if that was what he intended. She felt awful enough about having loved and lost. She had too much pride to take his pity as a substitute.

"You can keep your pity!" she shouted brokenly, giving the ringing phone a scathing look. "I don't accept consolation prizes, Mr. Locke. If I can't take first prize, I retire from the competition."

She stumbled out of the cottage and half ran to the gymnasium, fumbling with the lock repeatedly in a teary-eyed effort to get the door open.

She sighed, hoping for relief a few moments later as she sank down onto the familiar mats. She sat in the cold darkness, trying to push the pain from her mind, trying to remember the good feelings of being here. But all she could remember was Adam's face the day he came and saw her with Jim Reeves, the tone in his voice when he convinced her to spend the day with him. "You'll feel better," he had promised her.

"I don't feel better!" she cried angrily, wiping away another tear. "This was the only place that ever comforted me. In all my life it was the last resort. It never failed . . . but now you've taken that too! You've taken it all."

She cried brokenly until she was nearly exhausted. No more tears would come. She was empty. A shell.

Nothing really mattered anymore.

She put on her coat and locked the gym as she left.

She wandered slowly up the hill, not thinking of where she was going. She hesitated at her cottage, then continued on.

This is really great, she thought sarcastically, punishing herself some more. *I can't bear to go in my own home. I can't stand to go to my old hangout. Here I am all grown-up and no place to go! What kind of an idiot acts like this?*

The infusion of anger helped thaw some of the emptiness a little, but it didn't help her come up with a solution to her most pressing problem: where to go.

She sat down on a bench near the Inn. She looked up at Locke's terrace. Grief stabbed her again. Then she noticed something else. A tiny flash of light . . . like a small candle passed in front of the terrace's glass doors. And then it was gone.

That was odd, she thought.

As hard as she tried to repress it, a tiny thought forced its way into her consciousness. Perhaps he'd come after her. Maybe he really could explain.

She shut her eyes tightly and groaned.

Don't you dare think that, she warned herself. *Not even for a second! Haven't you had enough? What does it take to teach you to listen?*

Her wounded soul and righteous conscience ranted and raved.

But her heart . . . her heart was willing to believe anything, as long as there was a promise, however faint, that its love would return. No hope was too slim for it to grasp.

Ariel succumbed to her heart.

She leapt off the bench and went into the Inn. She ignored the startled desk clerk and went straight up in the elevator.

She was about to knock on the door when it opened, much to her surprise. Ariel stood there, frozen to the spot, fist suspended in the air, mouth open in surprise.

Jim Reeves, dressed in dark clothing, grabbed her and pulled her roughly inside.

"Make a noise and you're a dead girl," he vowed coldly.

Catherine stood at the curbside and watched her brother jump into the driver's seat, still warm from her occupancy.

"But, Adam, what's going on?" she called out, perplexed.

He pulled out of the drive shouting something that sounded sort of like, "I'll tell you later." Then he disappeared into the streets of Georgetown.

"Gosh, sorry I was a little late, big brother," she murmured apologetically.

When Locke arrived in Annapolis, it was close to midnight. He'd made the hour-long trip in record time and had the speeding tickets to show for it, unlike Ariel.

He was halfway across the parking lot when a figure rushed up to him and grabbed his arm.

"What are you doing back here?" Galway asked, not looking pleased about that at all.

"I need to talk to Ariel," Locke said unapologetically. "Don't worry. I'll steer clear of the Inn."

Galway shook his head.

"What's that supposed to mean?" Adam asked pointedly.

Dr. Norris joined them.

"She still hasn't come out," Norris said worriedly, speaking to Galway. Then, noticing Locke, he added in surprise, "What are you doing here?"

"What do you mean she still hasn't come out?" Locke asked suspiciously, sensing that something was seriously wrong.

Galway and Norris looked at each other uncomfortably.

Locke's eyes narrowed as his suspicions heated up.

"Who hasn't come out?" he asked, trying the back door since the front hadn't produced anything.

Their faces were answer enough.

"Is Ariel in some sort of difficulty?" he asked sharply.

"Come on," Norris said, pulling the two men back toward the van that had been his listening place in tonight's stakeout. "We'd better explain, Robert."

It was cold on the ground at this time of year. Cold and hard and not at all where she wanted to be. Ariel was pinned down under her captor, who wisely did not trust her to lie still otherwise.

"If you stop wiggling," he whispered, "I'll stop pulling your arms back so much."

Her arms ached from the telephone cord he'd used to tie them behind her back. She nodded her head in agreement. Maybe he'd offer to loosen the gag.

He'd forced her out of the building at gunpoint, using the exit that had been closed for repairs for a week. He'd told her to keep quiet if anyone saw them or he'd kill her and the person they met. They didn't meet anyone.

The same rules did not apply in the woods to which he'd taken her. He'd bound her using things picked up in Locke's suite.

Reeves bellied over to the edge of the cliff, looking down into the river. He was swearing softly. Forrestman owed him a ride out of this. It was the only way he was going to get out

276

without being caught. That really burned him. If Ariel just hadn't stumbled onto him, he could have finished up and just turned in his notice in a couple of weeks with no one the wiser.

All of the planted information would be where it was supposed to be. The staff would be none the wiser. Gail Marlow had no way of tracing his accessing the computer banks to manipulate the word-processing unit or the library's files or the engineering department's graphics and modeling programs. When Locke filed his report, his clients would clap him on the back and throw money at his designs. Then, in a matter of a few months, maybe less, they'd discover that Locke was recommending the use of insulation that had been established as dangerous, posssessing carcinogenic chemicals. The subterranean homes would have ventilation systems inadequate to the task of removing the buildup of radioactive gases that was sometimes a by-product of their below-earth location.

He grimly searched the river with his binoculars.

Locke would be found to have a connection financially with the East Coast distributor of the dangerous insulation and a fiduciary interest in the company manufacturing the ventilation systems. Forrestman had taken care of that. Even if it didn't hold up in court eventually, Locke's name would have been tarred enough by the allegation. People always have a hard time believing that where there's that much smoke there isn't any fire.

And this was tantalizingly complex smoke Forrestman was blowing.

Ariel watched through the darkness. They were in the middle of the most heavily treed section of the stretch of property along the river. Unless someone stumbled right onto them, no one would ever see her.

She watched Reeves come back to her and hunch down, checking her bonds for tightness.

What or who was he waiting for?

*   *   *

Locke walked into the lobby of the Inn. Galway was talking to a stranger at the far edge of the terrace.

"Where are Carrollton and Fontaine?" Locke asked Dr. Norris.

"They haven't left their cottages," he said, relieved that his employees did not appear to be responsible for what had happened.

Galway approached them.

"It sounds like your two leading candidates flunked out," Adam said bluntly. "Carrollton may have worked for a firm that would have a conflict of interest with this project and he may have been offered an excellent job if he performed some industrial sabotage for them, but that doesn't mean he accepted it," he pointed out sharply. "And Fontaine may be struggling with the finances needed to provide health care and nursing for his mother, but that also doesn't necessarily mean he'd take a bribe even if one were offered."

Locke's steely eyes surveyed the men. They nodded in agreement.

"What did your technician say?" Adam asked Galway.

"The alarm system we installed had been cut. That's why we didn't know when he left."

"For God's sake, why didn't you post a man there?" he asked.

"We needed to leave an opening somewhere to tempt him in. We thought he couldn't detect it."

Locke was tempted to say something about that, but he was diverted first.

"Mr. Locke," the desk clerk interrupted. "I have a message for you."

It was from Marge. Walter had found out who owned the ketch. It was Grant Forrestman.

He shot around to the other two men.

"Who was your third leading suspect?" he demanded.

"Jim Reeves."

"Have you got someone down by the riverfront where that sailboat keeps mooring?"

"No," they both said, looking as if Locke must have lost his mind.

"That's where he must have taken her," he said, turning to race across the lobby and out into the night. But as he plunged into the forest a few moments later, he was crying out silently, Why did you have to go? An echo from another tragedy. If this one ended the same way . . .

He wouldn't let it!

Reeves crawled to the edge of the cliff. This time he liked what he saw below. He pointed his flashlight toward the shadowy, silent form of the ketch. He flashed it on and off twice. Then he crawled back to Ariel's side and untied her arms.

"We're going down," he whispered harshly. "Try to get away and you'll go down so fast, you won't know what hit you."

He yanked her to her feet and pulled her roughly after him toward the edge. She could see a man climbing into a small rowboat from the sailboat on the river below. Was that her destination, then?

Reeves jammed his gun into the small holster strapped on his back. When he looked at her again, Ariel saw no vestige of the carousing mail clerk. He was a dangerous stranger. His face was hard and cold.

She thought fast. If she climbed down the cliff face with him, she knew that she'd have no chance. She'd be entirely at his mercy and at the mercy of the unknown man in the rowboat. Reeves didn't look like the merciful type.

The farther away from Athena she got, the slimmer her chances of escaping unharmed would be. She had to try to get away from him while she was still here. The sooner the better. The climb down the cliffside was beginning to look like her best chance.

"Come on," he ordered, using the same harsh rasp. He jerked her down over the side by her foot.

The rough cliff offered an unattractive descent to the river.

279

The overhang was cut away about a foot below the edge, forcing the climber to stretch feet and legs forward against gravity, seeking toeholds until he could get entirely onto the face. Rocks and roots protruded over the craggy surface until it was swallowed by bushes and shrubs at the base. Trees encroaching from the forest all around left it in perpetual shade and hard to see.

It had been for these very reasons that Reeves had selected it for meetings with Forrestman. No kids or casual hikers were likely to stumble onto them here. There were too many easier places to get to.

Reeves focused his full attention on getting a good handhold under the edge of the cliff. He'd gone down first, pulling Ariel along with him. He was concentrating so hard on steadying his precarious position that he didn't hear the sounds signaling human approach . . . footsteps in the leaves and twigs, softly snapping in the darkness.

Locke saw Ariel just as she climbed down. He crouched low, still half hidden in the forest and underbrush. He could see that someone had her and was pulling her down. Her captor's head had just disappeared below the edge. Ariel was still visible.

Locke ran forward, keeping low. Ariel didn't see him until she was almost ready to let go of the edge.

Then she saw the figure of a man running stealthily toward her through the shadowy forest night. She couldn't quite make him out, but he moved like someone very familiar. Ariel yanked the gag down over her mouth with one hand and pulled up her foot sharply, crying for help at the same time.

Her violent movement and piercing cry threw Reeves off-balance. He cursed viciously and struggled to retain his grip on her ankle. When she'd jerked away, she'd pulled him dangerously wide of the cliff face. Another centimeter and he could not have recovered. He'd have fallen all the way to the bottom.

In furious retaliation he pulled her leg down as hard as he could. If he'd had better leverage, it could have been a fatal move. Fortunately for Ariel, he was still scrambling for a secure toehold.

"Take the fast way, bitch!" he swore at her, yanking again.

This time he had his toehold *and* the leverage.

Just as Locke leapt over the last stretch of ground to the edge, Ariel felt the ground being jerked out from under her. Her hands and feet poked helplessly into the air. In slow motion she felt herself begin to slide down the rough surface of the cliff. She kicked out blindly, trying to find a hold. Her foot connected, slowing her fall just enough.

Reeves screamed. She'd connected with his side, throwing him off-balance. He fell shrieking to the ground below. His silence was swallowed by approaching voices.

Locke cried out in anguished outrage, reaching down in a desperate effort to grab her before she, too, was gone.

Their hands connected in the dark.

"Hang on!" he cried sharply.

Ariel scrabbled for toeholds in the rocky dirt face. Their hands weren't in good position to hold her for long. They were gripping palms, not wrists. Her left hand closed mercifully over a tree root. Then her toes located tiny notches in the dirt. She leaned her head against the cliff and breathed a sigh of relief.

"Come on," he said, sounding tremendously relieved as he grabbed her by both wrists.

She grasped his, and he pulled her up and over the edge.

Adam pulled her into his arms and crushed her to him. Then he started swearing and pulled away enough to glower at her in utter fury.

"You almost got yourself killed!" he shouted furiously.

Ariel started shaking. Stumbling onto Reeves, being kidnapped and dragged through the woods at gunpoint, being rescued split seconds before sliding down the face of a cliff by her lover whom she'd last seen in the arms of another woman . . . it was more than she could take in one day.

Ariel started to cry. That only made her feel worse.

"Yes!" she shouted back at him. "I nearly got myself killed! I had planned to surprise you Saturday night, but you surprised me instead! So, I had this time to kill, if you'll pardon the expression, and I just happened to stumble onto the creep burglarizing your suite. I really *do* apologize for all the trouble!"

Her hands were clenched with rage. Tears streamed down her cheeks. The wind blowing across the cliff whipped her hair and chilled her to the bone. Somewhere a voice asked how he had gotten here, but she was too upset to heed it.

"What in the hell were you doing in my suite?" he roared, still so upset that she'd come so close to being killed that he was beside himself.

"I was looking for you!" she cried angrily, wiping the tears away with the palm of her hand. "I saw a light in your room and I thought . . ."

The words died in her throat. She stared at him like a wounded doe as all of the pain came back in an avalanche.

"You thought I was there?" he asked, for the first time not shouting at her. He hardly dared believe it was true. It would mean that he still had a chance. She might listen if he explained.

She looked at the ground. The wind whipped her hair around, covering her face.

He stepped forward, his anger and fear subsiding, something else taking their place. He sank his hands into the tangled, silken strands, pushing the dark mass away from her face, pulling her head up so he could see her clearly.

"I'd give anything to have been there instead of Reeves," he told her quietly. "When I got here and found out that he'd taken you with him, I lost ten years of my life." He scanned her precious features, a little smudged with dirt. "And when I heard you scream and saw you start to fall—" His voice cracked. With an effort he forced himself to go on. ". . . I lost another ten."

His eyes locked with hers, and she saw what she needed so

282

desperately to see there. Anguish, suffering, and a deep, abiding love.

"I love you, Ariel," he said, pulling her close and holding her tight. "Sometimes it feels like I've loved you forever."

She closed her eyes and leaned against him. She needed his strength, and he gave it to her. She cried softly against his jacket and slid her arms around him, sobbing from gratitude and love, from reaction to all the awful things that had happened that night, and from relief that it seemed to be over at last.

He kissed her hair and rocked her gently in his arms, drawing comfort and reassurance from her nearness.

"But . . . why," Ariel asked unsteadily between sniffles, "was . . . she there?"

Adam held her tighter, as if he were afraid that she might try to leave him again.

"She's getting married. She wanted to tell me before the official announcement was made. And she wanted to see if she could buy the portrait I painted of her," he answered. "When you came, I had just given her the painting as a wedding present and was giving her a vintage bottle of champagne for her engagement party."

He buried his face in her hair.

"You've got to believe me, Ariel," he said, almost pleading with her. "That's all there was to it. I swear to you. That's all."

She wanted so desperately to believe him. But a tiny, recalcitrant part of her was still afraid. It had hurt so badly to see him like that.

"But she was kissing you," Ariel said, tears welling up again at the memory.

He sighed and pressed them closer together.

"She kisses everyone. She came to Washington as a teenager with her parents. They're in the diplomatic corps and were assigned to the embassy here. When they went back to Brazil, she stayed on, going to college at Georgetown University. She has an effervescent, warm personality. She blends

Brazilian warmth and charm with a relaxed American life-style. But she's not some kind of femme fatale, if that's what you're worrying about."

He kissed her temple and rested his cheek against hers.

"Raquel was a faithful, loving wife to her first husband. She married right after graduation. He was quite a bit older than she. Her fiancé is a good man for her. I'm sure she'll be as loyal to him."

Ariel could feel herself letting go of her last fear.

"But the painting . . . the way she looks. You couldn't paint a woman like that if you weren't her lover," she whispered, so afraid to hear his response to that.

She had had to force herself to ask. But she knew that if they were to have any chance for the future, she had to know it all.

"Raquel and I were *not* lovers," he said emphatically. "If the painting is good, it's because I'm a fair artist. Period."

He grabbed her by the shoulders and looked down at her, his face drawn with uncertainty.

"I'll be happy to show you a whole stack of portraits that are ten times more provocative than that one. They're all of the same woman. They're all done from the memory of one night. They were all done before we became lovers. If you want, I'll show you tonight. They're in my cabin. In that closet you found so fascinating. And they're all of you."

He looked at her in pure anguish.

"Ariel, what else can I say? You've got to believe me. Please . . ."

She saw the tortured look in his eyes, and the last vestige of fear faded from her. She lifted her hands and tenderly cupped his face. Warm brown eyes gazed up at him adoringly.

"I believe you," she said unsteadily, "but even if I didn't, I would still love you with all my heart."

Her words stopped him cold. Then, when their meaning had been thoroughly registered, he sighed with relief and pulled her close. His mouth found hers, and he made a deep, animal sound of satisfaction as their lips and tongues fused in a deeply intimate kiss.

"I love you," he gasped, breaking the kiss with an effort.

His sweet words made her glow with happiness, and she smiled at him radiantly.

"And I love you," she said softly, planting a warm kiss on his mouth.

"Damn it, Ariel, stop that," he said with a growl, holding her head against his chest. "I've been through quite a night. I can't guarantee my control right now. Keep kissing me like that and you'll end up on your back right here in the forest."

She hugged him and laughed.

"I can think of worse things," she teased, feeling giddy with newfound happiness.

He shook his head and eyed her with rueful affection. His acute mental health problem was as permanent as they come. That idea had been threatening him for quite a while now. Admitting it to himself came as a wonderful relief. Why fight it? he asked himself.

He leaned down and kissed her gently on the mouth.

"You know, I don't think I can go through many more of your Cinderella acts," he said teasingly.

"No?" she answered in surprise.

"No." He was quite firm about that. "But I think the prince came up with an excellent way to put a stop to that."

"Really?" she said weakly, staring at him in wide-eyed fascination. "How did he do that?"

He gave her a princely grin. "He married her."

Ariel forgot to breathe. "Oh," she said weakly.

"Do you think you might consider a proposal of marriage, Ms. Radnor?" he asked softly, rubbing his lips softly across hers to strengthen his case.

As far as Ariel was concerned his case didn't need any strengthening at all.

"Oh, yes, Mr. Locke. I certainly would." She moaned as a fiery trail slid from her throat to her abdomen.

He slid his hands underneath her coat and massaged her back slowly and sensuously.

"Will you marry me?" he asked huskily, kissing her ear and letting the tip of his tongue court the sensitive folds into ecstatic submission.

Silver fires ran through her from head to toe.

"Yes." She moaned again.

"When?" he asked, a man who knew when to push his advantage. He ran his hands up her front, cupping and caressing her breasts. The fabric tortured them both with its annoying presence.

"Whenever you want." She gasped, twisting against him helplessly.

"How about the day after tomorrow?" he suggested in a strained voice. At the moment that seemed like an eternity to him.

Ariel's eyes flew open.

"What?" she asked, startled.

"I'd prefer tomorrow," he admitted with a frustrated sigh, "but the Alexandria courthouse is closed on Sundays."

He looked at her seriously.

"I mean it," he said. "I don't want to spend another day of my life apart from you if I can help it." He grinned. "Remember, you've already taken twenty years off my life. We'd better hurry up and make good use of what I've got left!"

"You are crazy!" She laughed.

He sighed in resignation. "That thought has occurred to me," he admitted.

"My job . . ." she said uncertainly with a questioning frown.

"You could do the same thing in Washington," he pointed out. "But, if you like it here, we could work out a commute . . . buy a house halfway between my office and yours."

"Oh, Adam," she said gratefully, "you really are a prince!"

He laughed and hugged her.

"Listen, it's got to be better than sneaking out of your cottage every day before dawn!"

He frowned slightly as a new thought assailed him.

"If you're worried about your parents," he offered, "we could wait. . . ."

She laid her finger across his lips.

"They're not getting married. We are. And I don't want to wait, either. But, do you think we could go back to your house tomorrow morning? I don't want us to spend Sunday around here answering questions. I'd rather spend it alone with you."

He laughed and swung her up in his arms, resting her on his chest.

"Of course we can." He kissed her soundly. "But I think we'd better drive your car back to Georgetown. If the State Police see mine again on Route 50, they'll probably impound it on principle."

Robert Galway looked up the steep face of the cliff.

"Good thing Locke told us where to look," he said.

"Yes," Dr. Norris agreed as he watched the authorities put handcuffs on Grant Forrestman.

"And it was lucky he got to Ariel in time," Galway added.

"It certainly was!" Dr. Norris agreed with great feeling.

The stretcher bearing Jim Reeves had already been taken by the Coast Guard launch to the nearest hospital.

Galway frowned.

"I haven't heard anything, though, since they disappeared over the rim," he added, worried. "Maybe I should go up and see if they need some help," he suggested.

Norris looked at Galway in astonishment.

"Robert! I always thought you were more perceptive than that!" he said admonishingly. He cracked a smile and shook his head, gazing knowingly up at the clifftop. "They don't need any help, Robert. They're going to be just fine."